Lady Lazarus

by

Judith Shoemaker-Hill

PublishAmerica
Baltimore

First printing

ISBN: 1-4137-3789-7
PUBLISHED BY PUBLISHAMERICA, LLLP
www.publishamerica.com
Baltimore

Printed in the United States of America

This book is dedicated to my husband, George Hill;
my hero, my friend and my inspiration.

Acknowledgments

I wish to thank my friend, Lonnie, the founder and solitary member of my literary fan club, for her unflagging enthusiasm and encouragement throughout the years. To the Gustavus Adolphus College Class of '62, my thanks for giving me the opportunity to hone my writing skills on our alumni class letters. Your rave reviews kept me going. To my mother, Hazelle Flom, bless you for your patience and your vow to stay alive and well to finally see me published. To my son Matthew, who never lost faith no matter how many rejection notices he found in our mailbox, I offer my everlasting love and gratitude. And to my sister Mary Gail and brother Scott, thank you for believing in me and in the power of prayer. And to my brother, Larry, "I appreciate your putting in a good word for me from your heavenly home."

Chapter One

Only one second. That's all it takes. In one second a life can be given. Or taken. Or changed forever. How many times had Leigh Barnes heard her mother say, "Don't get too cocky, my dear, or God will show you in one second just who's boss." Had she gotten cocky? Had she begun to believe she, not God, was in control of her life? Well, she wasn't feeling very cocky right now. She was a scared little girl again, and like a well-behaved child who had been taught to be seen but not heard, she muffled her screaming senses as Jude Orcus forced his way through the front door and into the foyer of her parents' home.

His all-knowing smile ambled leisurely over the curves of her body as he moved steadily toward her. Only when she spoke did he momentarily stop his advance.

"Jude, what a surprise to see you…" With a strength she didn't know she possessed, she kept her voice from rising, her words from tumbling out like loose pebbles. She could give no indication in either voice or manner that she thought it unusual for a homicidal maniac to escape from the asylum and pay a visit to the woman who put him there. She finished, "here in Beaver Lake."

Her bare feet grew numb on the cold marble floor of the entry. Her stomach rolled over and over as the reek of his breath and the discharge of venomous spittle at the corners of his mouth assailed her senses. She willed her legs to lock and commanded her eyes not to betray her fear of the man who had once posed as a national hero; a God-fearing rescuer of lost souls; a courageous righter of wrongs. To millions of loyal readers of his column in the *Twin City Sentinel*, Jude Orcus was the savior they had been promised.

And I was the one who nailed him. Leigh shivered involuntarily. *Please God, give me just a few more seconds to figure a way out, to weigh my options*. Jude would leave her few, she knew that, since she had been the one who had exposed the man's deceit to the world, stripped him of his dignity and his admirers, destroyed his career, and then made sure he was denied the freedom to live alongside honorable men and women. She had been rewarded with her own newspaper column and the promise of a career she'd always dreamed of having. While she was being lauded, he was being taken away in handcuffs.

The hatred she saw in his eyes told her that he needed no reminder of who had tallied up his sins in front of God and the whole world. They were the same eyes that had remained fixed upon her as she sat on the witness stand and told nine incredulous jurors of the horror of the night she discovered Jude Orcus was a cold-blooded killer. All nodded sympathetically as she explained why that particular day would be forever emblazoned on her memory: it was also the day the man she loved, the man who had just asked her to marry him, was killed. The quaver in her voice had caused the judge to ask for a recess, but she had somehow managed to compose herself and calmly respond to all the questions asked of her. The story she told was one that had all members of the jury on the edge of their seats; a gory tale that *they* had promised would assure Jude Orcus's conviction and incarceration in a secure institution in which he would remain until his death. That man was now pointing a gun at her heart. Apparently, *they* had lied.

Chapter Two

"Johnny, the children! Where are they?" Grace O'Regan's scream pierced the quiet of the forest and bounced off the walls of the log cabin they had built as a fortress.

"They were just out there, by the well. Now they're gone, Johnny!" Her eyes pleaded with the mountain of a man who was silouetted in the bathroom door.

"Gracie Girl, don't get your pants in a bunch," he said, zipping up his own. "They're probably just down by the stream, angling for something or other."

His calm voice did not reassure her as it had from the moment she first met him nine years ago, when like a heavenly apparition he had appeared out of the clouds of smoke and pulled her from the building burning around her. "Go find them, please!"

Without stopping to put on his shoes, he crossed the great room, swung open the front door, and hurried down the path leading to the stream. Her eyes followed his broad back and muscled legs until they disappeared into the thick redwoods. He was gone only three or four minutes before he reappeared with two blond, blue-eyed eight-year-olds who burst into the room like human firecrackers, their faces bright red and their voices pitched high enough to break glass.

"Wait till you see this!" Buddy rejoiced.

His sister Bess opened her hands and beamed with the joy of their discovery. "We found another mutant frog. Look this one's got two heads!"

"Our science project is going to win for sure," Buddy said, his voice deepening with seriousness.

"Your science projects always win, even without the help of a two-headed frog." She stroked her daughter's flushed cheek and addressed Buddy, the older of the two by four minutes. "You and Bess might want to compare your discovery with that article we just read in *Science Magazine*."

"But that article was boring. It said the frog isn't really a mutant, just a dumb frog who got sick from eating something rotten on a lily pad. That's not as cool as being a mutant."

"If you're looking for excitement, Buddy, facts are usually stranger than fiction." She took a deep breath. "And you can find a lot of excitement closer to the house. I've told you not to wander so far into the woods unless your dad or I are with you. You know how you two can get so preoccupied with some new discovery, and suddenly you're in the next county," she scolded. "Please assure me that you'll respect my decision on this."

"Are you scared he'll find us?" Buddy asked, more out of curiosity than fear.

Grace blanched at the question, as well as her son's attitude of unconcern. She and Johnny had determined early on that the twins would not live in fear, but at the same time they did want them to be alert to danger: the kind the children's birth father presented. Their birth mother, Bitti, had done everything possible to keep her twins' birth a secret from the man who had forcefully fathered them. She had failed in that, but she was adamant that the children's whereabouts and the identify of their adoptive parents remain unknown to him. It was the only way she could assure the children's safety. And her own.

Keeping the secret meant the O'Regans had to move away from San Francisco, from Johnny's job with the fire department, and from everyone and everything that would give a clue as to their whereabouts.

"Bitti called. She'll be here in a couple of hours." Gracie kept her voice light.

"Is she worried too?" Bess asked.

Fooling her children was too unnatural a practice to be convincing. They read her correctly every time she tried to hedge her answers. "Just anxious. To see you, of course, and to bring us up to date on…things."

"On him, I bet," Buddy persisted. "Why doesn't she want him to see us? Why is it such a big deal?"

"Your birth father is a very possessive person," she began. "He loves too much. It clouds his judgment."

"How can he love too much?" they'd both asked at once, confused by the contradiction they found in her words and those they read daily in the Bible; words which they never doubted. Johnny and Gracie had seen to that.

Gracie flipped her long, straight hair behind her ears and attempted to explain what she herself would never understand. "His mother and father never taught him about God. Maybe because they never knew about Him themselves," she added, giving the benefit of the doubt to people she knew didn't deserve it.

"Maybe we can tell him about God, then Bitti won't have to be afraid anymore," Bess offered excitedly, her pale green eyes wide with the prospect.

"Bitti has tried to tell him, but he won't listen. We have to trust her judgment on this one. She knows him better than anyone." She played nervously with her wedding ring, taking comfort in one of the few certainties in her life. That her husband had been sent straight from God.

That momentarily satisfied their curiosity about a man they seldom thought about. But only until Johnny boomed, "He is never going to get close enough to talk about anything, Buddy! Ever!"

His intensity had the opposite effect on his children than the one he'd intended.

Bess grabbed her father around the waist and wound herself around his legs, gazing up at the tower of strength that reached almost to the sky, to God. "When you hurt my ears, it scares me, Daddy."

Johnny took a cleansing breath and absently brushed a wisp of white gold hair from his daughter's forehead. "Don't be frightened, little munchkin. We have God on our side. That makes our team very strong."

"Bitti says our birth dad's real strong too. She says he used to hold her down, that he's still holding her." Buddy's face was infused with the frustration of a child trying to translate adult expressions.

Gracie jumped in. "She didn't mean holding her physically, honey. She means she can't put him and his bad behavior out of her mind, and it keeps her from moving on in her life."

"None of us has to worry about him, because even if he wanted to, he could never find us out here. We're safe, Buddy, trust your old dad on this one."

The flush of heat to his face was as intense as any he'd experienced fighting fires. Just thinking about that man could raise his temperature several degrees. He desperately wanted to believe his own words. He wished he could be sure that the monster would never see the outside of the institution in which he was locked. For all his training as a firefighter, Johnny had no idea how to battle a man capable of doing such unspeakable things. He did know if he ever encountered him, he too might be capable of performing unspeakable acts. What he did trust right now was Gracie's instinct. It seldom proved false. And at this moment, her nerve endings were charging all the molecules in the air.

"Bitti told us we should scream and run like hell if we ever see him," Buddy volunteered.

"She didn't say hell, Buddy," Bess argued, her eyes narrowing.

"I'm sure Bitti didn't mean to frighten you like that." Grace's voice was gentle, but her unstated thoughts were anything but. "She knows that we will always watch over you, and that there are plenty of people watching over him, so there is no need for you to concern yourself with the man."

Not completely convinced but getting bored with the subject, the two budding scientists raced to their rooms, bickering over who had first dibs on the frog.

Johnny approached his normally stalwart wife, now huddled in a corner of the kitchen, her face hiding in the palms of her hands.

When she looked up, her soft brown eyes were wide and wet and her unpainted lips were trembling. "I feel danger, Johnny. I feel it in every bone and every limb."

"I'm not going to try to convince you you're wrong, Gracie, because I know you, and I know your intuitions. But I also know the state hospital is a very secure one. Remember, Bitti pretended to be writing an article on the hospital and researched their security measures. She came away feeling certain that he would never have an opportunity to reach our kids. Besides, we're not the only ones who want him locked up until the day his rotten carcass burns to ashes. Everyone who knows him or has heard about him would prefer he be permanently removed from the earth, but we've got to settle for having him locked up for life. We really have nothing to worry about."

Their exchanged looks denied it.

Gracie took his mitt-sized hands in hers and pulled him toward her. Her voice was a whisper. "You just can't keep that kind of evil contained in an earthly vessel. No cell has bars strong enough to hold him." She shivered. "I wish his father had succeeded in killing him."

"Gracie, even if he were dead, no urn could keep his filthy ashes bottled up." Johnny used every inch of his bulk to surround her, hold her close. He didn't need Gracie to tell him that they were powerless against such raw evil, that only God could keep the devil known as Jude from fulfilling his promise.

"God help us all, we know how determined he is to get both his revenge and his children. We need to pray, Gracie."

As they bowed their heads and held hands, neither of them knew just how close they were to joining Leigh Barnes, a woman they had never met, in Jude Orcus's personally-designed hell.

Chapter Three

Leigh could see that two years behind hospital bars had altered the distinctive facial features that had for five years accompanied his award-winning newspaper column. Once clear-eyed and serenely sovereign, his countenance was now shadowed by jutting cheekbones and cavernous scars. The new face was feverish with rage and smeared with stubble, as if a razor were unable to traverse the irregular features now pocked like the surface of the moon. Tiny rivulets of blood were staining the whites of his dead eyes.

She held her breath, trying not to inhale the filthy fragrance of unrefined evil that was his essence. Jude Orcus kicked the door shut behind him, the imprint of his dirty sole adding insult to its freshly painted surface. He secured the lock, his malevolent grin mocking her, daring her to protest any action he may take to seek his rightful vengeance.

Leigh's heartbeat kept a weird syncopation with her shaking hands. Fiercely hot blood flashed through her body, causing her brain cells to bump against each other so loudly she could barely hear him through the din in her head.

"I'm here to visit you, of course," he answered, again perusing the length of her body, using his gun to trace the curves and crevices.

She crossed her arms over her chest and slouched slightly, hoping to minimize the rise and fall of her breasts beneath her silk shirt.

"I wasn't offered the opportunity to congratulate you on your promotion, Leigh. For some reason my name was left off the list of well-wishers invited to your farewell party." He pouted his lips and saddened his rheumy eyes. "So, I decided to organize my own farewell party here, in the cozy Barnes family nest," he threatened, glancing first into the living room then leftward into the dining room.

Her mind raced around the rooms in search of a weapon to use against him, but nothing here was familiar. Why had her mother chosen this particular time to redecorate? The home in which Leigh had spent so many years of her life was now foreign territory in which the enemy had as much advantage as she.

He caught the involuntary movement of her eyes and took a step closer, his broad smile revealing yellowed teeth and a white coat of film painted on his bloated tongue. He slipped the gun back into the pocket of the expensive designer coat that had once looked made for him, but now hung like something from the sale rack.

"I'm sorry, Jude, the party really was a surprise. To me, anyway. I'm amazed you heard about it." She forced a smile, cringed when it became a twitch. Surely he would notice, see that he was succeeding in terrifying her. Leigh straightened her back and focused on her tormentor, despising her transparent fear even more than his recognition of it, his delight in it. "How did you hear about it, Jude?"

He disregarded her question. "Seems a little odd to me, rude even, that I, the mentor who brought you along all the way from copywriter to nationally recognized political columnist and now…NOW," he hissed, "a staff member of a national magazine, would not be invited to bask along with you in your limelight. But then maybe I'm being presumptuous to expect gratitude instead of ridicule and betrayal." His pupils were dangerously dilated and the splatters of blood that had dotted the whites of his eyes were now viscous smears.

The thought that he had been following her career, taking credit for it, while he was locked in a padded cell hundreds of miles away, made her shiver. Every accolade she received, every promotion she got, must have whetted his appetite for revenge. She was well aware that he attributed his fall to her rise. He'd stated that at the trial. He honestly believed he'd mentored and inspired her, that his trial was merely the product of her relentless pursuit to undermine his excellence and elevate hers.

She appealed to his once rational mind. "I didn't set out to betray you, Jude, I swear to you. I was only doing my job. My assignment was to write a piece on you. I was as eager as your readers to know the man so idolized for coming to the aid of the defenseless." She saw a small glimmer of reason brighten his eyes. "You were hailed for exposing the evil in the back alleys of Minneapolis and St. Paul and down into the black holes where the underclass lived. I never for a moment suspected that man would be anything but noble." She didn't have to lie about that. It was true.

His eyes were filled with fury. "I was nominated for the Pulitzer Prize, little missy. But after you got your fifteen minutes of fame, they took it away! Took me away! That hurt!"

How could she reason with a sociopath? How was it possible to communicate with an alien being who lived in his own private world, spoke in a foreign tongue?

His jaw locked in anger. "I was the one who set the example of excellence in reporting, and what do I get in return for my generous contributions to humanity? Fired! Humiliated! Locked up in a friggin' padded cell! Treated like some no-good bum instead of a revered member of the press club."

His frail frame was taughtly hung. There was no evidence of any softness about him, either in his body or his manner. How could she appeal to him, dissuade him from doing what she was now sure he was planning to do?

"You need help, Jude. You were getting it at the hospital. They could have put you in a regular prison, but they didn't."

His response was to give her the finger, its yellowed nail bitten down to the quick. She had no choice but to keep trying. "You were right to come to me, to talk with me face to face. We didn't have a chance to do that at the trial, and I'm sure we both need to clarify some things. Ask me anything, and I'll try to answer as honestly as I can. It's clear that you have issues that have never been resolved, issues involving me."

She felt a trickle of perspiration at her hairline. She brushed her hair from her forehead, hoping the light auburn strands had not darkened with tell-tale sweat.

He thoughtfully watched her struggle for self-control. He wasn't in any hurry to do what he came to do, that much was obvious. That was one thing in her favor. If only she could use the moments he was savoring, she might have time to calculate his next move. But that would mean diverting his attention somewhere else; to someone else. Her heart lurched. That someone was her mother, who was in the kitchen, blissfully unaware of their uninvited guest. Leigh shoved her clammy hands into her jeans pockets, hoping he was too preoccupied with his own festering anger to pick up the stench of her fear. But how could he not? It was so malodorous she nearly gagged on it.

"Who is it, Leigh?" her mother called out.

Chapter Four

Sebastian Vanderhyde's wide body filled the picture frame back of his leather swivel chair. His heavy forearms were in stark contrast to the delicately scrolled cherry wood arms on which they rested. When he'd had the chair designed, its dimensions allowed ample room for growth, but Sebastian's appetites were abundant and insatiable. Foremost among them was his passion for the truth, whether it be the word of a politician, a forecast of global warming, or the will of God. To provide the energy necessary to seek out all these truths, he needed fuel — preferably premium. He secured it at the best restaurants in San Francisco and in his own gourmet kitchen. Life was short. God would be pleased to see that Sebastian was appreciative all of the earth's bounteous blessings and diligent in exercising all the options the Lord provided his children.

Thrasher Cole sat across the desk from the man he considered to be the wisest he had ever known. Sebastian had walked into his life at a time when he wasn't sure he wanted a life. If it weren't for him, Thrasher would probably still be stewing in the fire department, literally and figuratively. That reminded him: he'd missed lunch. His retirement from the department must be complete; real firemen never missed a meal.

Despite his growling stomach, Thrasher sat patiently. He was not normally a patient man. Patience was no virtue when leading fellow firefighters into a raging inferno on the steep slopes of Telegraph Hill or Pacific Heights. Nor did it serve any purpose when a criminal needed a swift application of justice, and he was the attorney in charge of seeing that it was meted out. If and when he became Judge Cole, patience would have to take the form of an immovable rock, withstanding all onslaughts.

"How did you do it, Sebastian?"

The venerated publisher of the most widely-read political magazine in the United States looked incongruously puzzled, an expression his bearded, aristocratic face seldom wore. "Do what?"

"Convince the governor to appoint me."

He waved his hand in dismissal. "I had little to do with his decision. I would imagine your stint as deputy attorney general had more to do with his decision than anything else. You proved yourself to be the man you purported to be."

"I still can't believe it, Sebastian. How did I get here?"

It was not a rhetorical question. Thrasher needed affirmation from the man whose snow-white hair testified to the many years he'd been on the earth. His serene and unlined face contradicted the fact of those years, while his erudition confirmed them.

"Belief is what it's all about, Thrasher. Belief in God, in ourselves, and in the Constitution. Those beliefs are more difficult to sustain here in California than in most states, as you are well aware. Religion is so little tolerated, and the Constitution is considered a work in progress. But I take heart in the promise of the prophet Isaiah: '*Here is my servant whom I have chosen, the one I love, in whom I delight; I will put my Spirit on him and he will proclaim justice to the nations. He will not quarrel or cry out; no one will hear his voice in the streets. A bruised reed he will not break and a smoldering wick he will not snuff out, till he leads justice to victory. In his name the nations will put their hope.*'

"I just may get crucified too, you know, Sebastian." Thrasher's faith in himself and in mankind in general had been shaken too many times to be on sturdy ground.

"Keep in mind, dear friend, that once you are actually sitting on the bench, your faith will be restored and the Constitution will make a comeback. Here," he said, redirecting the conversation to a clipped article from the one of the smaller piles on his desk. "I want you to read this, Thrasher, see what you think." He tilted his chair back and watched closely for his response.

Thrasher took the offered page. Before reading it he said, "Sebastian, no one brings the English language to life like you do. Even on your worst day you can induce any functioning brain to sit up and take nourishment."

Sebastian accepted the compliment with a shrug and a wry smile. "Hyperbole doesn't suit a judge, my friend."

"I don't exaggerate. Besides, I'm not a judge yet and probably won't be if certain members of the Commission on Judicial Appointments can find some way to block me."

Sebastian agreed with a grim nod.

Thrasher cleared his throat, crackled the newspaper with a flourish and began reading. He was unaware that his friend was watching for his reaction, also needing affirmation that Thrasher Cole was the man for the job someone had to do. And soon.

Thrasher's posture was ramrod straight; his hands steady. His nails were well-trimmed and strong, his hands large enough to grasp people from the edge of death. Unlike his face, the skin on his hands was dry, crinkled, and prematurely aged, a result of the blaze that had burned the hands and blackened the lungs of this former San Francisco Fire Department Captain.

"Mm, Leigh Barnes. I recall reading a few of his articles in *National Review*. He's pretty good."

"As a future member of the Ninth District Court, counselor, I'd advise you to be sure of your facts before you render a decision. *He* is a woman, and an attractive one at that."

"He is? I mean, she is? Well, wrap my knuckles and call me a chauvinist," he said with a exaggerated twang. "I guess those newspaper editorials are right. I really am just a redneck in a cashmere jacket." He scanned the page again. "This is from a Minneapolis paper. Was Leigh Barnes the reason for your frequent trips to fly-over country?"

Sebastian hesitated, obviously editing his response. "Yes and no. I saw Leigh Barnes two years ago when I went to Minneapolis to pursue a personal project. As it turned out, Leigh Barnes provided me with several vital pieces of a puzzle I've been trying to put together for eight years. She's a good writer, maybe even a great one. And she's a damned brave investigative reporter with a unique take on politics and politicians. I've seen her pick up B.S. from an opposite coast."

His smile was that of a proud professor applauding his pupil's acquisition of all the knowledge he imparted. Or perhaps that of a doting uncle. It puzzled Thrasher. "How long did you say you've known her?"

As if he didn't hear the question, Sebastian said, "She also has an old soul, a very good one, I believe. I sat daily with her at the trial of a most brutal murderer. We became quite good friends in those weeks."

"Ms. Barnes is lucky. She didn't have to battle a four-alarm fire to get your attention."

Sebastian's face fell; his mustache with it.

Thrasher failed to notice. "*America in Review* was the only magazine I ever read consistently, and all six of your books were part of my library, so when you walked into my hospital room with that bottle of vintage wine in your hand, I nearly had a relapse."

"Certainly not my intent," he said gruffly.

"Meeting you was one heck of a shot in the arm for this wounded old firefighter."

Sebastian's eyes focused on something beyond Thrasher. "Real heroes are a dying breed. I was determined to meet you before another blaze further cut the herd."

Thrasher ignored the compliment, leaned forward, his elbows resting on his bad knees. "I found it hard to believe you thought it necessary to introduce yourself when that face of yours is as familiar as Ernest Hemingway's in the literary world. And eerily similar in appearance, I might add."

"Personally, I don't see the resemblance," he puffed, smoothing his thick beard with mottled hands. "But I'll consider it a compliment; that is, if it is his younger years with which you make the comparison."

"He died when he was sixty-two. By my calculations, you've already got five years on him."

Sebastian cleared his throat and switched positions in his chair, trying to get comfortable, which was impossible whenever he was talking about himself. "I will neither confirm nor deny your calculations."

Thrasher was once again reminded that his friend dealt only with facts in his magazine and his books, but as far as his past was concerned, it remained as sketchy as an artist's pad. No matter what polite interrogation techniques he'd used in the years he'd known Sebastian, Thrasher had gotten little more information than what was written on the inside cover of his six book jackets.

"Now, you want to tell me why I'm here?"

Sebastian cocked his head like a wary spaniel.

Thrasher's eyes narrowed. "Leigh Barnes isn't going to be one of your matchmaking projects as well as your assistant is she?"

Sebastian looked genuinely startled. "What would ever give you that idea?"

"Cynthia Hardaway. And the numerous other single and attractive women you seem to be able to produce as the need arises."

His eyes crinkled mischievously at the corners. "Suggesting that you have an occasional dinner with a beautiful blond is not normally considered a bad plan. And from what you've told me of Chandler, she would not choose a life of solitary celibacy for you."

Thrasher shifted uneasily in his chair. "My wife never made choices for anyone but herself. She never would have told me what or who was best for me." His pause was significant. "But she should have."

"Her death is still very fresh in your mind, isn't it?"

"Still fresh, still incomprehensible." He shook his head as if to remove the awful images of her lifeless, bleeding body lying in the street. He veered away from the site. "How is Cynthia doing? It's been a while since I've seen her."

Sebastian's expression was unreadable. "As beautiful as ever. As determined as ever. Cynthia was born to be in advertising. She's a true believer, so she can sell like a son-of-a-gun. Her predecessor lacked imagination — and any discernible core beliefs. Those things are essential when you're selling a philosophy. I'm very lucky to have her on the payroll."

"She started here when she was very young, didn't she?"

He was quiet for so long Thrasher worried that he'd been too candid. Sebastian was very protective of the woman. Strangely so.

"Very young, very needy."

"I don't think I'd call a beautiful blonde worth a considerable fortune needy, but she gives you full credit for her success in the business."

"Her parents' money bought her nothing but pain, I'm afraid."

"It bought her father one heck of a lot of power. There's no one in San Francisco who doesn't kiss his behind with regularity for fear being of getting on the wrong end of his power."

Thrasher had good reason to distrust Leif Hardaway. He had to wonder what reason his daughter had. "Is Leigh Barnes young and needy as well?" He realized how indifferent that sounded. "I mean, there are hundreds of well-known writers and reporters who would give their souls to work with you. Why this woman?"

"When you meet her you'll understand that she would give up her soul for no one and that she needs very little direction from me or anyone. I would have hired her two years ago, but we both felt a little seasoning and a healthy dose of experience would be beneficial before she became my assistant editor."

"So this seasoned beauty is arriving when?"

"She'll be on a flight early this evening. Leigh's spent the last few days with her parents in Minneapolis. They're not very happy about seeing their only daughter settle on the left coast. I visited with them on my last trip to Minneapolis. Very lovely people and quite vocal in their distaste for

California's 'progressive' political and cultural agendas. The only thing in which they take comfort is that she will be thousands of miles farther away from Jude Orcus."

"Jude Orcus," Thrasher repeated, frowning. "Oh, yes, the columnist who killed all those people in order to concoct heartrending stories on the homeless. The Orcus trial was the one you attended for all those weeks with Leigh Barnes, right?"

Sebastian closed his eyes and nodded.

"A mass murderer nominated for a Pulitzer," Thrasher said, shaking his head. "Profile fits. Only difference is that this designated hero made sure other people's hearts bled more profusely than his own." His smile was rueful. "There I go again, being judgmental. Forgive me; guess I'm just trying to get the feel of it."

"This is one case you would have judged far more harshly than the silk-robed woman who let him off so lightly. But I'm getting ahead of myself. Leigh Barnes was indeed the one who uncovered the heinous deeds of our latter day saint, Jude Orcus. Wasn't too pleasant a discovery, either, according to her and the trial evidence. Says she still has nightmares. Can't say I blame her, especially since while she's tossing and turning, Orcus is sleeping peacefully in a posturepedic hospital bed instead of on a cot on death row."

"He killed all those people and he didn't at least go to prison. Amazing."

"Not unusual, especially in that state. Many of those fine citizens brought very liberal philosophies with them from their Scandinavian homelands. Along with other distasteful things, I might add. Like lutefisk," he said, holding his nose and puckering his lips. "Being forced to politely digest that gelatinous fish even once is what I deem capital punishment. In this case, the jurors opted for the lesser sentence; life in a cushy hospital with Jude serving as a real-life case study for a whole lot of compassionate doctors armed only with a battery of Rorschach tests. Or perhaps in this case, the Minnesota Multiphasic."

"Doesn't seem that long ago that I was a case study and a candidate for the loony bin." Thrasher pulled himself slowly out of the chair and stood, appearing almost as indomitable in his tailored dark suit as in his firefighter's uniform. "I failed all the tests the first time around."

"That was years ago, my friend, and they don't nominate failures to sit on the bench. You proved that not only can you survive a terrible personal tragedy, you can revise your goals and then proceed to attain them without losing focus or faith. Becoming a successful lawyer, a partner in a winery, and soon a judge, all within the space of eight years, does not fit the MO of a victim or a candidate for the loony bin."

"Jake Malloy is the brains and the taste buds behind the winery. After his stint in Washington my friend, the Senator, decided that growing grapes was a lot more fulfilling than growing the government. Pays a lot better too, if you know what you're doing, and Jake always knows what he's doing, whether it's being the 49ers best-ever receiver or the most informed and principled politician you can find. He's had even more careers than I," he said with a laugh. It quickly dissipated. "And lost a wife and two children. Being a successful survivor is not all it's cracked up to be, Sebastian. I'd still rather be a lowly civil servant and have my wife and child. Jake wouldn't think twice about making the trade either." Thrasher headed for the door before his memories could reach flash point. "I'm leaving before the self-pity really piles up. I hope Leigh Barnes turns out to be as much of an asset to you and the magazine as Cynthia."

"Thrasher," Sebastian said softly. For such a large man he was graceful in pulling himself from his chair. He came around the desk and followed Thrasher to the door. He put a delaying hand on his broad shoulder. "I'm going to ask you to do something you normally don't do."

"Buy season tickets to the opera?" he deadpanned, trying to leave on a lighter note.

Sebastian chuckled without smiling. "No, and not the symphony either. No, it's more, uh, well, sensitive."

"I've been accused of being sensitive on occasion," he grinned.

Although he was only a couple of inches shorter than Thrasher, Sebastian was twice the girth. The former firefighter had urged his heavyweight friend to start working out, but Sebastian's response was, "Exercise is not one of my passions. Whereas you, my young friend, exult in lifting heavy weights, winning racquetball games, and beating just about everybody at everything athletic, I remain comfortable in the belief that if God had wanted me to run myself silly, he would have given me feet sans hammer toes and ingrown toenails." After that, Thrasher kept his council.

"I'm referring to a sensitive area; a discrete investigation into the fire that killed Cynthia's brother, Jason, and nearly killed Cynthia and her friend Gracie. You and Johnny could have easily have been casualties as well."

"That blaze nearly destroyed the entire China Basin area." His thick brows arched. "Why now, after all these years?"

"I can't be specific, but trust me, this could have repercussions that will resonate all the way from the China Basin to China."

The cynic in him held back any enthusiasm, while the attorney in him started itching to chase the ambulance. "You know what my suspicions were at the time, but I couldn't get anyone to listen. But, okay, I'll start digging around again. Now that the reign of corruption in the fire department has waned, I think I can get more definitive answers than I got eight years ago."

"I don't want you jeopardizing your career, Thrasher. I don't want you to get on the wrong side of the right people. Just nose around a little, and if you don't come up with anything, don't worry about it."

"What makes you think anyone would listen now?"

"Time has a way of revealing secrets. Emotions were running very high at the time. You were blaming the fire on arson, Leif Hardaway was blaming the fire department, and the Chief was blaming you for bringing the department's incompetence to light, making any charges Leif made that much more serious. As you suggested to me then, arson would have benefitted only Leif Hardaway, the grieving father. Although, finding himself with two blocks of prime San Francisco real estate on which he could now build would hardly compare with losing his only son and nearly losing his daughter as well. Besides, a very wealthy and generous man is normally spared scrutiny in this city. There isn't one charity I can name that hasn't benefitted from his largesse."

Thrasher's eyes flashed. "He's generous all right. Especially when it comes to his friends in China. The press gave about one week of tepid news coverage to his sale of top-secret nuclear technology to the Chinese Communists, despite the fact that he also sold them the ammunition to blow us all to hell. If he has his way, our country will be as defenseless as he is rich."

"Nor does he lose any sleep over his Chinese business partner's practice of 'crowning' helpless babies in an effort to restrict families to one child. How anyone could do business with men who condone plunging a syringe full of formaldehyde into the soft spot on the head of a baby at the moment of birth, is incomprehensible."

Thrasher had no intention of getting into a debate on that subject with Sebastian. His friend lost his cool whenever the topic came up. It seemed to be the only thing that could puncture his composure. "I don't like his politics from the ground up to his missile trajectories, so you know if I can put a crimp in his style, I'll help in any way I can." Thrasher massaged his jaw, then ran his smoke-cured hands through his coarse black hair. "I was burned so badly, literally, that I thought I'd never survive. I'd already suffered with Jake through the loss of his wife and kids when I lost my own wife and daughter, so I was hanging on to my sanity by a thread." Then, taking a deep breath and straightening his shoulders he said, "I'll help in any way I can."

"Leigh Barnes could be of some help to us on this one too."

"What could she possibly know about that fire? Or Leif Hardaway?"

"Probably more than she realizes." He reached up and put his hand on Thrasher's back. "I've taken up enough of your time." He glanced down at his watch. "I'd like you to meet Leigh Barnes once she's settled in, Thrasher. I think you'd like her. In fact, she should be contacting me any time now to let me know when her plane is scheduled to land. She's had a rough go of things for a very long time. I hope she hasn't had any complications in her travel plans."

Chapter Five

"It's a friend from the *Sentinel*, Mom," Leigh shouted, hoping the brusqueness of her tone would dissuade her mother from interrupting. *Please, Dear Lord*, she prayed silently, *keep my mother in the kitchen.*

But Ellen Barnes heard the anxiety in her child's voice. She didn't even take time to wipe her hands before her sixth sense and low-heeled sensible shoes clicked into gear. In the seconds it took her to reach the front entry she had dried her hands on her blue- and yellow-flowered apron and brushed wisps of graying hair and traces of flour from her guileless face. When she saw Jude Orcus standing so near her child, her face became as bleached as the flour that powdered it. She swallowed the lump in her throat before saying, "Hello, Mr. Orcus."

"I'm flattered, Mrs. B., I don't believe we've ever met. Formally, anyway. Guess my reputation has preceded me." He tapped his head with one dirty nail in a gesture of bringing forth an answer. "Of course, you were in the court room watching your darling daughter carve me up like a Thanksgiving turkey. Reminds me, I don't believe I've had lunch yet."

The smile he spread on his face was as oily as his complexion. "I'd be delighted if you and Leigh would join me in a little light lunch, Mother Barnes," he fawned, reaching for her hand and licking his swollen lips.

Ellen offered it reluctantly, pulled it away too quickly.

One hand cupped his chin and the other balanced on his hip in an introspective pose. His grinning lips were as full and red as if they'd been slathered with lip gloss. He licked them again as he ran his slender fingers through his hair. It was dirty blond and tightly curled around his head like a woolly stocking cap. *A cap well-suited to a stalker*, Ellen thought with new alarm.

Leigh smiled weakly at her mother, trying not to project her fears of what offal Jude's decaying brain might dump on them both. Anger began to clear her head, free her mind. Judgment day had come for Leigh Barnes, but that didn't mean her mother had to suffer for the sins of her daughter. Ellen said too brightly, "Leigh and I would love to have lunch with you, but we were just going out, Mr. Orcus. To visit her aunt and uncle," she added. "I'm sure Leigh would rather not cut your visit short, but they are expecting us. For a barbecue," she lied brightly.

"Yes, I'm sorry, Jude," Leigh agreed, thinking, *Nice try, mother, but Jude has no intention of aborting his mission just because of a Barnes family cookout.*

"I have very little time with my family before I head to California, Jude, and I haven't finished packing, and…" She self-consciously ran her slippery hands down her hips, wishing her size-10 jeans were size-20 bib overalls. "I know you heard that I have a new job there as assistant editor of *America in Review*, in part thanks to you, Jude, since you were always so kind to me, supportive of my work and—"

He cut her off in mid-sentence. "Moonbeam."

"Excuse me?" Leigh felt prickles of fear scampering up her spine.

"You heard me, Leigh. I said, Moonbeam. That nickname really caught on after you used it to describe me in your exposé."

Ellen quickly responded. "Oh, Leigh wasn't referring to you, Mr. Orcus; she merely mentioned that poor woman who wandered the streets of our former hometown, Buffalo Falls, for so many years." Her frightened eyes shifted to her daughter. "That's the Moonbeam he must be referring to, dear," her mother offered, prompting Leigh and trying to deflect the daggers Jude's voice and body language had aimed at her child. "I recall that she mentioned Moonbeam's name only once, then the press made the connection. The poor dear passed away several years ago," she added, obviously hoping that the woman's death might somehow end the comparison between the two.

Leigh nodded, silently thanking her mother for buying them precious moments, moments she could use to gauge the type and degree of attack she knew would be coming. She silently prayed for a miracle. No mere mortal could take down Jude Orcus and keep him down. The fact that he was standing in her mother's living room instead of squirming under restraints in a mental institution was proof of that.

She took a step backward and affectionately put her arm around her mother's waist, drawing her close. She wasn't sure which one of them was trembling more, but she was sure of one thing: Jude would have to go through her to get to her mother.

Leigh tilted her head and smiled, as if reminiscing over a childhood friendship. "Moonbeam was sort of a street performer we used to follow as children. Well, actually, she performed mainly for her own amusement; she delivered her monologue all day and well into the night, oblivious to her audience. She chose to be an observer rather than a participant in life. She was harmless, sort of a unique institution in our small town."

As soon as the word *institution* was out of her mouth, she wanted to rip out her tongue and wrap it around her throat.

"I'll lay odds she was in one too. An institution, I mean. That's where they usually put crazy people." Jude's voice rose higher and louder with each word.

"No, no, she was just eccentric; there was no need to put her in an institution," Leigh assured him, keeping her voice even. "The similarity was that you were also an observer, which is what made you...makes you such a talented writer."

But it was clear he couldn't hear her above the cacophony of his breaking brain. "I forget, how did you describe me then, Leigh? Eccentric? Slightly mad? How 'bout whacko?"

He moved toward them, forcing them to back off the marble and onto the hardwood floor, and then onto her mother's new Persian rug. A few more inches and he would be desecrating the hand-made rug her mother had scrimped and saved to buy after pressing her nose against the store window for more than a year. Each bit of territory they relinquished he captured, as he continued to invade the privacy and precious space all rational humans reserve to ward off bodily threat.

It was clear he was enjoying their increasing desperateness. That didn't surprise Leigh; Jude knew fear and desperation better than anyone. He'd described it in great detail every day in his column in the *Twin City Sentinel.* Under his byline, Jude solved crimes the police could not, revealed monsters never before unmasked. *Crimes of the City* had been the most widely read column in the Twin Cities. When it became syndicated, the entire country got hooked on it. He'd even been nominated for a Pulitzer Prize for his expertise in chronicling real crimes, real criminals, and the victims upon whom they preyed.

While Jude Orcus bided his time, all the events of that horrible time fast-forwarded across Leigh's mind. She was reeling with the recollections she thought had faded in those two years since she'd last seen him. Yet every scene was as bright and clear as if each had been played out only yesterday.

Chapter Six

Leigh had been thrilled when she was assigned the job of writing the piece. She was as impressed and in awe of Jude Orcus as the rest of his readers, and curious as to his background. But in researching, she found his résumé both confusing and porous. The blanks were more tantalizing than the facts, so she dug a little deeper. What she unearthed would, at warp speed, change the course of both of their lives.

With the ignorance of youth and the confidence of an innocent, she had poured over manuals on reconnaissance, donned dark clothing, and played Sherlock Holmes to the hilt. Her subject was either very innocent or incredibly arrogant, because in her two-month *Nancy Drew* adventure, Jude never once looked back. If he had, he surely would have seen the amateur sleuth as clearly as a patrol car's flashing lights. In only sixty days she discovered more about evil and Jude Orcus than she had ever wanted to know. In her interviews with the street people the compassionate columnist was supposedly saving, she discovered large rusting chinks in her hero's armor.

"Ma'am, that creep ain't no friend of ours."

The homeless man sitting on the curb was a study in gray; gray pants, gray shirt, gray hair, and a gray complexion. It would be impossible to tell what color all had been previous to the years of neglected hygiene, drug and alcohol abuse, and filthy cardboard beds.

"I seen him kill an old woman and blame it on my friend Jimmy, who was snoring behind the garbage can right next to hers." His voice, words, and stance were shaky, yet he was able to convince her that his account was truthful.

"You saw this man" she asked, showing him the picture that headed Jude's column, "kill the woman?"

"He stuck her good with a knife, then he put that knife in old Arnold's hand. Arnie slept with it real comfortable until the police got a tip and found him with the murder weapon. I shoulda done something when they took him away, but that guy Orcus was always lurking around, and I thought he'd get me next if I showed myself or got too nosy. He don't think anyone sees what he does to get stuff to write about, but we do. We may be drunks and druggies, but we ain't blind. He's gettin' so sure of himself, he don't even look before he kills. That's one cold and cocky SOB. But don't tell anyone I told you," he begged. "I'll swear you're lyin'."

Gus Theron's story was not unique. Once he talked and lived to tell, the rest of his nocturnal buddies opened up to her. She interviewed at least twenty homeless people with poor nutrition but excellent eyes.

She had her story; it was time to go to the police. And time to tell her boyfriend Bill what she'd been up to. Naturally, he'd begun to assume the worst; that she was seeing someone else on all those nights when she was so busy washing clothes, hair, floors, and her car that she didn't have time to see him.

He was understandably livid. "Why the hell didn't you tell me what you were up to?"

"You would have given me all kinds of very good reasons for not doing it. And I was afraid I might agree with you," she added sheepishly.

He shook his head, but a little smile crept into his boyishly handsome face. "I should take you over my knee and spank some sense into you."

"Nothing kinky till after the wedding. We agreed," she teased, hoping he'd forgive her duplicity.

He put his sinewy arms around her and hugged her so tightly she could hardly breathe. When he let her go there were tears in his eyes. "I can't lose you, Leigh. We belong together."

"You're not going to lose me."

He roughly ran his fingers through his hair but, as usual, the light brown wisps fell back onto his forehead, giving him the little Dutch Boy look she adored. "We're notifying the police right now, Leigh. This is a lot more than you bargained for if you can believe Gus and his friends. And God, Leigh, I do believe them. This guy may be a prize-winning writer, but he's certifiable, and crazy enough to come after you if he hears that you've been asking questions. When he knows you got answers, he's going to make sure you don't pass them along to the police."

"I'm not as stupid as I've made myself sound with all this cloak and dagger stuff."

He took her shoulders and held them tightly, a testament to his determination.

"We're not going to wait any longer, Leigh. I realize this isn't the best time in the world with the Olympic trials coming up, but life is too damn short and I love you too much."

"Is that a proposal?"

"Yes. And there will be no long engagement. I'm calling Reverend Thoreson right after you call the police."

"So my life has to be threatened for you to make a commitment?" she taunted.

"Here's another threat, Leigh. If you don't agree to marry me, I'm going to….to…" he searched for the proper punishment.

"To what?"

"Keep right on asking until you say yes," he said, crushing her to his chest and kissing her as if there were no homicides, no Jude Orcus, and no tomorrow.

She pulled away long enough to answer, "There is nothing in the world I want more than to marry you. I've loved you since the tenth grade. Even before Mr. Smithback began the family life section in our biology books, where all the wonders of the human body could be seen in living color. I couldn't wait to see if your wonders were that colorful."

"Then why did you?" He colored with his prurient thoughts.

"Attending colleges hundreds of miles apart sure helped."

"Speak for yourself. How many cold showers did you take?"

"Hey, I was the one taking the big gamble. A handsome track star at the University of Minnesota was the catch of the day for half the coeds I saw lusting after you in your short shorts and sweat-soaked t-shirt. Then when you made the Olympic trials, I was afraid you'd dump me like a hot rock."

"How many times did we break up?"

"Three, I think, but only one breakup lasted for more than two days."

"We just couldn't stay apart, could we?"

"And now we won't have to. Enough is enough." She snuggled against him. "I don't want our lips to be all shot to heck before we ever make it to the altar, or we'll have to mime our vows."

"I'm tired of reigning in all the passion I feel for you, Leigh."

"It will be worth the wait, my darling."

He grinned like the teenager she'd fallen in love with, but held her at arm's length. "I'm not kidding, Leigh, pick up the phone, cuz I'm not leaving here until I hear sirens and see uniforms."

"Okay, I'll save the metropolis from Jude Orcus, but what about you? Don't you have to be at practice?"

"Damn, I didn't realize what time is it. But I can't leave you here. I'll just wait till the cops get here?"

"Believe me, Jude doesn't have a clue that he's been found out. Now go, please. Since I'm going to be taking your name, I want all the glory that comes along with it when you win that gold medal."

His eyebrows formed a question mark. "I guess you're right. I don't want to screw up my tryouts. But I just don't feel comfortable leaving you."

She kissed him soundly on the lips. "Very soon you won't ever have to leave me again, Bill. I promise."

Leigh waved good-bye, then did exactly as he'd advised her. The inspector to whom she told the story was incredulous, but handled the bizarre information with professionalism. He advised her to stay put until they got there and promised they would put out an all-points bulletin and make certain Jude was fresh out of material for his column.

Minutes after she hung up she began processing the words that would appear in her next column. "The victims about whom Jude Orcus wrote so passionately and caringly had in actuality been created then destroyed by him — which explained his prompt arrival on so many crime scenes. Like an arsonist, Jude provided his own fireworks. He designed his own sets, chose his own actors, and choreographed their beatings and killings in a brilliant orchestration of the resulting chaos. He had murdered for his material, brutalized for the edification of his readers, and basked in the glory of his perceived goodness. Not only were his words a lie, his entire life was a lie." She would have to wait several hours longer to add, "The police discovered all his current personal documents were falsified. He too had apparently been created out of whole cloth."

It was ten o'clock. The police had come and gone, except for the stocky patrolman outside her door. When the phone rang, she knew it would be Bill.

"That's incredible, Leigh," Bill said after she'd read him what she'd written. "There's no stopping you now, honey. Whether you like it or not, you're destined for fame and fortune. Once the national papers get a hold of this, you'll be off and running."

"Then that will make two of us. How did the practice go?"

"I don't know if it was the adrenaline rush from finding out about Jude Orcus or your saying you'll marry me, but I knocked four seconds off my time."

She could hear the pride in his voice. This day had truly been the best of times and the worst of times. "That's wonderful, Bill. There's no doubt in my mind you'll qualify."

"What did the police have to say? Have they picked him up yet?"

"They said they'd notify me as soon as they do."

"Can I come over now? I will never get to sleep after all this. How 'bout I pick up a combo pizza from Tony's?"

"I won't sleep either, and I've got a chaperone right outside the door, so how can I say no?"

"I've got an engagement present for you, Leigh."

"Already? What is it?"

"You'll see when I get there. I love you, Leigh"

"I love you too, Bill. Now and forever."

At that moment in time she had it all: the man she loved, the career she desired, and the prospect of national recognition for her investigative reporting. The only thing she didn't yet have that night was Bill's engagement gift.

She did receive it, eventually, only not from Bill. She still had it: the large gold medal with the image of a runner in the middle, hanging from a red, white and blue ribbon. Tucked in the back of the frame was his note: *When I make the Olympic team, I'll have to take this back and replace it with the real thing.*

The policeman who gave her the engagement gift was very kind. He had first wiped off the blood.

Chapter Seven

Leigh was now paying the price for having it all, even briefly. She was paying for her diligent reporting, her crafty sleuthing, her innocent belief that her future was secure. She had been so sure of everything. Now she was sure only that the price was too high. No amount of awards from the police department and praise from her peers, no offers of choice editorial positions and fast-track career opportunities could compensate for her loss and the impossible position in which she now found herself.

Leigh nudged her mother farther away from the mass of throbbing veins and twitching muscles that Jude was becoming. The transformation was occurring too rapidly; he was allowing her too little time to think, to act. She pulled her mother along with her, their steps silenced by the thick matting under the expensive rug.

"Where is everybody?"

All three started at the sound of his voice. None of them had heard Larry Barnes drive up and enter the house through the garage door, despite the fact that his bulk made stepping lightly virtually impossible. Her father's massive six-foot, two-hundred-pound body suddenly filled the room and offered her hope that somehow they could get out of this alive. In his thirty years of coaching football, first in his hometown of Buffalo Falls, and for the last six years at Beaver Lake High, Coach Barnes had kept in shape by shaping up hundreds of uncooperative young men who continually challenged him, themselves, and his methods of discipline. Those years had not deprived him of anything but his hair. He was still strong in body and faith. Leigh saw her father hesitate, taking careful stock of the situation before moving confidently toward them.

"Daddy, I'd like you to meet Jude Orcus," she said in a shrill introduction, her eyes pleading with him. "I know how much you enjoyed his column in the *Sentinel*," she encouraged.

"Of course, of course," he nodded enthusiastically. "What brings a Pulitzer Prize nominee to our little town of Beaver Lake?" he asked, playing along.

"A shiny black Mercedes SLC, Coach Barnes." Jude's oily smile had gone dry, and he was eyeing her father with unconcealed hostility.

Larry accepted the sarcasm with a convincing chuckle. He'd counseled too many disturbed high school teens not to recognize a possible hostile takeover, and Jude Orcus was not only hostile, he was crazy as a loon. "A mode of transportation we'd all choose — if accompanied by a pile of cash to keep it running and rust-free in these harsh Minnesota winters," he joked. "What year is it, may I ask?"

"This is 2001," Jude responded, without a trace of humor. "Two years to the day since your charming daughter put me on sabbatical. Now, why don't we all sit down," he suggested. Strongly. "Level the playing field, so to speak."

My God, she thought, *he even knows my father. He's been researching my entire family*. "What game are we playing, Jude?" Leigh's bright blue eyes were no longer blinking spasmodically, her long legs were no longer coltish. God help her, she would stand up. She would hold up. She had to.

"How about musical chairs? You take those two!" he abruptly ordered Larry and Ellen. "Please, I insist!" His smile was menacing as he indicated the two club chairs on either side of the antique table which had once belonged to Ellen's great-grandmother. Strangely, that piece of her heritage brought everything into perspective for Leigh. The inevitability of it all — the living and the dying, and the joy and suffering in between — it was not hers to control. There was no stopping the force of nature, the passing of time, and the will of God. Or Jude Orcus. He was hanging onto his sanity by a thread, and once it broke, she knew he would take her down into the depths of hell along with him.

Leigh stiffened her back. She had feared this day would come as soon as his sentence was pronounced. The judge, in sonorous tones, stated her belief that many radical Christians took the Bible too literally; that an eye for an eye was open to interpretation in a diverse society, but in her courtroom such medieval notions would not be tolerated. So, instead of being sentenced to the gas chamber, Jude settled into a softly padded and very expensive room in the best psychiatric hospital in the state. Insanity was an automatic get-out-of-jail-free card; Leigh knew that. But who had given him the get-out-of-the-nuthouse-free card? Why hadn't someone notified her that he'd either escaped or been released, especially since he'd boasted to everyone in the courtroom that one day he would come back for her?

"I am a genius, Leigh. My IQ is higher than all of your family's combined. I didn't like being called Moonbeam, Leigh. Not one bit," he said, playfully pinching her chin. He slowly raised the gun and aimed it at Leigh's head, bringing a chorus of gasps from them all.

"Now, let's all get comfortable, shall we? I want everyone to have a good seat for the show." He paused, like an actor readying himself for a big line. "How sad that Bill couldn't be here with us today. I guess you would be Mrs. Anderson now, wouldn't you, Leigh. Instead you're still unwed and probably missing the dickens out of that cool dude, right?"

"You didn't know Bill." A cold new dread crept up her spine. "Did you?"

"We met briefly," he said, pausing once again for effect. "Or rather my fender met his head. It was too brief an introduction, but then I was in a bit of a hurry. I had just learned from one of the chattier homeless bitches that you had stuck your perky little nose into my business, and had in effect closed the doors on it. You definitely put a crimp in my life plan, so I thought, what the heck, an eye for an eye and all that. I knew Billy would want to be close to his little sweetheart, so I waited at your apartment. I watched the police do their thing. So predictable. So are people in love. I didn't have to wait long at all for young Bill to come running."

"You murdered Bill." She whispered the words reverently, as if she were once again in the chapel, looking down at her beloved Bill lying in a satin-lined casket; the man she had loved, the man who had loved her. And, she now realized, the man who had died because of her.

"Enough of this morbid reminiscing. Let's all focus on the present. Just do as I say and we'll all get along just fine."

Once her parents were uneasily seated in the club chairs, Jude forced Leigh down onto the sofa across from them. He sat down beside her and snuggled cozily, one arm clutching her, the other clutching the gun. Out of the corner of her eye Leigh saw her father glancing warily from her to her mother and back again, begging for some sort of signal from either his wife or his daughter.

All she could offer him was a prayer. Not even Larry Barnes — the strongest, smartest dad in the world — could save them now. She knew her mother would be praying. She hoped her dad was too.

Helen gasped, and Larry jerked forward in his chair, spreading his arms in a signal of surrender, his palms up. "Let's just talk about this, Jude. I know my daughter very well; you know her too, and you know she would never knowingly hurt anyone. She is not bad person. Nor, of course, are you," he added judiciously. "Everyone makes mistakes, and I'm sure you would do things differently too if given the opportunity to change circumstances. If she made reference to Moonbeam in her articles or in the courtroom, she merely meant that the woman also was sometimes, ah, misunderstood. She lived happily in another galaxy none of us could reach, thus the name Moonbeam. I remember your being interviewed once on television when you said that you often went outside your head and moved into someone else's — usually the criminals you described and analyzed so well in your columns. So well, in fact, did you enter other's minds, that you were nominated for a Pulitzer Prize for your insights." He quickly added, "The fact that you didn't keep it does not negate its importance. Really, Moonbeam was a harmless nickname, even an affectionate one. Now, please let me have the gun, Jude. You once cared about Leigh; you helped her on several stories at the *Sentinel.* You were a mentor to her. You don't want to frighten her, do you?"

"No, I don't," Jude answered. His smile oozed with sincerity. "I want to kill her."

Hearing the harsh intake of breath from her father and the helpless groan from her mother, Leigh realized she would have to act. Now. "Jude, we need to talk. Alone. Can we take a ride? Please?"

"No, Leigh! No!" her mother shouted.

As Leigh rose from the sofa, she reached out for Jude's hand. The moment she did, Larry sprung out of his chair and lunged. Grabbing Jude's arm, he fought to wrest the gun from his grasp, or failing in that, at least point it away from his daughter's head. As they struggled, Leigh pushed her mother out of the line of fire and reached for a brass lamp that sat on the table on her left. She hurled it at Jude, but not before the gun went off.

The lamp crashed loudly against the wall. Leigh fell softly to the floor in graceful slow motion, like a dying swan in a ballet, her arms furled out like wings, and her legs curled unnaturally under her.

Jude kept his balance and re-aimed his gun as both mother and father rushed to their fallen child. "Dear God, please let my child be all right!" Helen cried, kneeling down and using her apron as a swab, frantically attempting to stop the flow of blood in her daughter's temple. She sobbed softly as she pressed the wound. She pressed harder while the deep-red blood transformed the pale yellow and blue of the apron into muddy shades of orange and green.

"Sit back down! Both of you!" Jude shouted. He pointed the gun at one and then the other, until they were forced to obey. He glanced down at Leigh, her still body softly curled, her slender arms and perfectly shaped legs at grotesque angles on the floor at his feet. His fascination with her body was palpable, drawing low moans from both Larry and Helen. He glared at them as if they were the ones who had created the mess in which he found himself. Grabbing the apron from Helen and handing it to Larry, he ordered, "Coach, I want you to tie little wifie to the chair. Tight! Oh, excuse me. Tightly! Good writers are always conscious of proper grammar."

Larry shook his head at the man's degree of insanity, refusing to do the devil's bidding. Jude punished his disobedience by yanking his arm, pulling him down, then striking him on the back of the head with the butt of his gun. Larry swayed but remained on his feet, the light of hope that always shone in his eyes flickering, fading into nothingness. Tears fell from his eyes and filled the deep creases in his face; anguished sobs escaped from his pinched lips.

Jude supervised the procedure closely, his breath on Larry's neck and his finger on the trigger, as husband bound wife. When at last Larry pulled the knot on the apron sash, Jude checked the tightness. Satisfied, he commanded, "Now sit!"

As if he'd rehearsed it a hundred times, Jude pulled out a pair of pantyhose from his pocket, like a magician pulling a silk from his sleeve. "Just call me a souvenir-seeker," he snickered, waving the stockings in their faces. "One fair-haired nurse is going to find herself minus one pair of pantyhose. I always like to take a little something to remember them by. The ladies, I mean."

He used the pantyhose to tie Larry's hands behind his back, then he pulled a handkerchief from his pants pocket and stuffed it roughly into his protesting mouth. Not satisfied with his security measures, he pulled a roll of rope from the seemingly endless supply of articles he had stuffed in his pants pocket and retied them both. He then snatched a crocheted doily from the end table on which the lamp had stood and roughly thrust it into Helen's mouth. He didn't stop shoving until she started to gag.

He laughed delightedly as he watched her choke and sputter. Her eyes were wide with terror. "Know how they make paté, Helen? You'll find this interesting. Leigh once told me that you're a gourmet cook, so this is something you really should know. The manner in which you force-feed a goose is to stuff her all the way to her gullet until she's plumped and primed. Then you slaughter the little bugger, slice up her liver, cook it up, and serve it on a silver platter with some tangy gherkins, maybe a nice Chardonnay. Sound kinda tasty to you, Helen?"

His madness was complete, Helen realized. He would let her daughter die unless they did something. Helen's eyes pleaded with her husband's in a silent invocation.

His eyes mirrored her pain and fear, but there was something else there that was more horrifying. Resignation. Larry Barnes had dealt all his life with unbalanced young people, many of whom did dreadful things no matter how much or how well he counseled them. He had watched as one of his students, Darnel Jones, rushed into his office, pulled out a knife, and cold-bloodedly murdered the pretty young classmate Larry was counseling. The revered coach never even had a chance to shield her or call for help before she was lying at his feet, ghostly white and bleeding. As his daughter was now.

Both of them struggled against the bindings that made them impotent, but Jude was thorough as well as clever. The bonds refused to loosen, no matter how hard they worked at them, yet they continued the struggle as they watched the horror show.

The prize-wining killer began ardently undressing Leigh, playing happily with the rag doll he'd made of the Barnes' little girl. He laboriously unzipped her jeans, fondled them as if they were made of satin, then undid each button on her shirt. With each accomplishment, he breathed a rapturous sigh. His technique of removing her bra was practiced. It took him only a few calculated twists and turns of her lifeless body. He lovingly licked each of her nipples as they were revealed to him, then lingeringly dipped his tongue into her naval, savoring it as if it were filled with ambrosia. He moaned, "Sinny, sin, sin. Oh, sin, I love you." The words were as incomprehensible as the man.

Finally, with agonizing deliberation, he removed the last piece of clothing — her delicate lace panties — while they watched in horror and loathing. Helen wept silently, and Larry clenched his teeth and hands until their tears and rage and Leigh's snow-white nakedness mercifully blinded them.

Jude put one gangly arm under Leigh's waist and hoisted her on his shoulder, like a choice piece of beef. "We'll take that ride now. Sorry I couldn't stay longer, but I have a lot of work to do. Nice seeing you again."

He was nearly out the back door when he looked back at their incredulous eyes and said, "She shouldn't have called me Moonbeam." He disappeared, his precious pack still on his back.

Chapter Eight

The four customers and two bank tellers turned in unison and stared in disbelief as Selmer Torgeson burst into the Security State Bank of Buffalo Falls. Even Hilda Norquist, who was legally blind and stone deaf without her hearing aid turned to full blast, swivelled around at the sound of his wail. Arms jerking like a puppet whose strings had been severed, he sputtered in an uncanny imitation of his 1950 Ford pickup, finally cranking out, "God help us, sweet Jesus! It's crazy! He's crazy!" He shook his head in denial, even as he begged, "Dammit, somebody, call Chief Jacobson! The man outside in the fancy car, he's...he's half naked."

"Which half?" Hilda asked, scrunching up her forehead and adjusting her hearing aid.

"Naked to the waist. And the woman with him, I'm not sure, but I think she's starkers. It's got to be 5 degrees below zero, and she's naked, for Lord's sake."

These startling observations were coming from a man whose human interaction had for seventy plus years been limited to sharing communion at Buffalo Falls Lutheran Church on School Street and standing resignedly in line at the post office. Only his prize-winning hogs had felt the warmth of his hand on their flesh, or heard from his lips any words of affection. Only those who had watched him promenade with his porkers at the Caulfield County fair saw what pride and emotion simmered within his unused heart.

"What are they doing?" Hilda shouted.

"For Goodness sake, not so loud, Hilda! They're parked right outside the bank," he warned, as if the walls had suddenly turned to cellophane. In a lowered voice he explained, "I would have walked right by them, even though that fancy car made me kinda curious, but the feller rolled down his window and motioned me over to the driver's side. He asked me which way to Rochester. When I bent down to the window I just about croaked."

"We'll all be in danger of croaking if we go back out there. I called 911. We should just wait in here until the police arrive," Arvid Musjgerd, the Ford dealer in town, advised. "The man's obviously dangerous, and the woman... well, God only knows what's up with them two."

Selmer ran back to the door, opened it a crack, and peered out. "No, we can't let him get away. That woman, she looked kinda familiar, kinda nice. Naked but nice," he explained. "And too soft to be with such a hard-looking fella. I don't think we can wait for the sheriff." He grabbed a map from the counter and dashed out into the street just as the Mercedes started to pull away from the curb. "Wait, wait, Mister, I've got a map."

The car stopped. Selmer hobbled as fast as his spindly legs would allow until he reached the car window, still rolled all the way down despite the frigid temperatures and the driver's and passenger's state of undress. Selmer shoved his head and the map through the window, hoping to get a better look at the woman. He didn't need his bifocals to see that the poor thing propped up against the window was very white, very still, and as naked from tip to toe as the day her mother birthed her. Although her face was turned away and her neck was at an awkward angle, he could see a round crimson spot on her left temple.

"Uh, see here, you take this highway all the way," he directed, nervously fingering the line on the map and praying Thorvin Jacobson would come screeching up in his squad car. God help them all if he was out at Gerry Gustafson's farm again, drinking coffee and dunking one of her fresh-baked ginger snap cookies, while all hell was breaking loose here in town.

Selmer's adrenaline was pumping like high octane, but he refused to retreat. He'd never been able to save anyone's life before — not even his prize hog, Mame — and he didn't have much time left on the earth for another crack at bein' any kind of a hero, so he damned well wanted to at least give a description of the guy if he did get away. That's the least God would expect of one of his children.

While he watched the pervert checking out the map, Selmer was checking him out. Both fascinated and repulsed, Selmer stared at the man's rubbery lips. His stomach turned over like a trained pup at the sight of them; they were like two big boils that when burst would surely scatter shards of encrusted dead skin to hell and back. When he couldn't stomach the lips anymore, he studied the eyeballs. They were rolling in all directions like cat's eye marbles in a puddle of sewer water. When they stopped and landed square on his own face, he felt a chill pierce his parka like a pitchfork.

When explaining later to the police what happened then, Selmer omitted one fact. The man was not a man at all. He was the Devil, sure as there was a heaven and hell. Even knowing that, Selmer didn't run. He knew that wherever the Devil was, the Lord was there too, keepin' an eye out.

While Selmer was trying to stall the man he later termed "the perp," the driver, without thanks or warning, stepped on the gas and screeched away from the curb.

The hog farmer raced back inside the bank, hoping the Chief and his deputies were already on the case. That poor girl was probably already a corpse, but there was some loving mother or father out there who would want to collect her remains and bury them properly, he was sure.

"Did anyone get ahold of Thorvin?" he asked Emil Thorsrud, the bank's vice president, who had just returned from the Koffee Klatch, where he met daily with Chuck Johnson, the town's farm bureau rep.

"No," Arvid answered, "but Officer Towson called into the station. Apparently he saw a car of your description doing a U-turn at Main and Spruce. He's on it."

"Sure hope he remembered to bring his gun," Selmer said, his normally half-lidded eyes clear and wide.

They wouldn't have the answer to that question for another two hours, when Officer Joe Towson conducted his first television interview for Beth Benson, anchor of the *Ten O'clock News* on Channel 9. Half the population of Buffalo Falls, most of whom had heard the details within minutes of the incident in front of the bank, were tuning in. News travels fast when there is so little of it to go around.

Joe's mind was still occupied with the task of assembling all the facts and faces relating to the arrest, putting them in the proper sequence and level of importance. He reflexively fingered the beard he had been urged by his wife to cultivate. It did help to conceal his relative youth, but it couldn't do a hell of a lot to conceal his inexperience if he screwed this up.

He would have to give his wife Ruthie a real special thanks tonight when he got home. If it weren't for her, he wouldn't be wearing a neatly pressed uniform, and he wouldn't have had the benefit of a bracing breakfast of nine grain toast slathered with gooseberry jam (which she put up with the berries she picked each spring), pulpy orange juice, eggs over medium, and a rasher of bacon. Who would have thought that when he'd begun this sorry day, it would prove so vital that he be well fortified, well-shaved, and well-dressed?

This was probably the most important day in his life. Who knew when he'd ever be in front of a television camera again. He'd never even had his picture in the *Buffalo Falls Leader,* and he'd been on the job nearly six months. Not many photo opportunities in a small town like this. And nothing more challenging than occasionally checking up on the neckers behind the rock quarry to make sure the hanky panky didn't accelerate into a higher statistic of out-of-wedlock births.

He took long, deep breaths as the camera crew assembled and focused on him. Beth, as she had introduced herself to him, showed a lot better in person than on the television, he thought. She didn't seem so untouchable. Not that he would ever touch any woman but Ruthie. It was just that the woman had one of those loose falling, almost messy haircuts Ruthie always complained she couldn't get anywhere but Minneapolis. Beth's pantsuit was cut real smart, like the seamstress really knew her business. He was sure Ruthie would never find one like it at Dottie's Duds. Speculating about clothes and hair would seem mighty fishy to most of his buddies, but he didn't want to forget a thing about this day. Even the smallest detail would be important in the retelling of it.

He stood straighter as the anchor picked up her microphone. She wielded it like a band conductor's baton, directing him where and when to stand, telling him when to start, slow down, speed up, and stop. She was all business, a real professional. But so was he, he reminded himself. He'd just captured an armed and wanted man. And he hadn't even drawn his gun. Of course, Joe hadn't known the U-turning lane jumper was armed and wanted when he'd flashed his red lights and motioned the car to stop.

"When did you first suspect the driver was not just a traffic offender, Officer Towson?" she asked, her voice anchored firmly.

He cleared his throat, arched his back. She was as crisp as a celery stick. And he was surely just as green. "I did my normal traffic stop, walked up slowly to the driver's window, and motioned him to roll it down. As soon as he did, I picked up the smell of alcohol; also noted several cuts and bruises on his face and bare torso. I leaned in farther and appraised the nude woman in the passenger seat. She was very pale and appeared to have a head injury. She also seemed dead to the world." He quickly fast-forwarded, hoping his observation would not be construed as insensitive, since the woman probably was dead by now. "Of course, I immediately thought of spousal abuse, domestic violence, so I pulled the keys from the ignition so he couldn't escape. I walked back to my car at a pretty good clip and called for backup.

Chief Thorvin Jacobson from the County Sheriff's Department responded." Joe put both hands on his hips, one hand fondling the handle of his gun, as if pantomiming his action at the scene. "I waited in my car until he arrived. The whole time I waited, I could see the guy watching me from his rearview mirror." He didn't add that only at that moment did it really hit him: Joe, pay attention, this is for real.

He coughed, cleared his throat. "When the Chief arrived, he tended to the woman, while I conducted a sobriety test on the driver. He failed. I cuffed him, put him in the back of the squad car, and arrested him for a DUI. Then I paged the Buffalo Falls ambulance. The young woman was still breathing, miraculously, when they got there. They took her to County General in Fairlawn. At this time, we do not know the extent of the victim's injuries, but the doctors have discovered a bullet lodged in her head. She's presently undergoing surgery."

"When did you learn of the driver's identity, that he was wanted for kidnapping and assault?" Beth's brown eyes narrowed. She and her microphone moved farther into his comfort zone. His eyes narrowed and his antenna went up. He was trained to keep suspects at arm's length. You never knew what they might pull.

"When dispatch came back on the radio, they asked if we had the suspect in handcuffs, which of course we did," he added, somewhat defensively. "They told us to hold the suspect, because he was wanted for a possible 10-89." He thought for a moment, removed his hands from his hips and self-consciously stroked his beard, thinking how best to put it. Heck, what was there to think about, he had to be honest. "We didn't know exactly what that meant, so we looked it up in the manual."

Beth's eyebrows spiked. Way too high to suit him. "That means possible homicide," she explained with noticeable condescension.

"Yes." He quickly went on, realizing that to Beth and the sophisticated Twin Cities' viewers, he must sound like a Gomer Goober. "Minutes after I made the arrest, SWAT team members stormed the Barnes's home and found the victim's parents, Helen and Larry Barnes, bound and gagged. The driver of the car, who we now know as Jude Orcus, is an escapee from the Sibley Mental Hospital. He's been charged with five felonies, which include one count of attempted murder in the first degree; one count of kidnapping; first degree assault; and two counts of second degree assault."

"Do you mean THE Jude Orcus? The former columnist for the *Twin City Sentinel*?" she asked the question as if this whole deal depended on his answers.

Nobody had mentioned anything about the guy being anybody important. Joe shifted from one foot to the other, trying to regain his balance. Not only was he not familiar with the name, he normally never read the paper. He affected something between a nod and a sad shake of the head. The good news was that she took that to be a yes.

"How does it feel to be a hero, Officer Towson?"

He could pinpoint nothing in her words that could be construed as making sport of him but, all the same, he thought from now on he'd watch the *Ten O'clock News* on Channel 5 instead of 9.

"Looking back on the events of the day, not knowing what situation I was involved with, I realize the consequences could have been far different. This incident will make me approach every traffic stop more cautiously." He wanted to explain to all the real heroes out there watching him that he wasn't one of them, certainly, but for a guy meeting up with his first live criminal, he hadn't done so badly. All the praying he'd done while he was waiting for the live drama to play itself out sure hadn't hurt either.

"Living in a small community such as Buffalo Falls can serve as an anesthetic for a suspicious nature. As thoroughly as I've prepared for the eventuality, I really didn't expect to confront a kidnapper and murderer in a routine traffic stop; nor do the people of this town expect to be asked for directions by a topless fugitive. I do want to commend Selmer Torgeson. He did exactly the right thing. He didn't try to get further involved, but he got the needed information; such as the color of the car, the license plate and a physical description of the car, the driver, and the passenger. He was neither trained nor hired to perform those duties, yet he did them without hesitation. I would nominate him as the hero of the day."

"Thank you, Officer Towson," Beth said, turning her sincerely serious face away from Joe's skeptical eye and into the more forgiving one of the camera. "This is just one more incident of violent crime that has been slowly seeping and creeping into the quiet, innocent lives of people for whom violence happens only in the movies or on television. This was Buffalo Falls' wakeup call."

Too bad the call came too late for Leigh Barnes, Joe thought. Instead of brushing it away, he allowed the tear in his eye to remain, in respect for and remembrance of the brief life of a beautiful young woman. He prayed God she'd gone straight to heaven without knowing what unholy things that maniac had done to her.

Chapter Nine

"Johnny!" Gracie was breathing hard when she reached him in the barn, just as he was starting to milk Sadie.

He methodically pulled and squeezed, hoping the hypnotic rhythm would calm him during the storm his wife's worried tone predicted.

"Bitti called."

"Jude," he said simply.

"He escaped!" she cried, shaking her head wildly until her pony tail swung around like the tail of their horse, Blackie, who was eyeing the scene from his stall at the far end of the barn.

"He doesn't know where we are, does he?" He felt an unnatural impatience with his wife. "Tell me, Gracie, for God's sake!" he barked. Sadie immediately responded to his unconscious roughness. Milk splattered in his eyes. He swiped at them, and with an anger he didn't know where else to direct he demanded, "Just tell me what Bitti said."

"He may have killed a woman, Johnny. He kidnapped her. He went to her parents' house, threatened them with a gun, and carried her off right in front of her family. Oh, God, Johnny, he could do that to the kids too, to us."

"Where did this happen? Surely he's nowhere near here."

"Somewhere near Minneapolis. The woman he took was Leigh Barnes."

His denial was a whisper. "No."

"He vowed he would get her. He has. He also vowed he'd get his children back. Our children, Johnny."

He tried to formulate a plan as once again he pulled rhythmically on the cow's teats. "No one knows where we are except Bitti, and the last thing in the world she wants is for him to find us and the kids. She loves them as much as we do."

"And fears Jude as much as we do."

"Even more, because she knows better than anyone what he's capable of doing to people he supposedly loves. In his diseased mind, betrayal gives him a motive for doing anything that will satisfy his own need for justice, no matter how cruel or deadly that justice seems to normal people. Well, he may have motive, but he won't have opportunity. I'll see to that."

"Oh, Johnny, I feel so ashamed."

That was the last response he would have expected from her. "Why would you feel ashamed?"

"I've begun taking everything God has given me for granted. Even you." She was rocking back and forth on her heels, eager to run, if only in place. "I should never for a moment have forgtten to thank Him for sending you to pull me out of the fire." She looked down at the splatters of milk on her boots. "And out of the self-destructive life I was leading. It's hard for me to believe now that I found both you and the Lord that day. Before then I was so lost, doing things I can't even imagine doing now. Sleeping with men I didn't love, didn't even know very well."

The pain she saw in his eyes made her stop.

"We've all made mistakes, Gracie. God forgave them all. So did I."

"I did so many wrong things, Johnny. Now I have to make sure I do the right thing."

"The right thing would be to make sure Jude Orcus is taken off the face of the earth. He has no conscience, he feels no guilt. Taking a life, or our children, would mean no more to him than taking a pee!" he cursed, causing Sadie to shift her weight in protest of his rude behavior.

"Bitti will help us, " Gracie said, smoothing Sadie's back.

Johnny continued to milk, now more gently. "Too bad she couldn't help Leigh Barnes." He knew he had to make plans, take precautions and then take action, but he remained hunched on the milking stool. He wanted to pretend, if only for a few minutes, that life for the O'Regan's would go on as usual. That it would go on at all.

Gracie shivered under her down jacket. "God help us."

Chapter Ten

As Thrasher was leaving Sebastian's office building, Cynthia Hardaway arrived. He had to admit the long-legged blond striding toward him was breathtakingly beautiful. He was rudely reminded that the sight of a beautiful woman could be a potent aphrodisiac. The stirrings in his groin were proof of that. His flesh suddenly felt as hot as if he were standing in a burning high-rise without a hose.

He hadn't been with a woman since his wife's death; hadn't wanted to be with anyone. For the first few months, his sex drive had been in reverse; in the following nine months it switched to neutral. After a year, he couldn't deny that he was all fueled up and ready to roll, except he had no place he wanted to go and no one he wanted to take along for the ride. *I don't know if I deserve another ride*, he told himself. Besides, this was the era of HIV and STDs and all sorts of other deadly initials. A good lay wasn't worth the going price of promiscuity.

He stuffed his hands in his pockets and smiled. He could just hear Chandler saying, "Get the lead out, Babe. You're a man; do what's expected of you. Do what you were created to do. There are plenty of good women out there waiting to love you. Wasting one of God's beautiful creations on an unappreciative eye is a sin." Damn, he missed his wife so much.

"Thrasher, I'm glad I caught you," Cynthia called out.

He watched the heads turn all along her approach pattern. Even in her haste, her walk was lazily seductive. Cynthia Hardaway knew how to use her God-given gifts. He wondered again why Sebastian would hire a young woman with no experience and a crooked father for such an important position on his magazine. Her pale green eyes seemed too wide and innocent to belong to any child of Leif Hardaway. Either she had deliberately perfected the childlike innocence, or she was longing to recapture it.

Beauty notwithstanding, her father was reason enough right there for him not to get involved with her. Definite conflict of interest. If he did make it to the bench, Thrasher was sure that Leif Hardaway would surely one day come under his purview. So far, no one from the State Department on down thought it prudent to investigate a man who employed millions, made money for every stockholder in his company, and donated considerable amounts of money to politically correct causes — and the current administration.

Some very powerful people chose not to see his aiding, abetting, and selling out to America's enemies as traitorous. Thrasher did, and if his nomination to the bench was approved, he intended to remedy that oversight.

Cynthia moved within inches of his chest. Breathing hard and looking flushed, she asked, "Were you with Sebastian?"

"Hello, Cynthia? How have you been?"

"Is he in his office?" Her tone was brusque. He thought he knew why.

"I'm sorry I didn't return your call last week, Cynthia. This judgeship thing has had me camped out in the law library. I meant to tell you what a good time I had at that charity thing you invited me to, but…"

His conceit lasted only until she said, "I have some very bad news for Sebastian." She was plainly agitated, her eyes were puffy. If he hadn't been so absorbed in fanning the fires of his vanity, he would have noticed her distress immediately.

His frown asked for details.

"The new editor he hired for the magazine, Leigh Barnes?"

"What about her?"

"She's in a coma, not expected to live."

"My God, what happened? A plane crash?" he asked, remembering Sebastian's comment on her arrival later today. No, a plane crash would have been all over the news.

Her voice was strangely without emotion, but her expression was pained. "She was attacked, kidnapped by the man she exposed as a serial killer."

"Jude Orcus?"

"You know him, know the story?" Her normally unlined forehead was crisscrossed with concern.

"Sebastian refreshed my memory only a few moments ago. Apparently both the story and Leigh Barnes made quite an impression on him. The only other woman I've ever heard him talk about with such reverence is you."

Thrasher could have sworn he saw a tear forming in her eye, but she smiled so quickly and sincerely that he must have been mistaken. "Sebastian is the most wonderful man I've ever known." Her voice broke.

"Are you all right, Cynthia?" He took her arm and steadied her. "Did you know Leigh Barnes?" Thrasher had never seen her exhibit any real emotion for anyone or anything but Sebastian and her job. She was tireless in promoting the magazine and Sebastian had been proven right; Cynthia Hardaway had more inventive means of getting *America in Review* on people's lips than Revlon.

"Do you want me to go with you to break the news to him?"

He had expected her to wave off his offer. "Would you mind, Thrasher? I'm having a hard time with this one." Her voice broke once again.

"Of course I'll go with you," he said, touched by her vulnerability and the sadness and uncertainty he saw in her eyes. For the very first time since he met her, Thrasher really saw her. As they rode together in the elevator, he studied her more carefully, concluded that there was another side to the woman he'd perceived as one-dimensional. It was probably the firefighter in him coming to the fore, but at this moment, he felt very protective of the new Cynthia, even though he had no intention of feeling anything else. As they walked together into Sebastian's office, Thrasher hoped he would be able to find the proper words to tell his friend that the talented protégé he held in such esteem did indeed have problems with her travel plans.

Chapter Eleven

Six Months Later

The daily habit of writing in her diary had stuck. While in the first stages of recovery, Leigh Barnes did it only to get the hospital's psychiatrist out of her partially-shaved hair. Dr. Patton had insisted that keeping a journal would help her clarify what had happened to her: her near death and her miraculous survival. Neither could easily be explained, even with the expert analyses of police psychiatrists, brain surgeons, spiritual specialists, and well-meaning friends and family. Leigh would have liked to help them sort it all out, but she'd been absent that day. And the next. And the next. When she did return, she was not the same person she had been. That woman had not survived the trip to hell.

The woman who emerged from the wreckage was someone she would have to get to know better — when she had the time and the inclination to revisit that wretched pit of Acheron into which she'd fallen. Right now, she was loathe to reacquaint herself with Buffalo Falls, Jude Orcus, or the bitter victim who had written in the diary: *My name is Leigh Barnes, and I'm a recovering victim and emerging vigilante who must wage war against the system that almost cost me my life; one that cost the lives of people I loved. I am on the road to recovery, but there is still a good chance that I could become a woman I despise — one who would rather die than fight. Or displease. Or disappoint. Or make a fuss. The dead-eyed devil who chose me as his unholy bride counted on that woman not making a fuss. I didn't disappoint him. I was his willing accomplice. I followed him to Hell and back while God stood idly by and watched.*

The words were filled with loathing — for herself, the legal system, and for whoever was supposed to be in charge of this sorry world. This certainly was not the tone of a "Lady Lazarus," as her brain surgeon, Dr. Merchant, had christened her. How ungrateful he must have thought her when she didn't immediately appreciate the fact that although she should have died, or at the very least suffered permanent damage to a brain and body ravaged by Jude and the Minnesota chill factor, she was whole again. Unfortunately, he was only half right.

Half dead, Leigh's body had been taken for a hell of a joy ride in a vehicle of the damned: windows rolled down, radio blaring, and flesh freezing as Jude flew down the highways and byways on a maniacal high where the mind and the body take leave of one another. A few of the many experts that surfaced following her rescue claimed that it was the freezing temperature that kept her alive; others scoffed that nothing but God's will could have saved her. Sebastian Vanderhyde was of that opinion.

Leigh had no opinion: only a patent on exposing impostors and seeing that they paid big time. Thanks to Sebastian's faith in her ability to sniff out phonies in the political arena, she was indulging in her passion. That passion stopped short of any emotional investment. Love was out of the question. Loving and being loved had once produced heady highs. Now she was well acquainted with the lows. They were unendurable; the price paid for loving someone was not worth risking such huge and unredeemable losses.

The doorbell rang. She put down her journal. It would be Cynthia. Before the door was fully opened, Cynthia Hardaway rushed in, her expensive perfume trailing behind the flowing skirt and unfurling waves of thick, blond hair.

"You can't stay for dinner, right?"

The roommate/keeper Sebastian had assigned her after her release from the hospital lighted momentarily on the sofa. The fact that they had become friends had not been his mandate, but he was obviously pleased. Leigh sat down beside her, hoping to keep her in one place for at least a little while. "I wanted us to do some catching up. I haven't seen much of you since I moved out of your house and into my own. Finally! What was only supposed to be a couple of weeks turned into a couple of months. I miss you."

Cynthia was visibly touched and seemed at a loss for words.

" I guess I got too used to the pajama parties we had when we bared our souls and did our nails."

"I've missed you too, Leigh, but you haven't missed a thing in my life. Work is about all I can manage to fit into it." She unwound the bright silk shawl from her long neck and swirled it around like a banner. "The house is beautiful, Leigh. You've done a fabulous job of decorating. Makes me think I should do something with my place."

"Yours is a perfect jewel, Cynthia. You'd be crazy to change a thing. It exudes warmth and peace. And I'm not saying that just because I so desperately needed those things when I first moved in with you."

"Are you serious? You think my house exudes warmth and peace?" Her pale green eyes were incredulous but grateful.

"All the soft-toned colors and fabrics and cozy corners are a refuge from all the hard, sharp-edged realities of life. But I suspect you know that."

Cynthia looked as though she were squinting into the sun. "Yes, I suppose I did have an escape in mind when I decorated it. On the other hand, my mother says my house reminds her of a moldy old English cottage filled with fake cabbage roses and somebody else's dusty memories."

"Why would she think you would want anybody else's memories?"

The question obviously took her back. She clasped her hands together and brought them up to her chin. "Probably because it's true. My mother's perceptions are unusually sharp. Probably all that therapy she's had." She let her hands fall to her lap.

Leigh wasn't sure if that was an accusation or a compliment, but agreed. "My mother had this irritating habit of reading my mind too. I couldn't hide much from her. And what she knew she shared with my father, so I didn't have a prayer of getting by with anything. They were always in cahoots," she said. She surprised herself by the ease with which she spoke of her parents. Until recently she had been unable to even think of them without being overcome with either sadness or anger.

"They sound like a wonderful couple."

She couldn't argue with that. "Your mother and father seem very close too. Their names and pictures are always in the paper, pioneering projects, raising money. They must be quite a team."

"Yes, they're perfect for one another."

"Perfect couples are a hard act to follow. My mother and father were inseparable, a real Ronnie and Nancy."

"Don't ever compare my parents to the Reagans if you want to be invited to their home," she warned with a grimace. "Like most of San Francisco's movers and shakers, they are liberal to the bone."

"Thanks for warning me, because I'm going to have an opportunity to offend them tomorrow at their annual Green Grocers' Gala."

"To which only the most environmentally safe people are invited," she explained.

"Sebastian and I are invited into their inner circle not as members, but as press, of course."

"Consider yourself blessed. Circles can tighten into a noose."

Whatever messages Cynthia was trying to send were too subtle for Leigh to pick up. "I guess they were pretty strict with you growing up. By the way, will you be there?"

"In answer to both questions, no and yes. Leif and Lydia were very involved with their various businesses and charities during my formative years. Being strict takes a lot of time and energy. Our nanny did most of the disciplining in our family. Looking back, I guess she could have pulled the reins a little tighter on both me and Jason. And yes, I will be there, also as a member of the press as opposed to a member of the family. In my capacity as an advertising manager for the magazine I can say and do things I would never be allowed to do as a Hardaway." Her smile was genuine, but her words held a soft rebuke.

"My mother chose a different route than yours. She stayed at home to raise me. Of course she did a lot of volunteering like your mother, but I don't think she got her picture in the paper even once. She liked working behind the scenes, I guess."

"Leif and Lydia are hardly camera shy and are extremely cause oriented. That may be one reason I never even joined the Girl Scouts. My way of rebelling."

"Anyone who has even a remote knowledge of new technologies or has followed the NASDAQ knows your father."

"The original DotCom guy, that's my dad."

"I saw your mother and your beautiful home in *Architectural Digest,* so I'm anxious to see it in person. That must have been quite a place to grow up?" she said, recalling the glossy three-page spread of opulence that few in the world had seen and less could afford.

"Yes, it's pretty impressive. But the house you grew up in sounds more exciting. I felt like I was back in the 1800s when you told me about your taking a sleigh to your grandparents' farm for Christmas dinner, caroling all the way."

Her eyes were lit with wonder. Cynthia's mother was right about one thing, Cynthia did need to borrow good memories.

"Did you have all the carols memorized?"

"Yes, sure, didn't you?"

"I never knew anyone who went to church regularly, so the Christmas songs I knew where strictly secular stuff. Did you really recreate the nativity scene in front of the Christmas tree at your grandparents' farm?" She had seemed in such a hurry when she arrived, but Cynthia now seemed content to figuratively page through Leigh's family album, eager to put herself in a few of those poignant photographs.

"Every year."

"I can just see all those cousins scrambling to see who played Mary and Joseph. I think I would have liked the part of the angel."

"Those papier-mâché wings were beginning to droop quite a bit by the time the last cousin was grown."

Cynthia looked like a child herself as she listened raptly to Leigh's description of Christmas on the farm. It was if she were being read a wonderful fairy tale. And Leigh, without realizing it, was bringing to life parents who made June and Ward Cleaver look like the Adams family.

"It's nice to know families like yours really exist. It gives us all hope." Her tone, however, was far from hopeful.

"I suppose you're right. Although no family is perfect. But it is true that my mother and father were very much in love." Her own smile surprised her. "I remember hollering at them to 'keep it down' when I heard springs squeaking and Mom giggling behind their closed bedroom door. What a bratty teenager I was. I probably did a good job of snuffing out a fiery moment of passion."

Cynthia laughed like a bratty teenager too. "What a come-down that must have been for them," she chuckled nastily, "especially for your dad," she added, laughing harder. And then, suddenly, she was crying.

Leigh's arms went around her automatically. "What is it, Cynthia? Did I say something…"

"You must miss them horribly, don't you?" Without warning, tears streamed down Cynthia's cheeks and sobs racked her body. She flung her arms around Leigh and sobbed, "I am so sorry you lost them. And Bill, too. It never should have happened."

Before Leigh could respond, Cynthia was wiping her eyes, clearing her throat and chatting away as if nothing had just occurred.

"I've got a hot date with two prospective advertisers in…" she looked at her watch. "about twenty minutes, otherwise I would have loved to stay for one of your gourmet dinners. Between you and Sebastian, I don't know who would win the ultimate cookoff. But I will definitely take a rain check. I not only miss your cooking, I miss having you around." There was no doubting her sincerity or the tear Leigh saw lingering in one corner of her friend's tenderized eyes.

Cynthia gestured toward the journal. "Still writing in your diary, I see."

"Trying to write the kinks out of my life."

Her offhand words had an unusual intensity. "If you have any luck, let me know, okay?"

Normally, Leigh didn't choose to speculate about things that were none of her business, but she couldn't help wondering what Cynthia's relationship to Sebastian really was. It definitely went deeper than employer/employee. "If Jude Orcus weren't one of the kinks, I'd be in pretty good shape. For the shape I'm in," she added ruefully.

A look of pain once again crossed Cynthia's lovely face, as intense if she had been the one Jude Orcus had hurt.

"I'm so sorry you had to suffer, Leigh. That man's cruelty was so extreme that it's hard to believe anyone could have survived it."

"And yet I did. Against all the odds. Which frightens me almost as much as Jude does."

"Why?"

"I was slain. By the jawbone of an ass. Then I was resurrected. But certainly not by God, because if I ever did believe in the guy again I'd have to despise him for what he did to me and my family. In this second life I don't intend to leave anything to chance. I'll make my own history. That is if Jude Orcus isn't Houdini reincarnated."

"Don't worry, God is keeping a close watch on both of you."

"Sebastian's gotten to you, hasn't he? He's notched another convert on his belt."

She smiled shyly and blushed slightly. "Yes, I guess you could say that. Yes," she repeated, "Sebastian has definitely gotten to me. He'll get to you too, you'll see."

Now she was even more curious, realizing how little she really knew about Sebastian, Cynthia, or their pasts. "You have quite a lot in common. From what I've read, you were both born to very wealthy families, went to all the best schools, lived what many would call charmed lives."

Cynthia flinched as if Leigh had slapped her. She hurriedly backtracked. "I'm sorry if I sounded like I have a case of class envy."

"You're too smart to envy anyone, Leigh, especially me."

She moved away so quickly from her and the subject that Leigh was left with her mouth slightly agape.

"I almost forgot. Your favorite, I understand," Cynthia said, taking a pie from the shopping bag she'd set near the door upon arriving.

"Rhubarb! How did you know?"

"Sebastian may have mentioned it."

"That's funny. I don't ever remember telling him that. Oh, well, I am going to have fun pigging out tonight, even though the salmon I had planned for our dinner will probably stay on ice."

Cynthia looked flustered. "I'm sorry. Goodness, look at the time. I'd better get going. I don't want to keep our prospective advertisers waiting." She slipped her periwinkle blue silk shawl over her fitted camel-colored suit. "I hope you enjoy the pie. There would have been a couple of pieces missing if I hadn't stepped on the scale an hour ago." She took Leigh's hands in hers and squeezed. Then, as she approached the front door, she glanced back over her shoulder and said, "Thanks, Leigh"

Before she could ask her for what, Cynthia hurried out the door. Leigh moved to the window and waved as Cynthia jumped into her Porsche convertible and sped away.

In the short time she and Cynthia had shared a home, they'd shared too little of themselves to be called more than acquaintances, and hadn't known each other long enough to be real friends. Yet tonight Leigh realized that they must have been forming a fragile bond; one that not even Leigh's heart-stopping night screams and periods of self-pitying weeping had severed. How could a virtual stranger understand her so well? Why would a rich, beautiful young woman like Cynthia prefer to live in Leigh's world of rusted sleighs and battered angel's wings when all her life she had Cadillacs and Jaguars in which to ride and custom-made clothes in which to play pretend?

She finished washing her one dish and fork and put away the rest of the rhubarb pie. She wasn't yet tired, but she washed her face, got into her chenille robe, and climbed into bed anyway. She picked up the diary, flipped back to the beginning and tried to find every mention of Bill: what he'd looked like on that last night, what he'd said, anything that would bring him back to her. It was getting harder every day to remember his smile, his kiss, the timbre of his voice.

There was no point in reviving painful memories, especially since she wasn't even sure they were still accurate. She began writing in the cursive her father had insisted she master, and wondered if schools even taught the

Palmer method any more. Probably not. The Palmer method wasn't nearly as provocative a subject of study in grammar school as the joy of sex of any variety and the proper application of a condom. Something between a sigh and a laugh preceded her reprimand. "Here I go again, making all these nasty, negative judgments that drive some people crazy. And incite millions to buy our magazine," she added with some satisfaction.

She had often considered abandoning the habit of making daily entries, but six months after her attack and many entries later, Leigh was forced to admit the doctor's advice had been helpful. Being a writer, it made sense to chronicle her thoughts, look at them in print, and absorb the impact of the words that bounced back at her.

She sunk deeper down into the foamy peach duvet that covered her goose-down comforter. Her queen-size sleigh bed faced the French doors leading to her bedroom balcony. The doors were wide open, inviting in the fragrance of the flowering pink cicada tree, now in full and fragrant bloom. The moonlight backlit a scene she would have thought surreal before moving to Camelot, which was what she called Los Altos, California. The soft breeze brushing her cheek came scented with jasmine. Nothing but good things, safe and pretty things, could get by the sturdy gate and alarm system that stood between her and her nightmares.

She went back to the diary. There were still mostly questions on the pages and few answers, but she would continue to write, despite the fact that she often felt she was merely ripping at the wounds, delaying the healing.

Sebastian disagreed. He had been by her side when she regained consciousness. It was then she learned that while she was in a coma, he flew back and forth from California to Minnesota weekly to be at her side. It was Sebastian who saw that she had the best doctors. It was Sebastian who buried her parents; first her father, then one month later, her mother. The cause of death was listed as heart failure, because no one died of grief, did they?

She would never be able to understand why he went to such lengths for someone who was a relative stranger at the time, a mere employee, really. And how ironic that it was Jude who had brought her and Sebastian together and opened up this whole new world she had entered.

Jude. When would she be able to purge that name, that face, from all memory? She thought never. Sebastian insisted that time would do that for her. Sebastian was good at dismissing her personal, private demons, but she knew he had battled a few of his own whenever he insisted that his past was just that, the past. He protesteth too much.

Sebastian knew everything about her, her family, Bill, Jude, but she still knew so little about him. Had he ever been in love, been married, ever wanted a family of his own? In this "tell all" world of publishing, the famous magazine publisher's life would normally have been mercilessly scrutinized by those who would have loved to see him discredited, those who would love to see a moral icon come tumbling down in a crash and burn scenario.

She put down her pen. It was Sebastian who had kept her job warm for her while she slowly and not so surely fought to stop her brain from atrophying, and had talked Cynthia into sharing her home with her until she found a place of her own and the strength to furnish it. He was the one who had faith that she would be able to regenerate the unplugged brain cells and rev them up to speed again. But even after she was working daily at her cherry-wood desk in the magazine's corner office, she was still not the woman Sebastian had hired. She was Lady Lazarus.

Chapter Twelve

"I think we've made some good progress, Jude?" the doctor said, scanning his notes and looking up at his smiling patient.

"Does that mean I can have visitors now?"

"Who do you think would visit you?" he asked gently, reluctant to too harshly point out his patient's unrealistic expectations. "You've never mentioned any friends or family. Only a woman you once loved and lost. Is there someone else in your life you'd like to see?"

This subject was always risky territory. So much of the man's problems were directly related to his relationship with a woman he refused to identify, and his lack of a healthy one with anyone else on earth.

"I have to have some secrets, Dr. Nesmith, otherwise you'd lose interest in me." He seemed to take joy in frustrating any concerted efforts to help him understand his illness and the reasons for his savage behavior.

He'd been practicing psychiatry for thirty years, and Dr. Eugene Nesmith had not developed a skin so thick that it could not be penetrated by demonic pathogens. He was not a religious man, but he did believe Jude Orcus was a carrier of all things evil, and no amount of counseling would change that or change him. He had lived too long in the world he had invented, the world to which he had been forced to retreat as a child and in which he now felt he belonged.

"I know there was someone you once loved, Jude. From what I've gleaned, she also loved you. You were there for each other when no one else was. She stood by you, encouraged your writing, helped fight your common enemies. But you betrayed her, Jude. You told me that. You can't expect anyone to condone or forget what you've done. By your own admission, you lack compassion for your innocent victims. That would seem on the surface to be incomprehensible, since you said you spent so many years being a victim yourself."

Dr. Nesmith wasn't deluding himself. He was no longer acting as Jude's doctor; he was operating solely as his jailer. It was up to him to see that this menace to society never left the confines of this institution. Jude was heir to an accumulation of abuses and neglect, and his blood was bad.

"Your job, Jude, is to come to understand the consequences of your actions. You cannot control anyone but yourself. You must be able to fully realize the damage your actions have done, not only to you, but to your victims. Do you understand?"

The patient considered the doctor's words carefully. His lips moved sensuously over his teeth, as if he were contemplating a tasty snack. "I understand perfectly, Dr. Nesmith. I know what you're trying to do, which is why I brought you this," he said, offering him a heart-shaped Waterford paperweight he had kept concealed under his oversized shirt.

The doctor hoped his alarm didn't show on his face. He held up one palm like a crossing guard. "It's very lovely, Jude, but you know the rules on such things," he apologized nervously.

Where the hell had he gotten it? "I'll be happy to take care of it for you." He turned his palm upward, motioning Jude to surrender his gift. Jude fingered it, having some fun with his crystal of power.

Someone must have smuggled it into him. But who? Patients were not allowed to have anything in their possession that could do harm to themselves or anyone else. "I promise to keep it in a safe place," the doctor urged.

"I wanted you to know my feelings for you, Dr. Nesmith, and this paperweight can express them far better than I."

The doctor smiled warily. His brain flashed a warning. "I've got just the spot for it, Jude. No one can get into this cabinet but me." He nodded to Jude and reached behind him. There was a gun in the low file cabinet under the bay window of his office. He'd never had to use it, but then he'd never had a patient like Jude Orcus. He moved quickly. But not quickly enough.

If Eugene Nesmith felt the pain of the paperweight crashing down on his skull, he made no verbal objection. He was unconscious before he hit the floor, his index finger caught in the trigger of the gun.

Jude moved quickly around the desk and took the doctor's pulse. Neither happy nor sad that he had stopped just short of murder, he turned Dr. Nesmith over on his back and began removing the white coat from the doctor's limp body. "Who the hell do you think I am? Moonbeam?" he hissed. "Am I some idiot savant you can follow and study like a fecal specimen? You were never going to let me out again, were you? You were going to keep me as your captive so you could play doctor/patient with me. Just like he did. Well, surprise, Dr. Nesmith! Surprise my love! Surprise Leigh Barnes! Surprise Gracie and Johnny! I'm baaaaack!"

Chapter Thirteen

Awakening, but still in that foggy state between sleep and reality, Leigh blinked the room into focus. The first thing she saw was the shapely vase of spring flowers she'd placed on the fireplace mantle the day before. They were lovely, but they weren't peonies or lilacs that perfumed the Minnesota springtime. She had searched every nursery in the area, but Leigh hadn't found one peony bush, and the California breed of lilacs paled in color and fragrance.

She threw off the comforter. She must not let herself dwell on all she was missing. She had to concentrate on what she had; which was a good job, one or two good friends, and a party to attend. She stretched her legs, then slung them over the side of the bed. She sat there for a moment, remembering the dream she'd had, grateful that it wasn't *the* dream: the one in which she was at a cocktail party making polite conversation when suddenly she realized she was naked. All conversation ceased and the people and the patio umbrellas disappeared. She frantically searched for something to cover her nakedness. She was so cold. Then there was only darkness and a voice shouting at her, clammy hands caressing her. "Moonbeam!"

She shivered, though the room as warm as toast. Last night's dream had a slightly different twist. The villain Jude didn't even have a bit part. A handsome visage instead had reached out to her, offering her warmth, guiding her back home and promising her peace and love. But at the end of the dream she again discovered she was naked and sitting under a patio umbrella. At the Hardaway mansion. Not difficult to analyze that dream. Today she would be exposing herself to the scrutiny of a very large group of very critical strangers who were either known or potential enemies.

She ran her hands through her tangled hair, trying to remember the last time she'd attended a party just to have fun. She couldn't remember, only that it had probably been with Bill. She was too busy to cultivate friendships. She had a career to grow.

She glanced at the clock on the bedside table. Only seven thirty. She was meeting Sebastian for lunch. He never attended a cocktail party on an empty stomach, explaining that he had once nearly starved at one at which only vegetarian fare was served. She hopped up and headed to the spare bedroom she'd converted into an office. She swung open the doors of the armoire that concealed the machinery all modern women loved and hated. She'd have plenty of time to put the finishing touches on her editorial on campaign-reform myths before she foraged through her closet to find something more appropriate to wear than the birthday suit she sported in her dream. At twenty-six years old and the youngest assistant editor of *America in Review*, — or any other national magazine — she had a reputation to keep polished, and appearing before her political opponents in the buff would definitely tarnish it.

Her fingers flitted over the keyboard. Like almost everyone else in this world of super technology, Leigh had come to depend on her computer and all its time-saving, knowledge-capturing features. She was grateful for the technology in her home and office, but dreaded browsing the buffet tables with the technocrats who now ruled the economy, most conversations, and the unaffordable housing market of the Silicon Valley. The home in which she lived was so overpriced that it should have been an exact replication of Tara, complete with columns and magnolia trees, instead of the modest Tudor that sat on one-quarter acre. Without her parents' insurance settlement, she never would have gotten in. What would they have thought of her new life, her new home? They probably would have encouraged her to wait before taking on the responsibility of a house. Wait until it was too costly for her to buy anything at all. Or wait until your husband can pick out one with you.

For the exorbitant cost, the house was still no Tara, and if Rhett appeared on his white horse, he'd be too involved in his new start-up company to saddle up and carry his lady off into the sunset. Well, fiddley dee. She'd think about that tomorrow. Or maybe not.

She finished the article, shut down the computer, and stepped out onto the balcony, breathing in the cool morning air and gazing out onto the Santa Cruz mountains in the distance. The morning fog spread a gauzy film over the real world, so all she saw was opportunity.

She leaned over the wrought iron railing and looked down onto the lush garden of vibrant azaleas and rhododendrons. Her mother loved rhododendrons.

Leigh's arms crossed automatically over her chest as if to stop the flow of self-pity. She rocked slightly from side to side in a comforting slowness.

Leigh's bare feet were dragging, and her heart had put on five pounds of dead weight by the time she entered the bathroom, where she fairly hurled herself under the shower's violent spray. "Stop feeling sorry for yourself, Leigh; you've got a party to attend, new friends to make, new enemies to expose."

And expose she would. *America in Review* was the best vehicle she could imagine for spreading the truth. By the time she was through, the whole world would be able to spot the devils, no matter in what heavenly mansions they lived or how many pairs of Gucci's they bought to conceal their cloven feet. Later that very day she would remind herself of what a crock that burst of bravado turned out to be.

Chapter Fourteen

"Don't you think it's time you started using some of your investigative skills to find out why you're still alive and well, Leigh?" Sebastian had warned at lunch. "The clanking of those skeletons must be keeping you awake at night."

Fortunately, he'd begun the lecture after she'd finished her sautéed scallops and black bean cake, and he'd finished his seafood risotto. One of the things she appreciated most about her employer was his pragmatism. Eat first.

"After spending an afternoon with Jude Orcus, a skeleton doesn't seem that sinister, Sebastian." She raised her brow for the beating she knew was to follow.

"Then why are you allowing him to continue ordering you around?" he asked more gently. "You beat him and all the odds. You were murdered. You were raised from the dead. Three times. You should be jubilant, not mad as hell."

She felt the skin along her hairline begin to perspire and was relieved she hadn't worn any blusher on her high cheekbones. She was probably as red and shiny as an apple. "I flatlined. I did not die. I didn't see a bright light or my great-grandfather Olaf, who died forty years ago, and…." Her head was hurting too much for diplomacy. "Save it for Elizabeth Kubler Ross, Sebastian. Even if I did die, which I did not, I didn't ask to be reborn. I didn't ask to take on this monstrous debt of gratitude you insist I owe, one that compounds each day I inexplicably continue to live and thrive against all the odds. You talk about pressure? You don't know pressure," she said, rubbing the back of her neck. "Have mercy on me, I'm going to be facing a patio full of antagonists in a couple of hours."

"No one would blame you for how you think and feel about Jude, but..."

"You're wrong!" she interrupted, her blue eyes blazing. "I don't feel anything. I don't think about him. He's a nut. Probably always has been, definitely always will be. And as certified nuts should be, he'll always be institutionalized, unless some kind-hearted psychiatrist decides to give society a spanking for not providing poor lonely Jude with the love and understanding he needed and lets him loose. Jude's got a full-proof, ready-made excuse for anything he does. He's blameless because he's nuts. And we're all going nuts because he's blameless. Simple."

"It's not simple, Leigh, and you know it. You've always paid your way through life, paid for your mistakes, your sins. But how do you pay for a miracle that was performed just for you? Don't good deeds like that require some reciprocation? After all, that was quite a service God rendered, quite a gift He gave you. Don't you think it merits at least a thank-you note, an acknowledgment?"

When she didn't answer, he said softly, "Please give a little thought to that note's composition? For your soul's sake, Leigh."

"Did you ever consider the idea that it wasn't personal? That I was just at the right place at the wrong time? That there is no God? And even if there were, does He think torturing people until they're a few intact organs short of a corpse is cause for appreciation and jubilation?" she finished angrily.

"He wasn't doing the torturing; Jude Orcus was, of his own free will, not God's."

"The only thing I do believe is that we're living in some kind of alternate, upside-down universe where good is evil and bad is relative. In the universe I once inhabited, I didn't require immediate gratification. I waited until Christmas Eve to rip open my presents, I planned to wait for marriage to have sex, I waited for this job until I was sure I was ready to handle it. My parents taught me that waiting was good, that all things come to those who do. And what did they do with their advice? When the chips were down they refused to wait. They were too anxious to die and join their God to wait for me to regain consciousness. They left me. They decided there was no point in waiting for their only child to return to them. I know, I know, I'm judging them harshly, and in this century of our Big Brother Knows Best, no one may be judgmental, therefore no one may be judged. Even Jude Orcus. Jesus Christ would certainly approve of that policy of forgive and forget, wouldn't he?" She hurled the words at him.

"You are a very intelligent woman, Leigh, one I respect, admire and care about as I would a daughter. But God is not the arrogant being here; you are.

My dear, you are not nearly bright enough to have all the laws of the universe adjudicated. You are not the master. You have not had so much of a glimpse of His plan."

"Maybe not, but If I had judged Jude Orcus as he deserved to be judged — with a loaded gun and a firm resolve to use it — I wouldn't have lost part of my skull, months of my life and…." She swallowed a sob. Leigh Barnes still didn't like to make a scene.

"You told me you didn't want to become that woman you despised, the one that would rather switch than fight, rather be red than dead. Well, unless you were lying to me and to yourself, you'd better put up your dukes, kid, and start fighting the good fight; against the things in society and ourselves that produce all the Judes of the world. And then stop denying the existence of the God who allows it all."

"Okay, Mr. veritable voice of reason and speaker of truth, has there ever been anyone in your life you just couldn't forgive?"

There was no hesitation. "Yes."

She waited for him to elaborate. His long silence was uncharacteristic. Sebastian Vanderhyde was never at a loss for words.

Finally, he spoke. "There was only one person I could not forgive, have not forgiven." His smile was enigmatic. "But I'm working on it."

Chapter Fifteen

"I need to talk to Chandler, Jake. How 'bout we make it a double date at the cemetery?" Cell phones were good for something besides irritating those who don't have them, Thrasher decided reluctantly.

Jake Malloy, his best friend and partner in the Golden Bridge Winery, was in San Francisco checking on their new wine distributor, and the cell phone seemed to be the only way they could connect lately.

"I'll be here for only a couple of hours, Thrasher. I've got to head on back to Napa to help Jose with our selections for the wine auction coming up. You planning to be there?"

"I've already forked over my $2500. I can't afford not to." His '56 Jag made for a fancy phone booth, yet he squirmed in the leather seat. "Jake, I know when we first started the winery I promised to be more than just an investor, so you're probably wondering just when I'm going to start playing more than a supporting role."

"Knowing a judge I can consult when those ambulance-chasing lawyers come around claiming damages for overindulgent wine tasters might be even more helpful than a full-time partner." His down and dirty laugh was still as therapeutic as it was when they were boys and in deep trouble with the aunts who raised them.

"The winery is doing great, Thrasher, don't worry about it," he said. Then, in a more serious tone he said, "No problems with your confirmation I hope."

"Not if I change my party registration, my life philosophy, and adopt a transvestite."

"Sounds a lot like Washington, only they wanted me to change my color too. I was too damned conservative for a Black."

"So remind me, why do I want to be a judge?"

"Don't ask me. I don't know why anyone would want to do anything but play football and grow grapes."

"I was thinking of asking Chandler. I know you go to see Rita and the kids whenever you're back in the area, so how about a double date? In an hour?"

"Sounds good. There was a time when I went to the graveside daily, then it became a weekly visit. And now..."

"The winery is over an hour away and you're coming into the city less and less, so don't be so rough on yourself. If anyone's to blame for your being so busy it's me. I've been an absentee partner as well as absentee friend, I'm afraid."

"Not so, good buddy. I'll see you soon."

Thrasher arrived before Jake. He sat down on the stone bench near the front gate of the cemetery, folded his hands between his legs, and released a labored sigh. What would he have done without Jake? What kind of a man would he have become? He was certain of one thing, they both would have been diminished without the other. Their life-long accusers said that their colorblind friendship was only a masquerade. The truth was that Thrasher had forgotten his best friend was black after their first fight in kindergarten. Thrasher's eyes were closed when he heard, "It's been too damn long."

He could see that Jake's long, dark lashes were damp as he sat down beside him

"I used to take flowers to the graves myself. Now I have someone do it for me. I guess because I feel as if Rita and the kids don't stay put in any one place. They turn up at the winery, the supermarket, the movie theater, or wherever I happen to be when they slip back into my life."

"What's Rita saying to you these days?"

"Get married again and raise a family, you idiot. What else? Same thing Chandler would say to you, I'm guessing."

Thrasher shivered involuntarily. "Chandler and I would have been celebrating our wedding anniversary today. Next week would have been our daughter's birthday."

"And in the best of all worlds Rita and the kids would be living with me in Napa, enjoying the success of the winery and all that open space, the warm summers, the cool dark caves with all those secret places for the kids to hide. But that's not the way it is, my friend, and no amount of graveside visits are going to change that. Our wives wouldn't want us to choose grief over a happy life. They'd want us to cherish their memories and thank God for the wonderful times we had together. They'd want us to go forth and multiply, Thrasher."

"That doesn't seem like an option right now."

"I know the feeling. At one time, living didn't seem like an option to me. You know, you were there when Rita and Mary and Robby were carried out of our burning home on stretchers. You know how much I wanted to go with them instead of trying to hang on to a life I no longer wanted." He wiped the glitter from his dark eyes.

"At least you have all those memories of the kids to hold on to. I didn't even get the chance to meet my daughter. I never got to hold her in my arms and tell her how much her daddy loved her."

"Maybe it's better that way, Thrasher. You don't see her face in every little coffee-colored girl that comes skipping down the street. You aren't reminded of her whenever you see a curly little head and big brown eyes looking up at you. You have only your imagination to tell you what your child would have looked like, what her first words would have been, when she would have taken her first steps. It's haunting, man."

Thrasher leaned sharply toward him. "Jake, here I am trying to one up you on the degree of hurt we're each feeling. Well, friend, I feel your pain," he said in a credible imitation of a former president.

Jake's smile was broad as he lightly punched Thrasher's upper arm. "Thank God that's one pain we don't have any longer. Now, how's the judging going?"

"I'm not looking forward to facing that committee. Chandler would have talked me through all my answers to all their questions. She would have told me to ignore the fact that half the people on that committee would rather see me dead than sitting on a bench making judgments they would disagree with one hundred percent of the time. To them, law and order means surrendering all our guns, all our rights, and all our opinions, and trading them in for the finer things in life, like bigger government and smaller families. Or even better, no families; only compatible groupings of individuals composed of all races, colors, and sexual persuasions, except fathers — those evil, tall men who say no to everything and work for tobacco companies or nuclear labs."

"Sounds like you need a woman in your life, Thrasher," he laughed. "You're becoming an old curmudgeon. And that's not the image we want for one of our youngest judges. Not to mention bachelor wine makers. We're in this year, you know. At the auction we're going to look damn impressive with all those wine connoisseurs bidding on our wine, picking our well-developed nose, applauding our nutty finish. Oh, by the way, Joe and Jennifer called to say they're going to be there."

"Oh, yeah, the Youngs have a home in Calistoga, don't they. Great, the more celebrities the better."

"How about bringing Cynthia? All that Hardaway money would sure boost the charity take at the event. That's the least old Leif could do to make up for his endangering our national security."

"Cynthia doesn't take anything from or ask anything of her father. Plus, Chandler spoiled me, Jake. The chemistry has to be more than just a combination of flammables. Beauty and a great body just isn't enough anymore. Not after loving a woman who could feed my soul and make my toes curl at the same time."

"Then just bring her to gussy up the scene. If you tell me she doesn't make your male libido want to reach out and touch someone, I'm gonna' start worrying, Buddy Boy. I'm not saying you have to get physical, but at least acknowledge beauty when you see it. Most men would be content to just show her off. Hell, even just gazing at that perfection is worth the price of admission. She's bright too, man, so it isn't as if you'd have to have her jaws wired in order to get through the day. My advice is to jump into the dating pool and get your feet wet; pretty soon you'll get the hang of it again. There is someone out there for you, Thrasher. Me too, I hope."

"I just don't have the energy to dive into anything right now except the law books. I've even resisted taking on new clients until after this judgeship thing is settled. But once it is, I'll try to keep up my end of our partnership."

"So, what kind of a work week do judges have? Can I count on you for Tuesdays and Fridays at the sales counter?" His wide smile was teasing.

"Now I know why I called you. I needed some comic relief." But he'd needed more than that. "I'm going to see Chandler now. Say hi to Rita and the kids, okay?"

But as he and Jake walked in opposite directions, Thrasher felt more and more alone. And more and more guilty. Not even Jake knew the extent and the reason for his guilt. It was too awful. It was too damn stupid.

He knelt down and touched the name carved in granite. Chandler Malloy Cole 1964-1994. In front of her headstone was a small marker. Baby Cole 1994-. He let his fingers dip and turn into each letter and number. If only he'd listened to Chandler, her name would not be etched in the cold, gray granite. If he hadn't been so obsessed with justice, his daughter would have a name, and he would have a life without gaping holes in it. But no, he always knew best. Even when she'd pleaded with him to postpone his investigation of the Channing Building fire until after the baby was born, he'd answered by giving her all the noble reasons for nailing the bastards who had started it. Only when she fell down the stairs did he realize how upset she must be to be so inattentive to her safety and that of their unborn child. But that was just prior to his getting a lead he had to follow, before it disappeared like all the rest of the evidence. One of his friends in the FBI, a man who had helped him and Jake take down a corrupt judge and her minions, told him they had a line on the arsonist, and that with a little more effort they might be able to link him to Hardaway. One day after the call, Chandler was killed by a hit-and-run driver. He was too grief stricken to make any connection then, but as time passed, he began to remember things. Like how Chandler had so suddenly and inexplicably changed from a happy, positive woman into a nervous, frowning worrier with fresh lines drawn on her lovely face. He'd asked her to tell him what was wrong, why she was so adamant about his stopping the investigation, but she just repeated what she'd said before; that she didn't want to have any extra worries during her pregnancy. He should have probed further, but instead he'd chalked her strange behavior up to the raging hormones that caused the mood swings; a normal part of a pregnancy.

It wasn't until he pulled into the Sutter Street garage that his speculations became certainties. His wife's death had not been an accident. He would find out the who's and the why's, even if it killed him too.

He grabbed the new report on the Channing Building fire from the passenger seat. He was looking forward to seeing the look on Sebastian's face when he showed him the results that the fire inspector hadn't shared with the media or that idiot former chief of the department. Now that Perry Prudden was out, corruption was slowly being replaced with competence, and the real firefighters left in the department were reestablishing a new freedom of information. The newly appointed Chief Wynn had decided Thrasher's hands were the proper ones in which to put some of that information, and he intended to use it to the advantage of the good guys this time around.

Chapter Sixteen

It hadn't been hard to blend in with all the other pretenders. The state hospital's doctors looked down and through anyone not at their elevated stature, and paid little notice to any of the nutcases with whom they were forced to share space. Even when all the qualifications of a consult were met, they were still reluctant to share any portion of their great brains with anyone not in their exclusive club. No, Jude had slipped through the ranks like KY Jelly. Like the rest of the club members, he wore a straight white jacket and an imperious look of disdain.

The starched white frock, borrowed from the good Dr. Nesmith, along with the clearance card Jude had pocketed, got him through the door. The hush money he received every month would soon get him to California. The supply of help and money was as infinite as the debt owed him. Of course he still despised his benefactor; that would never change.

His escape wasn't as difficult as he had anticipated, due to the fact that over the years he had become intimate with the hospital and the people who guarded it. He had done his research thoroughly, just as he had researched the subjects for his newspaper column. He had done his homework: he knew all the doctors' and aides' schedules, their idiosyncrasies, and their dirty little secrets. Only a person accustomed to keeping secrets could so easily discover and unearth those kept by others. Sex was always a fertile area of enlightened blackmail, so he'd begun his research there; he found no lack of it in the Sibley Hospital for the Criminally Insane. In fact, he could have accumulated enough porn to supply the Internet through the next millennium, but he wasn't interested in supplying anything. From now on, he would be given everything he needed, everything he wanted. His wishes would all be granted by those who owed him. And the first one to wave her magic wand would be Leigh Barnes.

She, like the rest, believed he would be locked up forever. Wouldn't they all be surprised? Especially Daddy Dearest. Papa should have paid more attention to all those tests he'd had done on his only son. The IQ test alone should have been fair warning that messing with a genius could be dangerous business. The psychological tests were irrefutable proof that it was also a deadly one.

Once outside, he walked directly to the parking lot, the car keys jingling in his pocket. He unlocked the door and slid behind the wheel of the shiny black Mercedes that had been left for him. It was the model he'd requested. All his demands had been met, albeit with a pained acceptance. But also, he knew, a glimmer of hope that the monster unintentionally spawned would be driving far away, never to return.

Oh, what wonderful memories he'd had of riding in an identical luxury automobile with Leigh. The engine purred, as did he, thinking of the fun he would have crashing the party — literally. All his favorite people would be there, according to the article in the San Francisco paper. Of course, he wouldn't be able to rub elbows with them, but rubbing their noses in their own excrement was even more fun. And Leigh. Wouldn't it be delightful to see her once again.

Chapter Seventeen

"Mom, look, it's Bitti!" Bess ran barefoot through the front door of the cabin and stretched her arms straight out so her birth mother could easily catch her in her own.

Buddy was right on her tail, a cookie lodged in his mouth and the third in a serious of mutant toads clutched in one hand. "Bitti, you gotta see this!" he said, handing the creature to a dubious but gracious Bitti.

She put down the bag she was carrying and took the gift he so generously offered, holding it gingerly and at a good distance from her body. "So this is your prize winner."

"Nah, he croaked right after he and I won first prize at the science fair."

"What's in the big bag?" Bess asked, bouncing excitedly.

"Children, is that any way to greet Bitti? She's not Santa Claus, you know." Gracie was usually glad to see the woman who had given her two of the greatest joys she would ever know, but this visit was one none of them looked forward to.

"Bitti? What a nice surprise. Always good to see you." Johnny rolled out from under the rust spotted car and wiped his greasy hands on his greasier jeans. "The Oldsmobile's acting up again. Should have driven the truck to Mendocino to pick up the necessary parts to fix it, but ..."

He didn't have to further explain his reasons for choosing not to leave his family alone.

Bitti's normally velvety face was pinched, her eyes clouded. "Buddy, Bess," she said, kneeling down to their level, "I need to talk with your mom and dad for a few minutes. Why don't you go into your bedroom and see what's in these boxes," she said, pulling two elaborately-wrapped gifts from the big Neiman Marcus bag.

"Wow!" Buddy said, grabbing both of them.

"That one's mine!" Bess protested, snatching the one with the pink wrapping and purple bow. They were her favorite colors, and Bitti made sure every gift that she gave Bess was wrapped in them.

The children romped and stomped into the house like frisky colts and disappeared behind their bedroom door, their giggles reverberating, their joy unbounding. Not even the specter of Jude could interfere with the opening of a present.

"They're very happy children," Bitti said, her voice conversely grave. She followed the O'Regan's into the house, and sat down in the only upholstered chair in the cabin's great room. She began. "I want them always to be this happy, but..."

"We promised you eight years ago that they always would, Bitti. We stick to our promises," Johnny said, more firmly than he had intended. "Can you keep yours?"

"No, I'm afraid I can't."

Gracie's intake of breath was like a gust of gale force wind. "I knew it. Even before I saw you drive up, I knew. In my morning devotions the pages of my Bible fell open to Revelation 12:7-9." She ran to get her Bible and began reading. '*Then there was war in heaven; Michael and the angels under his command fought the Dragon and his hosts of fallen angels. And the Dragon lost the battle and was forced from heaven. This great Dragon — the ancient serpent called the devil, or Satan, the one deceiving the whole world — was thrown down into the earth with all his army.*'

She set the book down, but kept her right hand on it. "Who is in his army, Bitti?"

"He had to have help to get out." Johnny didn't try to hide his anxiety.

Bitti did try to hide hers. She sat up straighter in the chair, her chin high with manufactured confidence, her normally pretty face distorted by anger. "It wasn't as easy for him this time. First, he had to take out Doctor Nesmith with a paperweight." Her voice wavered, but there was no other sign of what had to be great distress. "There's no longer anything Jude can do that will shock me. He was always doing things he tried to convince me were good and good for me; things I eventually understood were shockingly depraved."

"Is Dr. Nesmith dead?" Johnny whispered, hoping the children were not eavesdropping on the adult conversation, as they often did.

"No, for some reason Jude left him breathing. They think he'll be okay."

"That means he puts some value on a human life," Gracie said hopefully.

Bitti took her hand. "I don't think those homeless victims would agree, and I doubt Leigh Barnes would either."

"He wouldn't risk coming anywhere near you," Johnny insisted. "Besides, I honestly believe he wants to be found, needs to be found. He craves the limelight, all the attention he receives when he does something unforgivable. That's the reason he drove Leigh Barnes to Buffalo Falls, the town where her mother and father were born and raised, where she had lived for the first years of her life. He wanted to humiliate her in front of people who were important to her and her family. He wanted to literally strip her of her dignity, just as she had stripped him of his. And that's not my opinion of how his sick brain works, Dr. Nesmith agreed with my theory."

"Yes, that's true." Gracie sounded too eager to agree with anything that would ensure her children's safety. "He could have gotten away with it. All he had to do was take Leigh someplace remote, bury her body, and take off. We know he had access to money, so he could have flown somewhere, anywhere, and just disappeared. But he didn't want to disappear, and he didn't want to kill the people who could identify him: Leigh's parents. He only tied them up so that he'd have time to complete his plan."

Bitti reached over and touched Gracie's arm. "But he did kill them, Gracie."

"Not directly, not really." Her voice was breaking up as her words accelerated. "They both died of heart attacks, I know, but that wasn't his intention."

"It was the ending he hoped for, Gracie. In his mind, everything worked out even more perfectly than he had anticipated. He could not be blamed for their deaths. Leigh would. She was the one responsible for bringing him into their lives, and she would never be able to forgive herself for that."

"You don't know that, Bitti," Gracie said with little conviction. "That's diabolical."

"Yes," she answered simply. "It is. I know Jude, and I know he hasn't checked off everyone on his list of victims." She hesitated before adding, "That list also includes me."

Gracie hated asking, but she had to know. "You don't think he could have followed you here, do you?"

"I would die before I would lead him to you and the children." Her voice held as much hurt as fear.

"I'm sorry I had to ask, Bitti, but we have to know how to prepare," Johnny soothed.

"He hasn't had time to reach California, but I'm sure this is his destination. You'll be safe here, and I won't contact you again unless it's absolutely necessary."

"And under what circumstances would that be, Bitti?"

"If he kills again."

Chapter Eighteen

Leif Hardaway had been trying to reach his wife all day. She was normally prompt in answering his messages. That was one thing that hadn't changed. Lydia was still the consummate Organization Woman. If she had a schedule to follow and a project to head, she was happy. Which was why her calendar was always filled right up to the hour. If there was any down time on her treadmill life, she squirmed like a rat let out of her too-familiar maze and ran to her psychiatrist. He saw that as a healthy sign — for him. As soon as she stopped running and started thinking too much, he would be in trouble. And he had enough trouble as it was; he didn't need his wife adding to it.

"Mr. Hardaway, Senator Guttmacher is here to see you."

"Good, send him right in."

It wasn't good. He didn't like the senator showing up here so often. People would start wondering why they had so much to talk about. The senator was anxious to preserve his first position mortgage on the sale of arms to China. He had been instrumental in the initial negotiations and now he was determined to see it through to the end.

Leif twitched involuntarily. He didn't like to think about the end of anything, but people kept making it necessary for him to second-guess himself. Thank God he'd gotten rid of the evidence that would surely have convicted him as far as his son Jason was concerned. He could not expect his enemies or many of his allies to understand the man/boy relationship they had shared. The uninformed masses would have put a much different, much uglier label on it, and he just couldn't have that. It didn't matter that he was confident that such relationships benefitted both partners and educated them in the many ways of loving. But as long as main stream society frowned on it, he must pretend he did as well.

Lydia would be the first to accuse instead of trying to understand. She was too provincial to indulge in sexual practices not described in her sixth grade biology book. Even his own lawyer, who put no limits on private behavior, would find it distasteful. His experimentation was confined to women, unaware that men too could offer great mental and physical stimulation.

Unfortunately, Jason had decided to pursue his own agenda and his own lovers. At one point he had gotten quite nasty about it and threatened to divulge the deep relationship they had shared throughout the years.

Eventually Leif realized he had no choice but to have him gone. The Channing Building fire had served dual purposes: the removal of a historical building that did not fit his plans for revitalizing the block, as well as the removal of his son, who also did not fit into his plans.

His only concern had been that pyric hero Thrasher Cole and his hotshot fire fighting sidekicks. Fortunately, they had saved Cynthia. Just as fortunately, they were too late to save Jason. They made a lot of noise about the fire being deliberately set, and tried to make the case that the Hardaway empire would be greatly enhanced by the addition of those now available blocks of prime real estate. He had become outraged, of course. He had lost his only son in the disaster and nearly lost a daughter as well. How could they imagine a father being party to such a thing? The press came down hard on the two when no evidence was ever introduced. Of course only he and Fire Chief Prudden knew why. Prudden had been one of the first public servants to be put on his payroll. He enjoyed all the things in life one could pursue with more than a firefighter's meager salary.

"Leif," the Senator began his filibuster as soon as he hit the office floor, "I hear we've got some chatter from the whining patriots in Congress who want to stop all trade with China and deprive us and them of a more stable relationship." He didn't try to hide his disdain for anyone who would put patriotism ahead of profit. "What do you plan to do about them?"

Leif knew exactly what he'd like to do with the Senator, but Guttmacher was too high-profile to disappear conveniently. Besides, he suspected the Senator had a safe-deposit box full of incriminating evidence against him.

"My attorney has advised me to stall as long as possible, until the American people say, 'Stop' to all these tiresome investigations and independent counsels. They aren't going to find anything that proves we sold the Chinese Communists anything they couldn't have gotten by logging on to the Internet. Our tracks are well-covered, and there are one hell of a lot of people who want to help us make sure that they remain covered."

"Are you leveling with me, Leif? I've got a lot to lose too, you know, and you've been acting a little preoccupied lately. Lydia giving you grief again?" he asked, arranging his wide bottom on a straight-back leather chair facing Leif's desk.

"Lydia's good."

"Your daughter too?" He cocked his head, inviting elucidation.

Everyone suspected the same thing, that his only living child was a definite security leak in his operation. Her alliance with Sebastian Vanderhyde was the stuff of which exposés are made, and he had one hell of a lot to be exposed.

"She's no threat to anyone but herself," was all the explanation he offered.

"Lydia knows a lot, Leif."

"Not enough."

Once he'd purchased the bed and breakfast hotel on Post, he had successfully avoided any and all grief Lydia would have given him. As long as he didn't flaunt his affairs, she was happy to have him out of her hair. When one owned the building, one had no trouble getting a room, and there was no one to question what was done behind its closed doors. It was the perfect solution to what could be a sticky problem for less-affluent adulterers.

"As a matter of fact, I've been trying to reach her in order to discuss a few family matters."

"You both have had it rough. Your only son dead at such a young age. And under such tragic circumstances." Once again, that irritating cock of the head.

"Yes, losing a child is something one never gets over. Which is why we're watching Cynthia carefully. She goes to such extremes to prove her independence. One of these days I'm afraid she'll go too far in asserting it and find herself in a dangerous place."

"I would say right now she's putting you in a dangerous place, Leif. That pretty little gal is doing one hell of a job supplying ammo and advertising bucks to our biggest enemies. Sebastian intends to paint a pretty nasty portrait of you in that upcoming article he's doing on you and your company's close, personal relationship with the ChiComms and the current administration. Cynthia's providing the canvas, from what I've heard."

"On the other hand, it's useful to have a fox in the hen house."

"She's a fox, all right, but I think she's after you, not the hens, Leif. Even though it certainly wasn't your fault, you ever get the feeling she holds you responsible for her brother's death in that fire? I've seen the looks she gives you when you don't know she's eyeballing you. The expression 'If looks could kill' takes on new meaning."

"Cynthia is headstrong but not delusional." Leif was well aware of those looks. They worried him too. Just how much had Jason confided in his sister before his death?

Lydia couldn't possibly have told her about his father/son intimacies with Jason. She was too absorbed in her charities and too zonked out by pills and champagne by nine o'clock at night to hear or see anything. It still bothered him that Cynthia had been in the building when the fire was started. She hadn't spoken much about the fire or Jason, which made him nervous.

"I'm having lunch with the vice president at the Bohemian Club. Want to join us?"

"Oh, yeah, he's in town again to pick up another sack of soft money in his quest for campaign finance reform."

"Bite your tongue, Leif," the Senator chuckled.

"I almost forgot, I've got a board meeting scheduled. Sorry."

"What the hell, I'll swallow another one of his prevarications as long as I can wash it down with a martini. What do you think his claim to fame will be this time? That he's been chosen to serve on the committee to select the next pope?" The Senator's laughter rang like a cracked liberty bell.

Chapter Nineteen

While Jude was planning his party within a party, Leigh was appraising her pale-yellow suit in the restaurant's ladies' room. She was afraid that the exquisite lunch may have qualified her for a size larger. The suit had looked as sedate as it was expensive when she spied it on the store model. But a vision of understated elegance was not what she saw reflected in the full-length mirror. The light gabardine fabric emphasized her curves more than her trimness, and the slim, short skirt hinted more of tart than smart. What had she been thinking of to buy the goldenrod silk shirt that made her skin glow with unabashed femininity?

The mirror soundly disputed her contention that she was a little too tall at 5 foot ten inches, too healthy looking at 130, and too clear-eyed to be considered sexy. One of them was wrong. All these years she had believed it was only the color of her eyes that drew appreciative glances. The few men she'd dated after Bill's death had felt compelled to describe their color as electric, startling, intense, or vibrant. Mesmerizing was also right up there on the list. But when you're a tubular teen with buck teeth, great eyes don't do all that much to boost self-confidence. Braces eventually coaxed her teeth into what Sebastian called a charming overbite, but she still had always seen herself as she was before all the warts were removed.

Only at her mother's urging had she begun adding highlights to her naturally auburn hair. Applying a little mascara and eye shadow to further accentuate her eyes had also worked. She had even started believing Bill when he said she looked like Jeannie Crane, her favorite actress of the forties. She too had been insecure about her looks in Leigh's favorite movie, *A Letter to Three Wives*. She wondered idly whatever happened to Jeannie Crane.

An hour later she and Sebastian arrived at the Hardaway estate. Her quick steps made her hair bounce softly on her shoulders as it caught glints from the sunny-colored fabric of her suit.

"You look like the first warm spring day after a long winter, my dear. A lovely sight for these old eyes," Sebastian said, as they locked arms and faced the imposing entrance to the Hardaway mansion.

"Shouldn't there be a moat or something?"

They moved with the rest of the guests up the curving driveway that fronted the palatial home. "There would be, but the planning commission just said no. Of course, all the members who voted against him were soon out of a job."

She winced. "He's not an enemy you would like to make."

"Having second thoughts about your first public confrontation with Hardaway and his gang?"

"Where do you hide your mind probe?"

"I remember the first time I came up against the big boys."

"But I bet you weren't naked."

His mouth fell open. "Excuse me?"

"Last night I dreamed that I attended the party in my birthday suit."

"How did you get out of that predicament?" he laughed.

"I was saved by some knight in shining armor. Guess he'd brought along an extra suit. I don't really remember."

"What did your savior look like under all that armor?"

"It doesn't matter. I don't believe in saviors anymore. I did once, but that was one abduction and several funerals ago. To say the least, my faith has been shaken, not stirred," she said in answer to his pitying smile.

Both of them turned their attention and their direction toward the host just ahead. Leif Hardaway was acting as centurion at his own gate, enthusiastically and personally welcoming guests as they encroached on his turf.

Sebastian leaned in and whispered to her as they climbed the flower-laden path. "The air you are now breathing is completely free of pollution, thanks to our host's environmental sensibilities. Without his activism the earth would have been destroyed years ago."

Sensing Leigh's unease, Sebastian stepped up first to the distinctive gray-haired legend who was extending his hand. "Thank you for inviting us, Leif. Leif Hardaway, Leigh Barnes, my assistant editor. I don't believe you two have met."

The man was as charismatic as she had heard. Every movement of face and body was subtle but well-conceived. The scorch of his penetrating eyes seared her breasts before moving up to her face. His fingers squeezed gently and moved seductively over her hand. *The better to know you*, she thought. "Thank you for including me in the invitation, Mr. Hardaway. Your house is truly beautiful."

"It has served many generations well through the years," he said with a dismissive shrug. "It has been in my wife's family since the early 1800s. But I'm sure my daughter has given you a recap of the family history."

He seemed to be waiting for her to admit or deny it.

"Actually, Cynthia always showed more interest in my family home. She's a great listener."

His smile of apparent relief was puzzling.

"She's listening to everyone but me these days, I'm afraid. That may have something to do with working for you, right, Sebastian?" he said, not waiting for his reply before saying, "I can't thank you enough for keeping my young daughter gainfully employed and out of trouble. Our Cynthia is quite a handful." His wink was suggestive, vaguely insulting.

If Leif Hardaway noticed the hardened look in Sebastian's eyes, he didn't show it. "Please, Ms. Barnes, Sebastian, go right in and enjoy, although I would like to speak with both of you a bit later about the upcoming article on my company, which I understand you have in the works. Just want to make sure you have all the facts." Without waiting for their agreement, Leif began welcoming the next wave of guests.

Leigh's heels echoed through the enormous marble foyer, then were silenced by the Persian rug that covered half of the spacious living room. They followed the madding crowd out onto acres of brick, stone and yards of rolling lawn where white tablecloths, bright umbrellas, and beautiful people abounded.

Sebastian's normally placid countenance was stormy.

"What was that all about? I thought you were going to punch the man."

"Let's just say our host and I have some disagreement on what life's priorities should be. Myself, I would choose to devote my life to the raising of a child rather than to the saving of a tree, but then that's what makes me politically incorrect, isn't it? In any case, I intend to eat and drink very heartily and speak very candidly, all at our host's expense."

Leigh quickly accepted the first glass of champagne offered her by a roaming waiter. She sipped it so fast she started to hiccup. The host would be only the first of their adversaries, so it was vital that she not to be overwhelmed by the acres of expensive slate and brick that composed the Hardaways'outdoor living arena, as well as the throngs of rich and famous who roamed freely on the lavish preserve. "Let me know when we should start playing reporter. I want to be reasonably sober."

"You might want to go easy on the bubbly around this group. You throw blood in these political waters, and you can watch the raptors rise to the surface."

"And one of them is heading our way." She caught Senator Guttmacher's scowl before he could change it to a smirk. The two faces he always wore were both chatting away as he approached with an attractive woman, not his wife, on his arm. He was no doubt engaging in his usual dance routine of changing opinions as easily as he changed conversational partners. He kept all his constituents happy, his finger in the wind, and his hand in every deep pocket.

Reading her mind again, Sebastian suggested. "Try checking out prospective dates rather than probable felons."

"Guttmacher is not a probable felon; he's merely an unconvicted one. And I don't need a date, I have you."

"I'm referring to someone less long in the tooth, my dear; some nice young man who has all his hair and his original teeth."

"You've got the best head of hair on the lot, and you know it," she said, admiring the thick shock of hair as soft and white as moonlight.

The senator was prevented from reaching them by his fellow senator, Gloria Belzer.

"Both Guttmacher and Belzer would be serving ten to twenty right now if it weren't for circuit judges who believe in selective justice," Leigh fumed.

"Nothing we can do about that. Let's start mingling. I want to leave this party with some items for our *Believe It or Not* section."

Leigh squinted into the moveable feast, watching the guests and waiters carrying plates of artfully designed and displayed appetizers and confections.

"First, you must meet the hostess."

"I'd love to. Cynthia has got me very curious about her."

"The ubiquitous Lydia will be covering any bases her husband is not."

"Cynthia said that they are quite a team."

"They get along famously despite the fact, or maybe because of the fact that they despise one another; which has never stood in the way of their achieving their common goals."

"Cynthia didn't for a moment give me that impression."

"She wouldn't. Her family's business is a private one as far as she's concerned."

"I can understand that. Being so rich and famous, they undoubtedly have their privacy invaded enough."

Sebastian gave her a look she'd never seen before. It was patently hostile.

"When did privacy become an inviolate right?"

"Well, I guess you could say with Roe vs. Wade."

"The day freedom became a dirty word and life and death became relative terms." His sputter became a wrenching cough, and he held his chest as if he feared it would shatter.

"Let me get you some water," Leigh cried, grabbing the closest waiter and a bottle of Perrier water he was carrying on a silver tray.

He sipped it slowly, recovering quickly. "This is no time for me to be emoting on that issue. See Cynthia anywhere?"

"She'll be here, don't worry. There will be a lot of people here she can schmooze for advertising space in the magazine. Her dedication to the magazine seems to be an irritant to her father."

"Among other things."

Sebastian's glances around the area were concerned.

She wondered if the other *things* were the rumors that Cynthia and her boss were romantically involved, and that the prestigious job in publishing he'd offered her was in appreciation of her unpublishable talents.

"I guess I sound protective of her, don't I?"

Leigh knew how absurd those rumors were, but how many in this crowd believed that his feelings for Cynthia were more than avuncular.

As if she'd uttered it aloud, he said, "I'm flattered that people would even consider the odd coupling of me and Cynthia, and I care not a whit about anyone's speculations on my personal life. But I do care about Cynthia. Sadly, all she cares about is whether or not the speculators are buying and reading *America in Review*. If curiosity about the two of us causes more people to plunk down the subscription price, she's delighted. No matter that it probably discourages potential suitors from approaching her."

"You really are a matchmaker, aren't you? Has anyone tried to match you up with someone?" She didn't expect to get anywhere, but it was worth a shot.

His bushy eyebrows rose. "I never needed any help in getting what I wanted."

Subject closed. He attempted to wave down a server. "Quite a prized collection of Silicon Valley legends in attendance. And quite a large sampling of Hollywood's flotsam and jetsam eager to please and be pleased by the Hardaways, you'll notice."

Leigh saw one of the FJ's, Delia Packard, erotically arranged in a patio chair on the opposite side of the pool, obviously well into the initial throes of passion necessary to recreate her most infamous movie scene. Leigh wasn't the only one guilty of voyeurism. The actress was playing to a rapt audience of incredulous guests, and convincingly disproving the myth that her legendary long legs just didn't quit. Sebastian caught Leigh's eyes widening, then closing modestly as the myth was blatantly disproved once and for all. Every one of the guests invited to Delia's one-woman peep show saw exactly where her legs quit.

"Quite a performer, isn't she?"

Two famous attorneys, one noted doctor and several wealthy industrialists standing within earshot nodded their agreement.

Leigh wrinkled her nose and mumbled. "Yes, quite. No wonder I'm no longer hungry."

"Maybe a little kibble would suffice."

"Do I sound catty? Don't answer." Her crooked smile acknowledged her bad behavior.

"You can't leave your sense of humor at home at this kind of a party, my dear."

"At least I brought my clothes."

"Quick thinking, Leigh."

"Haven't you ever had that dream?"

"Of course. Classic fear of exposure."

"Or maybe merely a way of getting attention, having every man at this party lusting after me and my...whatever," she mumbled, glancing at Delia. "I think I'll try one of these things," she said, snatching a toast point topped with caviar and grabbing another before the waiter moved on. "Were you aware that there are no calories in food eaten outdoors on tiny paper plates?"

"I wouldn't waste a perfectly good cache of jealousy on that woman, my dear," he said, not letting her change the subject. "If our revealing little blond weren't married to Glen Packard, the owner of the *San Francisco Globe* — a man who has the means to provide her a platform for her artistic exhibitions as well her mental meanderings — I fear Pussy Galore over there would be doing her act on Broadway. And Columbus," he clarified, alluding to San Francisco's bawdy intersection. "I dare say, the notorious nymph is possessed of a mind so broad that there is nothing it cannot espouse or condone. Except, of course, an opposing point of view."

Bored by the show already in progress, Sebastian groaned, turned his attention to the buffet, made his selection, then popped a salmon spread mini-bagel between his well-trimmed mustache and goatee, just as the mayor of San Francisco offered his hand.

"I see you're hoarding all the delicacies again, Sebastian."

"The mayor's way of asking for an introduction," he explained to Leigh through his mouthful.

"Leigh Barnes," she said, shaking his hand. "I would be more flattered by your coming over to introduce yourself if I hadn't seen you trying to dodge the political consultant you fired last week."

He tried to look offended. "Apparently you are not familiar with my penchant for beautiful women?"

"This one also has brains, Mayor Jones, as I'm sure you're aware. That is, if you've read her article detailing Buckley Caen's plans to sue you and divulge some of the sweet deals you made in order to get re-elected?"

"I'm sorry to say I don't subscribe to your magazine or your points of view, Sebastian. And forgive me, Ms. Barnes, for not being familiar with your little columns. However, now that I've met you, I can't help but be more interested."

"I hope you mean that, Mayor. I would like nothing better than to know I had influenced your viewpoint even a little."

"I have a reputation to uphold, so I never make promises I can't keep, Ms. Barnes. But perhaps we may have an influence on one another. Say, at dinner some evening?"

"I'd be delighted, Mayor."

"You are truly charming. Please call me Frankie."

His farewell handshake was firm and protracted. With what passed for warm regret, he finally released his grip. His long-legged stride carried him quickly to his next conquest.

"He thinks I'm charming."

"No, he thinks he's charming. He's as crafty as they come, and he flaunts it. He's a clever crook. He steals other people's ideas, other people's thunder, and other men's wives, but he does it with a smile and his assurance that he's doing you a big favor by relieving you of these heavy responsibilities."

"It's ludicrous that Frankie Jones can remain in power and gain in prestige even after all the scandals, the larcenous deals, and the outright graft, while you're continually lambasted in the press for your *brutal* honesty. Why do they link charm with larceny and honesty with brutality?"

He didn't have an opportunity to answer. A new and improved audience, consisting of a former secretary of defense and secretary of state were offering their hands. Leigh chose to be an observer rather than a participant in the conversation. It was a good opportunity to watch the great one in action, the man who was as aristocratic as his name, and as revered and emulated in the literary world as was William F. Buckley. Sebastian had worked hard to merit both his well-developed ego and his legendary reputation as the nation's reigning political columnist and best-selling author. Leigh Barnes considered herself very fortunate to be included in even one chapter of the legend's life.

She had already learned a lot at his polished wing-tipped feet. She had learned to nose about for truth with one less prominent than his, which was aptly large and ruddy — a natural result of his relentless pursuit of the news and his refusal to give up martinis for lunch, even after a triple by-pass. Nearing seventy, he still had the energy of a young bloodhound sniffing barrels of tempting pork and howling triumphantly at the moon whenever he came upon rare sightings of honorable men.

Sebastian eschewed the offer of more champagne from a white-suited wait person, and instead reached over to the white-skirted wait person, plucking off her tray a tumbler with two large olives swimming about in the clear liquid. He eyed Leigh surreptitiously. She knew her fretting about his health was a source of both irritation and comfort to him. He'd once lamented that it had been a long time since a woman had taken his health to heart.

"How about playing doctor?" she whispered in a bad imitation of the very Germanic Dr. Woerner, who also fretted about Sebastian's health. "When it was suggested that a couple of glasses of wine would do you no discernible harm, mention was also made that a couple of dozen will."

He guffawed. "Your Dr. Woerner impression sounds more like the Godfather. I'm in bigger trouble than I thought."

"Okay, I'm not good at impersonations. But I am an expert at nagging. I want you around for a long time. I need this job."

He devoured the bagel and mopped cream cheese from his mustache with an already soggy napkin. "I want to stick around as well; long enough to make sure we'll meet again after the martinis and cholesterol have sent me packing for the Pearly Gates. It remains to be seen if I'll be allowed to unpack once I get there, but I have great hopes for you."

His joke was not that at all, judging by his thoughtful expression.

"I'm surprised to see you here, Sebastian. Is there a conspiracy afoot?"

Lydia Hardaway appeared, radiating wealth and superiority. Until Leigh looked closer. There was a glow on her matte-finished face. The light film of perspiration was telling, because women like Lydia Hardaway didn't sweat. Other than the fine lines around her eyes, the woman appeared impervious to the normal vestiges of age, whether by nature's or a surgeon's design. Her body was slim, her bare arms nicely defined, probably due to a daily workout in her private gym or on the tennis court. But her smile was strained, her laugh as thin as she. She had passed along her thick blond hair and fine features to her daughter, but whereas Cynthia's smile spread naturally across her face, Lydia's would have to be pried open.

"And you are?" she asked, studying Leigh with the eyes of a diamond cutter.

"Lydia, I don't believe you've met Leigh Barnes. Leigh, Lydia Hardaway, our most gracious hostess."

His emphasis on the word gracious sounded gratuitous, but she didn't let on. "Ah, yes, Cynthia's former housemate."

"Yes, Cynthia was kind enough to put me up while I looked for a place of my own. I also work with Cynthia."

"Leigh is my assistant editor, Lydia, but I'm sure you already knew that."

Her green eyes suddenly sparkled like the emerald earrings she wore to accent them. "I can't fool you, can I, Sebastian?"

"I'm sure you can, Lydia, and probably have."

The sparkle was gone. In its place was something akin to fear. She took a step closer to Leigh. "Cynthia has spoken of you. She thinks very highly of you."

The pain in her eyes was deep and permanent. Where had it come from? Her childhood? Her marriage?

"Please excuse us, Lydia. I don't want us to be guilty of keeping you from the rest of your guests," Sebastian said, pulling Leigh away with a brusque motion.

It was as close to rudeness as Sebastian had ever gotten in all the time she'd known him, and an obvious rebuke to the hostess.

Lydia's voice was so resonant that Leigh couldn't believe it came from such a fashioned face and such a flat belly. "Your chivalry is admirable, dear Sebastian, but your rescue is unnecessary this time."

With those incomprehensible words she whirled around on her spiky heels and floated away in a sea of green organza.

"So, that's Lydia Hardaway? What in the world did she mean by that exit line?"

When Sebastian only shook his head, she said, "Cynthia was fortunate to inherit her mother's looks, but thank goodness she dumped the attitude?"

Sebastian looked beleaguered.

Leigh led him toward the bar. "You look like you could use another cold glass of water. It's getting rather warm out here."

It took her several minutes to find any fluid not alcoholic, but when she returned with a bottle of water he emptied it without taking a breath.

"What is it with you and the Hardaways, Sebastian?"

"Most likely a fight to the finish."

"I give you the first round."

"I'm not so sure. Leigh, Cynthia could really use a friend; one she could trust. She's a very smart, very complicated young woman who doesn't know what she wants and usually gets it."

"You'll have to explain that."

"I wish I could."

"Cynthia means a lot to you, doesn't she?" What she wanted to ask and didn't was why. The two seemed to have little in common besides the magazine. If she didn't know Sebastian had extremely high moral standards, she would have questioned his concern for the woman's well-being as being something other than altruistic.

"Yes, she does."

His voice caught on the words. He quickly took another long sip, attempting to drown the emotion.

Something compelled her to ask, "What else did Cynthia do — besides work for your magazine — to so alienate her parents?"

As soon as the words were out of her mouth she realized she was the one doing the alienating. Sebastian answered not as her friend but as her boss.

"Making a hasty and unsubstantiated evaluation of another human being's life is generally a mistake, Leigh. Until you have proven facts and a firm basis for your indictment, it's wise to withhold judgment. I would have assumed as a well-trained reporter you would be unlikely to forget that basic tenet."

She felt her face turn crimson, clashing wildly with her yellow suit. "I'm sorry, I know that sounded as if I were blaming Cynthia for their estrangement. It's probably none of my business what went on in their family, but since you seem to want Cynthia and me to be friends, I think you might share a little more information about why she so desperately needs one, don't you think?"

"Suffice it to say that she needs someone she can trust, someone honest and ethical and compassionate. I thought that might have been Thrasher Cole. But not even the beautiful and eager Cynthia could entice him, for one moment, to forget his dead wife, Chandler. Cynthia has not been able to find the love that should have come easily to a woman so bright and beautiful. The problem is, she would probably not even recognize love in its purest form."

"Do you blame her parents for that?"

He didn't answer her question.

"Our job is to report, and let the public evaluate the results of that reporting. I plan to see that Mr. Hardaway's dealings with the Chinese government are examined under the very bright light of truth. His company's sale of technology to America's enemies will be fully reported. Then the criticism can follow and the nature of the man and his deeds will be clear. But don't confuse criticism with cynicism, Leigh. I don't hate Leif Hardaway, I just hate what he's doing. Misanthropes soon find themselves without a soul mate. Or a soul," he added, suddenly looking every one of his sixty-nine years.

At that moment Cynthia dashed through the patio door and down the stairs.

"I'll still bet that when it comes down to the wire she won't want to see her father hurt."

"And you would lose that bet." The certainty in his voice gave her goose bumps.

Chapter Twenty

Leif's responsibilities as host had been fulfilled to his satisfaction. Lydia, of course, would see to it that everyone there was sufficiently fed and entertained. She prided herself on making every guest feel honored and flattered to have been invited to a Hardaway event. That was about all she was good for. Only his need to keep her in his sights overrode his personal contempt for the weak woman who had such a strong interest in seeing him destroyed. She was the only other person in the world who really knew him. He paid dearly to see that she kept that knowledge to herself.

While Lydia was playing her part, he would be able to do some behind the scenes negotiating. Most of the businessmen and politicians at the party were beholden to him in some way, but it was vital that they remain so, which sometimes required large outputs of cash; often a favor that some idealists would label felonious, and occasionally a promise of a piece of the action. The action now was bigger than any he had ever imagined when he started his company and issued the first stock options. This action would determine the fate of a nation and the future of the world. And it was all in his hands, he thought, unconsciously rubbing them together.

"Tony, over here," he called to the man who at an hourly rate of $1000 had for the last eight years protected his ass.

Tony Angelico quickly excused himself from the gaggle of admirers flocked around the indecorous Delia.

"Any success?" Tony had complained several times to Leif that after months of trying he was still unsuccessful in getting her between the sheets of his canopied bed. The newly-wed star was still not sufficiently motivated to travel the short distance to Atherton and Tony's five-acre estate. Leif had never asked the barrister just how he got his wife to vacate the premises at those times when he did prove successful in a seduction. He might have a few innovations Leif had not considered; he should inquire.

Tony was tall, good looking, and totally devoid of morals. Just the kind of guy any astute businessman would want for a lawyer. He was never too busy to attend to his biggest and most powerful client, and was not too proud to admit it. Leif Hardaway was his meal ticket for life. And he was dining on only the finest of fare.

"What's up, Leif?" His features were as sharp as his mind, and he used both to maximum benefit for his client and for himself. He was a master at blurring the fine lines between right and wrong, and knew a million ways to withhold evidence that would clearly prove his client's disregard for the law.

"Sebastian Vanderhyde has managed to fire up a few senators and congressmen. The subpoenas will be coming any day."

"I know. I'm the one whose desk is starting to buckle from the weight of them."

"Should I be worried?"

"No. A little dragging of feet to go along with our f… you attitude is working very nicely. If they want information so badly, they're going to have to litigate for it, and that takes lots of time. By the time the independent counsel gets all the ducks in a row and all the court battles fought, you'll have everything you want, and the American people will be complaining that all these investigations are taking too long and costing too much. You know as well as I do how weak-kneed these types get when they feel public sentiment running against them. They'll back off eventually, I promise you."

"Sebastian has a way of inciting his readers, who in turn incite their congressmen, which eventually generates a little attention from the media."

"The media are on your side, Leif. They don't like Sebastian or the other holier-than-thou types any more than you do; they won't allow those right-wing Jesus freaks any press coverage. And if any one of them tries to make a real ball game of this, you can be sure I know how to strike them out. Fast."

"That's my man," Leif said with a smile and a pat to Tony's arm. "Now you can go on back to Delia and see if the honeymoon's over yet."

Tony's returning smile was as venal as his ethics.

Leif spotted Lydia by the pool. He hadn't seen Cynthia yet. Maybe she'd decided to stay away. Every time he'd talked with her lately she seemed ready to spring out of her skin. He wondered again what had happened to his quiet angel, the ethereal child who had been so manageable, so reasonable. She had vanished during her teenage period of rebellion, reveling in her promiscuity and defying all convention. That he could understand. But after the fire she had become another woman entirely. He was sure of one thing: working for Sebastian had driven her farther away from him. He did have to admit that since she had become the Advertising Manager for *America in Review* subscriptions had gone up by thirty percent. He was glad she was enjoying the sweet taste of success. He just hoped her success would not mean his failure.

At first Leif suspected the spread she offered prospective advertisers was more inclusive than the half page one they were originally seeking. She had been one hot little number, that little girl of his. His lips pushed out in thought. The thought of her beautiful blond body writhing in ecstasy kind of turned him on. Although he supposed the writhing had stopped, due to Sebastian's preaching. She'd found religion and joined the holy crusade against him and his business dealings with the Chinese government.

"Judge Benson, glad to see you up and around again. Did you get our flowers?"

The judge glared in response. "I'm not here as a guest, Hardaway. I'm here to gather intelligence. Not that it's found in abundance among any of your friends and business associates. One day at one of your parties, someone's going to have one too many scotches on the rocks and inadvertently say something that will nail your ass to the wall, and I want to be here when it happens. And don't think I don't know who was driving that phantom car that hit me and put me in the hospital. It was one of those phantom flunkies of yours who are paid so well to do your wet work."

Leif smiled as the judge limped away. He was pleased to see the judge had received his message. He'd think twice before ruling against him again, no matter how loud his bark at the moment.

His thoughts returned to Cynthia as he perused the partyers scooping up his caviar and scarfing down his vintage wine and booze. He didn't trust a damn one of them, but he had enough money and power to keep them in line. That wasn't an option with Cynthia. He wondered again what she thought about her brother, the departed but unlamented Jason. At times they'd seemed very close. At other times she seemed almost afraid of her big brother. Strange, because Jason was such a docile sort; eager to please and slow to anger. Until the last, that is. He stroked the cold wet glass of wine thoughtfully. There were times when he missed the boy and his accommodating nature and blond good looks. He'd be a man now, of course.

"Leif." From behind him he heard his wife's cultivated voice. No matter how soft, breathy and well modulated, it irritated the hell out of him.

He turned toward her and away from the crowd so his glower would not be seen by the guests. "What is it?"

They could barely tolerate the sight of one another when there was no one to notice their lack of simpatico. By design, those occasions of togetherness were occurring less and less. His current distraction took up most of his free time. Tony would probably not be pleased to know that Delia had been a great help in relieving tension and keeping his juices flowing. She made few demands that were not sexual, and he rewarded her by lavishing her with expensive jewelry and gifts she would not have to explain to her husband. She didn't need money, since she had her own successful career, but she did need constant adoration and a heavy dose of naughtiness that a legal husband somehow distilled. She inoculated herself against morality like the plague she believed it to be. He liked that in a woman. The extra challenge of Tony on her tail was also a turn on to both of them. Poor Glen. He didn't know what he was missing.

Out of the corner of his eye he could see hurried movements and smell the scent of Cynthia. It always had the power to turn his head. But as his eyes drifted toward her golden body, he sensed more than her perfume. She had fear in her eyes and a determination in her graceful step. He decided right then and there to have one of his men follow her, see what she was up to and with whom. A little preventative maintenance wouldn't hurt.

Chapter Twenty-One

Sebastian knew the news was not good when he saw Cynthia's wild eyes squinting into the sun, frantically looking for someone or something upon which to rest them. Leigh and the other guests would see only the cool, stunning mannequin, perfectly made up, dressed expensively. She had revealed to very few the emotional bruises she wore like a coat of many colors.

He could tell Leigh was still smarting from his criticism. His eyes filled with pain. If Leigh only knew how blessed her life had been, even with Jude Orcus in it. She would know soon, however, how cursed Cynthia's had been. It would come as quite a shock.

As Cynthia approached, he remembered the first time he'd set eyes on the lovely young woman. With the first flow of her tears, she had endeared herself to him in ways he had never explained to anyone, including Cynthia.

He wanted desperately to talk with her, hear what she'd found out, but he didn't want to raise any alarms just yet. He had to make sure they were in a safe and private place when all hell broke loose. And he needed a little help getting there, he thought, motioning to Thrasher, who had just arrived.

"Now's your chance to meet Thrasher Cole, Leigh."

Her eyes followed his to the man who walked very tall indeed; at least six foot three inches, she estimated. She hadn't imagined that the man Sebastian spoke of so often and with such reverence would be so young. He couldn't be more than thirty-five or six. She'd just naturally assumed that someone who was about to named to the bench, a man who had earned successful careers as a firefighter, a lawyer, and a vintner would have been much older. And not as handsome as a movie star.

"I think you'll like him," Sebastian predicted.

His approach was as exhilarating as that of a jumbo jet. Her ears were ringing, her heart was throbbing and her legs were wobbly.

"Quite a nice-looking chap, wouldn't you say, my dear?"

She was mortified by the intensity of her visceral reaction to a stranger. Leigh turned to Sebastian to see if he'd noticed. She felt her face grow hot, her feet cold. Surely everyone around them would sense the synergy, read her impure thoughts.

Sebastian reached for her arm and began the introductions. "Thrasher, Leigh Barnes. Leigh, Thrasher Cole."

She was sure she had never met him, yet he was so familiar.

Thrasher smiled broadly and took her hand, pulling her slightly toward him in the process. "I've heard so much about you, I feel as though we've already met."

"Yes, I agree," she answered,

"Sebastian, I need to speak with you," Cynthia interjected, physically putting herself between the three of them. She looked shaken. Reluctantly, Thrasher released his grip on Leigh's hand, yet he made no move to put any real distance between them.

Sebastian quickly led Cynthia away without any explanation to either Leigh or Thrasher.

"Did you see how she was trembling?" Leigh had seldom seen Cynthia in anything but a becalmed state.

They watched in stunned silence as the two disappeared in the crowd.

"What was that all about?" Thrasher's look of concern was genuine. "I hope she's okay. Maybe I should go after them, see if I can help."

Leigh felt her face flush. She wasn't ready to let him go. He had to be aware of the effect he was having on her.

His smile was an innocent one, a polite one. Her heart sunk when she realized that she was seeing romance where there was only cordiality and feeling tingling sensations that had nothing to do with the champagne.

"Excuse me, Ms. Barnes?" The waiter held a silver tray on which lay a folded piece of paper.

"Yes, I'm Leigh Barnes," she answered.

"This is for you," he said, bowing slightly as he offered her the meager contents of the large serving tray.

She took the note, unfolded it. She stared uncomprehendingly at the one word written inside. Her eyes widened with fear and darted around like bats blindly searching for a safe haven.

"What is it, Leigh?" She was unaware of how long she'd been gone, but when her eyes refocused, Sebastian was standing there along with Thrasher. He reached for the hand that held the crumpled piece of paper. "May I see it?"

Her fist was a death grip.

Sebastian held her hand in his, rubbed it as if the warmth of his own would unfreeze her hold. "May I see it?" he repeated.

Still blinded by the horror of the word, she offered up the note, praying her eyes had played a cruel trick on her.

Sebastian's demeanor did not change when he saw the handwritten word stretched over the length of the page; large, legible and threatening.

"Read it aloud," she murmured.

Thrasher moved quickly to steady her. "What is it, Leigh? You look as though you had just read your own obituary."

"I have," she whispered.

"What is it, Sebastian?" Thrasher demanded. "What does that mean?" he asked, regarding the single printed word with confusion.

"It means Jude Orcus is back."

Leigh's head felt as if it were floating away from her body. She swayed dizzily.

Thrasher grabbed her before she fell. "Nothing is going to hurt you, Leigh; not while I'm around," Thrasher promised with a vehemence that startled all of them, especially himself.

Sebastian took out his cell phone, turned his back and spoke in hushed tones for several moments.

Cynthia remained standing on the periphery, watching. She had no questions to ask. She already knew the answers.

Chapter Twenty-Two

His mouth had grown as his face had shrunk around it, so that it now seemed to consume the entire lower half of his face. His eyes, in contrast, were red slits, the lids puffy as marshmallows.

"We can't let the children see this," Gracie insisted, crumpling the police photo of Jude into a compact ball. "This went out to all police departments in the area, according to Bitti."

"Bitti didn't fax us Jude's new mug shot just so it could replace the old one in our nightmares. We can't keep his escape a secret, Gracie. If we do, the children won't be able to protect themselves from him. They have to know the danger; they have to know him."

"Just because he knows where to find Bitti doesn't mean he can find us too. She would never tell him where we are."

"Bitti won't tell him, but he doesn't need her. He has his own sources. Though God knows who or why anyone would want to help him."

"Whoever it is may not want to. It's possible they have no choice. Jude's very talented at manipulating and intimidating. He learned that at his Daddy's knee. I'm sure he once desperately wanted Bitti's love, but I don't think he cares about anything now except claiming what's his." With effort he spoke the unspeakable. "Our children."

"So what do we do?" she cried, her trembling hands covering her mouth and muting her sobs. "Where can we go?"

"There is only one place we can go; you know that, Gracie."

"Yes, I know.

"We need to align ourselves with his enemies. There is strength in numbers, and it will take a lot more than two. I'll call Sebastian right now. He'll know what to do. He always knows what to do."

Chapter Twenty-Three

"Moonbeam." Sebastian said the word as heedfully as if it could invoke the devil. "It's Jude. I've called the police, Leigh."

Thrasher's eyes flashed angrily. "How could they have let him escape a second time?" His hand tightened on Leigh's shoulder, but she felt nothing, saw nothing but the piece of paper Sebastian was holding. She stared at it as if it might leap out of his hand and grab her by the throat.

"First, let's get Leigh out of here." With Sebastian on one side and Thrasher on the other, an obedient Leigh was led around the pool and across the lawn, circumventing the door leading into the house or any danger it may now hold. She stumbled along like a zombie, unaware of her surroundings, uncaring of who was steering her through the maze of people and rooms, then the rows and rows of parked cars.

Both Leif and Lydia were shouting after them, but Cynthia ignored their questioning cries, raced down the driveway and caught up to Sebastian. "I'm coming with you. You're going to need me."

Thrasher noted her ashen face, her frenzied movements. "Cynthia, if this guy's as goofy as they say, the best place for anyone not involved would be as far away from Leigh as possible." His tone was harsh, his tight mouth uncompromising.

"I am involved," she said, her pale green eyes pleading first with Sebastian, then Thrasher.

"How are you involved?"

Sebastian made a quick survey of the people and cars parked along the entrance road, saw nothing untoward. "Later. Right now we need to get the hell out of here."

He hurriedly led Leigh toward the car and shoved her into the back seat. Thrasher slid in beside her.

"I think it's time you brought me up to speed on this," he said, as Sebastian crawled behind the wheel. "I may not have lifted hose and ladder or executed the fireman's carry for a few years, but I still can contribute some muscle, if that's what's needed here."

"We're going to need a lot of things, especially God's guidance, if we want to keep Jude Orcus from reprising his old act. I don't know how the hell he does it, but this guy can out-Houdini Houdini."

"Not without an assistant." Cynthia buckled herself into the passenger and gave Sebastian a sideways glance.

In seconds Sebastian was weaving in and out between the cars and the frantically waving parking attendants.

"This is your car, isn't it?" Thrasher asked, looking back at the men left standing in his wake. "They're acting like we stole it."

"Yes. I made sure it was parked where we could make a fast getaway."

"You thought we might need one?" He saw Sebastian's eyes regarding him in the rearview mirror. He had never seen his friend's jaw set so firmly.

When he didn't answer, Thrasher said, "I think you'd better let me in on this, my friend. You might have information on this whacko that I don't have, but I have a heck of a lot more experience saving lives. And judging by your speed," he said, glancing at the speedometer, "lives are in danger here."

"Indeed they are."

"May I ask where we're going in such a damn hurry?"

"To my house in Woodside."

"I didn't know you had a house in Woodside?" Thrasher's head was spinning around like a lazy Susan as he tried to gauge the innocence or guilt of every other driver on the road. "I thought your only residence was the Victorian on Broadway?"

"There are very few people who know of the house in Woodside. Cynthia is one of them."

When Sebastian didn't elaborate, Thrasher's mind went racing off into territory as treacherous as it was unfamiliar. Neither Sebastian nor Cynthia had ever given any indication that they were anything but business associates. No looks of longing had ever passed between them. No unnecessary embraces or tender touches had ever occurred; at least none he'd witnessed. What the hell was going on here? Sebastian was a very strict arbiter of his own moral code. If he loved the woman, he'd be open and aboveboard about expressing it. In fact, he would have shouted it to the whole damn world.

"What did the police suggest?" When he didn't get an immediate response from either of them, he sternly advised, "I think you'd better explain all this to me before I start theorizing, because my thoughts are taking some pretty sharp turns too."

Cynthia and Sebastian exchanged looks, then weak smiles.

"I'll take your prurient thoughts as a compliment, Thrasher, but Cynthia and I share only a desire to keep *America In Review* a superior magazine. Our friendship is deep, certainly, but only platonic. It would be wise for you listen to all the evidence before you hand down your verdict," Sebastian advised.

Cynthia's laugh was mirthless, but it was a laugh, nonetheless.

"What's so damn funny?" Thrasher asked, not politely, still wondering what role Cynthia played in this increasingly dangerous game of intrigue. His tone startled Leigh, who until that moment had sat slumped and mute in the seat beside him, her head bowed.

She raised her head slowly, as if coming out of a hypnotic state. "Please help me understand all this," she said, animation returning to her voice. "How could he have known where I was?"

The state of her mind was as easy to read as a road sign. She was back there again, on that highway to Buffalo Falls.

"We don't know that yet, Leigh. I talked with the waiter who gave you the note. He said he got it from a man whose face was partially concealed by sunglasses and what looked like a fake beard. When I probed further, I concluded that his description closely matched Jude's. There's not much doubt; he was at the party."

Leigh cried out, "He can't do this again! I can't do this again! You know I can't, Sebastian. You of all people know what he's like. You were there at his trial. You talked to him."

Cynthia's voice sounded very tired and much older, "No, Leigh, I of all people should know!" Then, with a raspy sigh she added, "It's a very long story, and I'm afraid it began with me."

"And it must end with you, Cynthia. All of it. You know that, don't you?" Sebastian said softly, putting his hand over hers.

She nodded and was silent.

"I promise we'll tell you everything once we get safely to Woodside. Detective Ed Cadigan will be there. He's been a friend of mine for a great many years. I've been keeping him up to date on my research."

Sebastian's calm voice and reasonable plan was only momentarily reassuring to Leigh. "What research?"

"When we get to Woodside I'll explain everything," he repeated, taking the 280 exit at a very rapid speed. His passengers all leaned to one side and held on to anything stationary, silently concurring that it was best to allow Sebastian to concentrate on his driving right now and let the questions wait.

Just then Sebastian's cell phone rang, breaking the silence and signaling the beginning of the final battle lines drawn between good and evil.

Chapter Twenty-Four

"My God! What are you doing here?"

"Mother, it's not like you to ask rhetorical questions. Aren't you glad to see the prodigal son?"

Lydia Hardaway's jerky motions betrayed her outward calm. She moved away from her dressing table and confronted her son, Jason. He had managed to slip into the house and into the room without sounding any alarms. She shouldn't have been so surprised. He had been able to do that all his life. Stealth was something his father had taught him well. Escape was something he'd had to learn on his own.

"You didn't tell me you were coming here, Jason. You led me to believe that once I provided you with the car and the cash you would go where no one would find you again. By the way, how did you get out this time?"

"I'm smarter than my captors. Now, how have you been, Mother? Is old dad behaving himself? Or is he still up to his old tricks?"

Her eyes could not stay long on her child's face. "Leif hasn't changed. His sins are his own. I don't share them. Or bear them."

"Only your sin of looking the other way while he's engaging in molesting your son. Not to mention killing your son," he said, clearly enjoying her anguish. "I think some people — particularly those attending your lovely party — might find that blind eye untenable in a woman of your high social standing and your civic and civil mindedness. Some might even call you an accessory."

The hairbrush she was gripping with all her might began shaking noticeably. He would like that; seeing her out of control.

"Why, I really am frightening you, aren't I, Mother? Why in the name of God, or your current deity of choice, do I frighten you, Mother?"

Jude Orcus stepped closer, until his breath was hot on her neck and his hand clammy on her slender arm. "You shouldn't be, you know. I would never harm you. If anything happened to you I would be unable to complete my mission. Without your willing assistance and ready cash, I never could have so altered my appearance and forged, literally, a new life for myself after my death by fire. I also could not have escaped twice from a mental institution or a father who sought to forever rid the Hardaway family of its blackest sheep. Or should I say its sacrificial lamb?"

She flinched. Her hand flew up to her neck. Her eyes were wide and her mouth gaping. She was giving the classic "I'm choking" signal. He made no attempt to relieve her distress, but waited patiently for her to find her breath.

"I didn't know he was capable of such evil, you must believe me," she whispered. Even to her own ears the words rang false.

"Then you probably didn't know that I had to be tested for AIDS for years, that I had to live in fear of collecting my infectious inheritance. But then that disease was only a cause to you. You no doubt still believe the virus is spread by a lack of funding."

"I tried to help you! I was the one who warned you about your father's plans to destroy his own building with you inside. We should both thank God that I was listening in to his private phone conversations and getting into his e-mail, or you would not be here right now."

"There you go again, Mother, thanking God. Since when did you two get on a first name basis?"

Her breaths were short and shallow, and the veins in her pipe stem-neck throbbed.

"Never mind, mumsy. I thank you for the timely warning. Too bad you didn't issue one to your daughter. Imagine the inanity of a rich party girl burning to death while checking out locations for a charity ball. What do you think? Would her obituary have appeared in the death notices or the society column?"

"Were you the one responsible for Cynthia being there, Jason?" she asked, dreading his answer.

He eyed her, estimating her fear of him. "I was the only one in this family who ever loved Cynthia, mother. I never wanted her hurt. Ever!"

Lydia's look of relief was pathetic in its degree. "Of course you wouldn't. And certainly your father had no idea that she would be there. It was purely a coincidence that she was there. She told me, when I was finally able to see her in the hospital, that she was there because she thought the Channing

Building would be a chic setting for a fund-raiser, since it was located in such a bad part of the city. She was so cynical then."

"Runs in the family."

She continued as if she hadn't heard him. "She was able to speak only in a whisper, but her words were harsh and so angry. Even in all her pain she was chuckling at the thought of my socialite friends who would revel in slumming in their finest gowns, as the homeless drunks, druggies, and derelicts gaped from the periphery, watching the circus my friends and I had brought to their pitiful patch of land."

"And if the affair was successful, she and her partner, that idiot Gracie, would reap the professional accolades needed to boost their little company's credibility in the marketing and advertising field. Cynthia may have been a cynic, Mother, but she was a practical one."

"Yes, I'd almost forgotten about Gracie."

"What the hell, three scorched bodies for the price of one arsonist. Father would have been pleased with the guy's fiscal acumen if only his daughter hadn't been one of the expenditures. Cynthia was too beautiful, too prized a possession for him to let her go. I was the only one he wanted out of his way, out of his life."

"Whose body was it, Jason? Where did you find him?" In all these years she had never sought the truth. She hadn't wanted to know it, couldn't know it, not if she wanted to continue helping her son survive. And she couldn't possibly help him if she knew how pervasively evil had invaded his once innocent soul.

"Do you really want to know, Mother?"

Her dilemma was that she had allowed, even nourished the evil she saw in him. Through her benign neglect she had allowed her husband to sneak into his room in the dead of night and repeatedly rape her child. She had slept on as her son was being tortured by the man who had given him life. What a cruel twist of all reason that must have seemed to a small child. The man who was supposed to protect him from all danger *was* the danger. And the woman who had conceived him, carried and birthed him, had allowed his torture to continue for years. She had remained either unwilling or unable, she still wasn't sure which, to see her child dying before her very eyes: eyes that had pleaded with her, begged her to make her husband stop killing him one rape at a time.

"I found him where I found my later victims — near the dumpsters, lying in alleys and doorways. They were throwaways. Kind of like those fetuses you pro's choose to dispose of with such high-minded conviction. We sure as hell don't need any more of them, do we? Sure, it's a life, sort of, but what do those homeless people and those fetal masses do for society except mess it up and overpopulate it. I just used your rationale, Mother, and helped save the planet from all those unwanted, inconvenient throwaways. Although, I guess they could be considered recyclable. Now that's something the Green Grocers at your party today would certainly applaud." He clapped loudly.

"Incidentally, Mother, nice party. But I thought the guests would never leave. Although a couple left rather abruptly, did you notice? Leigh Barnes looked positively freaked when she ran out, with Cynthia and her boss joining the hasty exit. Yeah, and also the guy who felt so bad about not saving me from the fire: Thrasher Cole. Wonder what that was all about? But getting back to your question. It was easy to kill. You had taught me early on to devalue life. You made choosing death an easy one for me. So easy that I decided to make a career out of it. It's amazing how these brilliant ideas can come, isn't it? I could make myself a hero and rid the world of those worthless bastards at the same time. My writing talent must have come from all those years when I had nothing to do but study. Since I had no loving family, no devoted friends, I decided to make them up in short stories and novels. My first column was in the school newspaper. It was called 'Cudgel Your Brains.'"

Her gasp was soft and quick.

"It was composed of brain teasers, mother, not a method of doing in the homeless." He waved a cautionary finger in her face. "My English teachers were quite impressed and highly praised my prose, mother. They told me I could be a writer of renown if I set my mind to it."

She attempted to make her voice soothing, encouraging. "Yes, you were always very bright, Jason. Your IQ was scored at the genius level. I thought when we had you tested that your father might realize what a rare child you were, that he would appreciate you more."

"Oh, he appreciated me, all right. I can assure you of that, Mama!" he snarled.

"I'm so very sorry, Jason. Please forgive me!"

"For I know not what I do?" he mocked. "Don't give me that shit, Mother dear. You knew all right. You just didn't want to lose your cushy job as wife of the wealthy Leif Hardaway and leader of the Highest Damn Society in the Western World. You were born to fill coffers with gold, which you could then distribute to the underprivileged, the minorities, the gay people, the fat people, the chosen afflicted ones. They all benefitted from your compassion and love for your fellow man. I always wondered why churches were never your charity of choice. Or why Cynthia and I never were privy to your bountiful generosity of spirit. Then I figured it out. God can be a real drag, and he's got all those nasty rules and regulations. You try to get creative with that guy's words and he comes down on you hard. So demanding. So unappreciative."

She hid her face in her shaking hands and sobbed without ceasing, as he continued. "Only a daughter of the devil could let her son lie in bed night after night waiting for the footsteps that warned him he was only moments away from indescribable pain and violation."

When he pulled her hands away from her face, her eyes were shot with blood and her face was streaked with mascara.

"Mother," he said with saccharine sweetness, "you are going to try once again to pay for your sins against me. And what I'm asking is not going to be difficult for you, because if I succeed, you will remain a rich wife, or maybe become a rich widow."

His laughter drowned out her sobs.

When both had ceased, he sat there, watching her intently.

A feeling of déjà vu washed over her. She remembered his sitting at the foot of her bed watching her prepare for one of her charity events, quite content just to be in her presence. She hadn't remembered that until now. She hadn't thought of anything except how that little boy had become a heartless, calculating murderer, and how she had become his accomplice. It wasn't supposed to have turned out like this. All she had wanted to do was save her son's life. It was the least she could have done.

"Time to go, Mom. I require another withdrawal from my inheritance fund. This may be the last time I will ask you to do my banking for me."

She nodded her defeat and slowly slid her narrow feet into her Bali pumps. She stood, trying to regain her balance. Then she plucked her Gucci purse from the bureau and followed him. Jason/Jude followed her down the back stairs, so they could enter the garage without being seen by the servants. He said nothing. She had nothing to say. Her thoughts were her own. There was Cynthia to consider. She winced. Considering anyone other than herself was an unfamiliar exercise; one she was in no shape to do properly, but it was vital she try. She had never taken the time to know her children. Now it was too late.

My God, how could she have deluded herself so completely, convinced herself that her benign neglect harmed no one?

But the fact remained that full expiation of her guilt should not mean that Cynthia become a martyr as well. This was her cross to bear, one Leif would soon hang from, she vowed.

"How do you plan to find the children?"

"Mother, you don't know me at all. People cannot keep secrets from me. They can try, but they never succeed. In this computer age, no one is safe from inquisitive minds," he cooed. "I had all the time in the world to do my research. And whenever I got close to finding my children, the name of Sebastian Vanderhyde would pop up, just as he popped up at my trials. He is the key. All I have to do is turn him."

"Please don't, Jason. Please."

"You know, I actually thought you'd be happy when I told you about your grandchildren, Mother," he said, scanning the address and smiling. "Instead, you seem horrified that any woman I would impregnate would choose not to abort my child. Why would she not take the better option: hacking it up into little pieces and putting them back together like a little human puzzle? That's what they do, you know, Mother. When it's too late to just vacuum the kid out, they just pull off its arms, legs, torso, head — like I used to do to insects. And to make sure they got all the parts, didn't leave a little finger or toe behind, they reassemble all the little pieces. Wonder what that job title might be?"

"I'm sure your father knew nothing about your, ah, becoming a father."

"Well, thank goodness for that; the old man might have killed me," he said, a mock horrified look on his face. "Oh, wait, he did kill me, didn't he? Just not for that particular infraction of impregnating a woman. He killed me because I could ruin his stellar reputation."

"He would never have done such a thing but...," she said defensively before she realized she was trying to rationalize a father murdering his own child. She was as bad as he.

"Of course Dad couldn't have something like a charge of incest hanging over his head. He had to make sure the offender and proof of the offense no longer existed. Thus the fire, thus the funeral. Poof, no more Jason, no more problem. Sadly, that left him with no one to molest, but I imagine not for long."

"Jason!" she screeched in agony. "You don't think..."

"No, I don't think, Mother. At least I try not to. I may not have much left in the way of humanity, but I pity the poor kid or kids he chooses for his next man/boy lovefest."

"Jason," she pleaded, "why don't you let the children be? You said they were placed with loving parents. And who knows where they are? They could be living somewhere in Europe, anywhere. Everyone involved would have wanted them as far away from the Hardaway family as possible, Jason, you know that."

The memory of her little boy plunged her into her own self-made hell.

"Being able to see them was a condition in her adoption agreement with them. I saw the papers. The mother of my children is not like you. Eager to be rid of her offspring."

"I realize what I am and what I am not." She tried to keep tears from blurring the road ahead, and attempted to keep her contemplation of suicide from steering them into the sound-proofing walls that ran alongside them. "I should never have been a mother, but your father insisted that we start a family immediately. I was so young, only eighteen. I didn't even know how to be a wife when I became a mother. I know that's no excuse, but I wasn't ready then. Maybe I never would have been ready, I don't know. All I know is that having a child was the most painful experience I ever had, and caring for helpless infants threw me into a panic. When either of you cried I felt helpless, then I felt angry. How was I supposed to know what you wanted? You never wanted my milk, you both made that clear. You spit it out like it was rancid. I couldn't seem to do anything to please you. But your nanny could, so I thought it was better that she take charge."

"Well apparently Nanny was just as deaf as you were. Or maybe the sounds she heard coming from my bedroom were music to her ears. Guess we'll never know, will we? By the way, what ever happened to Nanny Sloan?"

She stared at him with eyes as questioning as a frightened doe. "You didn't do anything to her, did you?"

"Now why would you think such evil of your lactose-intolerant son? My, my, you are coming unglued, aren't you? We can't have that. You must remain as strong as your martinis, mother."

His slim frame was rigidly planted in the passenger seat; his eyes were narrowed by speculation and darkened with threat. He frightened her.

"I'm now confident, Mother Lydia, that this day I will become a real father, and whether you like it or not, you are going to help reunite our happy family. Of course, we can't have a real family reunion without including the grandfather, can we?"

"You're going to see Leif?"

"Yes. I'm going to invite him to dinner after his board meeting. I'm sure he'll be hungry after tossing all that bull around. It's a tough job turning all those facts and figures on their heads and mentally transposing right and wrong. Selling America's technology to the enemy, after all, is not only in the company's best interests, but also an inevitable result of research. The Chinese will master the technology themselves in time, so why not profit from their lack of scientific intelligence in the interim? It's all so very simple," he said with practiced nonchalance.

"Leif will kill you, Jason. You know he will. He did that when he had far less to lose." Lydia had no fear for her husband's welfare. She would be far happier with him dead, but Jason was no match for the man, and she and Cynthia would surely be caught in their crossfire.

"No, he will help me, you can bank on that."

"What do you expect to accomplish? Your arrival won't ruffle him for long. He's very good at improvising, as you are well aware. He's always prepared for any contingency, any threat to him or his business. You can't beat him at the game he invented. Please, let's go to the police. That is the only way we can destroy him. That is what you want, isn't it? To destroy him?"

"With 'No-Controlling-Authority-Tony' to defend him, he won't spend a day in jail or a moment in pain. No, the Justice Department didn't know where to bury the stake, so the police sure as hell won't. Only I know every crack, crevice and stench of his body. Only I know how to make him suffer."

Lydia must let him go, knowing full well that today she would pay full price for the life she had bought with her children's trust. She was so frightened that if she knew how to pray she probably would have done it.

Her knuckles whitened on the steering wheel. By saving Jason's life she would assure the deaths of others. She had made a deal with the devil, and he wanted his payment. For the first time in her life she realized she had never been in control of it. She had no idea where she was going. And once she got there, it would be too late to turn back.

"Let me off here, Mother," he ordered as she stopped for a signal on California and Pine.

When she hesitated, he said, "Don't worry, I'm used to being dropped," he said, kissing her tear-stained cheek.

Lydia knew then she had to stop him. It didn't matter that her life would end as well. Her life had had no meaning for years. What do you call someone who has no substance? A ghost? An empty suit? Her designer suits, her magnificent home, and luxury car were but mirages on the desert her life had become. If she blinked, they would all be gone and she would be left with only a face surgically lifted, a marriage devoid of love, and a future as desolate as her soul. Why had it taken her so long to see that? Why had it taken murder to open her eyes to what and who she was? Now she had no choice but to see, and what she saw was more death, more hate and horror beyond belief. Unless she stopped it.

Chapter Twenty-Five

"Excuse me, ladies and gentlemen. I had no idea you would be meeting so late in the day. Especially since you've been seriously partying. I didn't get the nod to the Hardaway mansion, but my sources say it was a blast."

Jason had found it easy to slip in and out of his father's office. He'd done it dozens of times as a kid when he'd sit in his father's chair, pound on his desk, and pretend he was in charge.

He stood before the board members confident that none of them would suspect that an escaped murderer had gained entry to their hallowed room, especially at this hastily scheduled meeting. They would assume he was one of them — an elitist. Someone privy to the reason for the emergency gathering of the Board.

Leif frowned his disapproval of the interruption. He put down the pen he had been waving. His hands lay flat on the table as his eyelids opened and closed several times in quick succession. He was obviously thinking, "Where the hell is my secretary?"

"May I help you?"

"I'm sorry to interrupt, but I'm here to deliver a very important message to you, Mr. Hardaway. You probably don't recognize me, but I was a very close friend of your son, Jason."

At the mention of Leif's dead son, all the members took turns clearing their throats, loosening their collars, or otherwise fidgeting in their own discomfited manner. Leif had paled noticeably. His hands unconsciously formed, "Here is the church, here is the steeple," until he realized what he was doing.

"Excuse me, ladies, gentlemen," he said, rising slowly. He didn't take his eyes off the stranger as he moved toward him. "I won't be long," he advised the board members, motioning Jude through the door at the far end of the boardroom and into the reception area of the office. His secretary was nowhere in sight. He closed the door behind him and gestured toward his office. "Please."

Jude smiled and entered the spacious room. It was much as he remembered it, except for the twenty-foot by twenty-foot Oriental rug which had replaced the smaller, more colorful one. "Nice," he said, sitting in one of the club chairs in front of the heavily-carved desk. It was the same desk he remembered from childhood. It had frightened him then: those fierce looking lions' heads and claw feet. But now he was the lion. He had the claws.

Leif sat down behind the desk in the familiar leather chair. Jason had sat in it once too, until his father discovered him and accused him of soiling it. Jason had not only been a bed wetter, but also had been unable to control his bowels until he was almost eight. The doctors could never diagnose the problem sufficiently and suggested sending him to a psychiatrist. Leif, of course, could not have a psychiatrist probing around in the child's brain for evidence of his so-called crimes against the minor. Some professionals would have understood his theory, which held that no discernible damage could be done to a child involved in a relationship with an older male. But most would not have been sufficiently open-minded. He let his father mull over his options for a moment before he asked, "You don't recognize me?"

"Should I?"

"Only the voice is the same. The face has undergone some radical changes."

Jude saw terror in the eyes that had so terrorized him all those years ago. It gave him more satisfaction than he ever dreamed. "Oh, don't concern yourself, Father, it wasn't as a result of the fire that I required plastic surgery. I just thought a new face might go better with my new life. The one you forced me to invent."

"Jason?"

"The one and only."

"You must let me explain, Jason. You know I wouldn't deliberately hurt my own son." The terror was still blinking his eyes, shaking his hands, but he was recovering nicely, as Lydia had predicted.

"There's no need, Father. I understand perfectly why you wanted the building destroyed. And we both know why you wanted me destroyed. But that's history. I'm more interested in the present and the future."

"What do you want?"

"I want your help."

"What kind of help?" His hand was below the desk. Jude knew his father was slowly pulling out the desk drawer in which he had always kept a gun.

"Both hands on the table, please." It was not a request. Leif quickly obeyed.

"I have a scoop for you, Father. You are a grandfather. You didn't know that, did you?"

"What are you talking about?"

"I'm the proud papa of twins."

Leif's smile was weak as he strained to make sense of what his son was saying. "I'm happy for you. So, you're married?"

"No, I'm afraid the mother and I fall into that new category of single parent."

"Where are the children?"

"Now that's where you come in, Father. You have unlimited sources that enable you to find people, lose people, torch buildings. I knew I could turn to you for help in finding my twins."

"How do you expect me to find the children if you haven't? They could be anywhere in the country, in the world?"

"Trust me, they are close and getting closer. You find Sebastian Vanderhyde, you find the O'Regans."

"Who are the O'Regans?"

"Buddy and Bess's adoptive parents. Johnny O'Regan was the fireman who saved Cynthia's life, as well as her slutty friend, who is now his wife, Gracie. It's amazing how that woman cleaned up her act when she thought it may be curtains. My children were bequeathed to a bell-ringing, pole-sliding savior and his Mary Magdalene, Gracie."

"Does your sister know you're alive?"

"She knows everything, except where I am at this moment. Which is why we must hurry. She will not tell the authorities until she has to. Whether she knows it or not, she still loves her brother, but she's hanging around with guys like Sebastian who are intent on putting me back where they think I belong. Fortunately, I have an ally too. My loving father."

"Jason, I'm in the middle of a very important meeting. The future of the company you'll one day inherit is in jeopardy."

Jude stood, towering over him. "Your life is in jeopardy, old man!" he roared. "Now, let's move it. Get all your henchmen in a row right now or that boardroom full of jurists will hear all the juicy details of how you contracted to have your son murdered and how you acquired those blocks of San Francisco real estate in one fell swoop. And then you will find yourself locked up like I've been for so long. Only you will be in a prison where the bed partners aren't quite as domesticated as I was."

Leif picked up the phone, gave precise orders to one after another "specialist" on his payroll. The two studied each other in silence until the calls were returned, bringing them the final solution. With an almost bored expression, Leif assured his son that, according to the last caller, the O'Regans would be located within hours.

"Until then, Father, we're going to be spending some quality time together getting reacquainted. Won't that be fun?"

Chapter Twenty-Six

Johnny set his cell phone on the console between them. "Sebastian knows we're on the way to Woodside, that we're safe." So far, he cautioned himself.

"What did Sebastian say?" Gracie asked, turning around to check on the children in the backseat. She was relieved to see they were each engrossed in a book.

He kept his voice low, pitched at the hum of the car's engine. "He said we should have a talk with the children before we get to Woodside. There won't be much time for explanations once we're there."

"But the police certainly have been notified, haven't they?" Her hands and voice were trembling noticeably.

"Yeah, Eddie Cadigan is up to speed on everything, including the new information on the fire. Thrasher finally got ahold of the original report, the undoctored one. Chief Prudden, the gay caballero, was beholden in many ways to Leif Hardaway." His eyebrows arched dramatically. "In ways I never knew until Ed Cadigan filled me in."

"You mean Leif Hardaway is..."

He proceeded to fill her in. "So you see, it makes a lot more sense that he refused to give any consideration to further investigation of the fire that started Leif's real estate empire rolling."

"I remember you talking about Ed Cadigan. I hope he's as sharp as you say he is."

"He's the best on the San Francisco force. Thrasher's known him since they were kids. And in Sebastian's mind, the guy can do no wrong."

"It's been so long since we've seen or talked with Thrasher. Do you think we were wrong to cut him out of our lives when he needed us so terribly? We left him as abruptly as his wife and child, and just as unreasonably. What must he have thought of us?"

"I sure as hell didn't want Jude after him too. I owe him too much already. Without him in charge that day, I would never have been able to save you. A lesser leader would have accepted the situation as hopeless and the living beings inside that inferno as expendable. That was the philosophy in the department then, 'save your own ass.' Thank God, Thrasher was of the old school. He was there to save lives. If I hadn't gotten to you first, he would have."

"I thank God every day for both of you."

He regarded her as he would a brilliant gold nugget. "I sure as hell didn't think I was going to meet my future bride when I started digging through that pile of debris," he laughed. "When the smoke cleared I had myself a real find."

His smile lasted only a moment. "Sebastian has been investigating the fire and Leif Hardaway for eight years. It was only recently that Thrasher helped him put the final pieces together, and from what Sebastian told me when I called him earlier, it's not a pretty picture."

"There's no reason to keep anything from me now, Johnny. What don't I know?"

He looked sideways at her beautiful, freckled face, a face free of any artifice or makeup. He had loved that face from the moment he saw it, partially buried under what remained of a conference table.

"Sebastian will fill us both in when we see him. What we all have to hope for is that no one else, including the police, know all the facts. So many lives depend on our keeping some things secret. Thanks to Jude, too many innocent lives have already been torched."

She looked away from him and out the window, her reflection sallow. If the meek truly did inherit the earth, Gracie would be a very wealthy woman right now. All the fight seemed to have been drained out of her.

"Don't you dare pull that on me now, Gracie!" he ordered. "I don't need a helpless, submissive little woman in the passenger seat. I need that gun-toting, fish-scaling, chicken-plucking wife I know and love. I can't do battle without you slugging away right next to me, Gracie."

She turned toward him, and for the first time in two days, her smile was honest. "Right. So, who gets to throw the first punch?"

"Age before beauty is what my mother always said, so I guess you go first," he said, praying for a flying fist or scathing glare to let him know she was back in fighting form.

Her smile became a throaty laugh. Bess and Buddy both looked up from their books. "What's the joke?" Buddy asked.

She sobered instantly, hating the thought of ending her children's age of innocence before they'd had time to enjoy it. She turned until she was facing them head on. "You've known for a long time that your dad and I weren't able to have children of our own, so Bitti did a very courageous thing and gave you to us to care for and love."

"Yeah, because she couldn't take care of us as well as you and Dad could," Bess piped up.

"Cuz she loved us enough to give us two parents who would love us and protect us always," Buddy said.

Gracie's heart leapt into her throat. Buddy's words sounded rote, rehearsed. What if the children had merely been repeating verbatim what she and Johnny had been teaching them for eight years? What if they had never really understood the meaning of the words they dutifully parroted?

"And our birth father was sick and might have hurt us without meaning to, so Bitti didn't want us to know him," Bess added. "We already know all that."

If only the O'Regan family could just keep on driving, never leave the safety of the cocoon in which they'd all felt safe. But that wasn't an option, she knew. "I'm afraid there are some things we haven't discussed with you. We hoped it would never be necessary, because they were things we felt had no real bearing on the life we have together. But something has happened now that makes it important for you to know everything."

Buddy studied her, his green eyes glistening. He knew this wasn't a game any longer.

"Jude Orcus is your birth father's name. It's the name he adopted when he turned away from God. When Bitti first knew him, his name was Jason."

"Was he sick when he was Jason?" Bess asked.

"Not in the beginning. Like all children of God, he was innocent and trusting. But that innocence and trust were taken away from him, quite brutally, and all the goodness inside him began to harden and crack and fall away in big ugly chunks. What was left inside was anger and hatred and fear."

Johnny continued when he realized Gracie could not.

"It was his fear that made him want to get closer to Bitti. I'm sure he didn't want to hurt her, but in his great need to find human comfort, he got too close."

"And that's when they made us," Buddy finished. His life had been a sheltered one, but education had been the rule, not the exception, so his questions were always answered, and facts were deemed essential in finding the truth. Also, sex was no big secret on a farm.

"Yes, that's when you and Bess were conceived," Johnny answered.

"Did that make them happy or sad?" Bess boiled everything down to the heart of the matter.

"I wish I could say that it made them both happy, but that would be a lie." Johnny now began measuring his words more carefully. "It was wrong for Jason to get so close to Bitti, to love her in a way that only husbands and wives should love." From here on in, he'd be praying for the right words to come to him. He knew he couldn't find them on his own. Please, God, he prayed, don't let my words hurt them more than help them.

Chapter Twenty-Seven

"Here we are," Sebastian announced, as they pulled up to a scarcely visible wrought iron gate surrounded by camouflaging foliage, several live oak trees, and bushes of raging red roses. It would be difficult for anyone to see that there was a gate supporting the roses, or even a house beyond the gate, if one didn't have personal knowledge of it.

"It feels like we're in Bavaria instead of a northern California suburb," Leigh said, gazing around at the lush abundance of green above and around them.

"I've had this property for forty years. I lived here for twenty of those years with my wife."

"Your wife?" Leigh's aching head was once more barraged; her mind reeled from the battering of each new and disturbing piece of information. "You never mentioned being married? What else haven't you bothered to mention?"

Cynthia had been long silent. Now she frantically ordered, "Hurry, Sebastian. Get us through the damn gate."

He pressed a button and the gate opened slowly, allowing them to pass through before closing again.

Leigh was too scared to be polite. "You obviously have your reasons for keeping this place, your marriage, and whatever else a secret, but if I don't get some answers soon there's going to be an insurrection, I promise you."

"I intend to tell you everything, and there very well might be an insurrection, my dear. In fact, you may want to put me and Jude Orcus in the same cell."

Thrasher squeezed her hand. She hadn't realized he had been holding it. It felt good. It had been a long time since any man had held her hand.

Sebastian pulled into a three-car garage, which housed a classic Dusenberg and a vintage Cadillac. "Another well-kept secret," Thrasher said, eyeing the immaculately-preserved old cars.

Thrasher got out, then helped Leigh out the other side.

"Ever drive them?"

"Every chance I get." Sebastian led them through a stone courtyard covered with thick vines and splashed with bright blue and yellow flowers. Only the sky above was visible from inside its deep green walls.

Massive carved oak doors opened into a house both contemporary and ageless. The furnishings in the large vestibule and living room were European in origin and feel, representative of several historical periods. Leigh felt as if she were on a mystery tour as they traveled reverently through the rooms that introduced them to the real world of Sebastian Vanderhyde: the world he'd kept to himself for at least twenty years.

Leigh noted the many fine and obviously priceless objects which stood comfortably next to some not so fine but equally intriguing, like the 18th century monkey band holding two candlesticks, along with one vase containing a yellow rose. The beamed ceilings and rough-textured moss-green walls in the family room made it appear as if it had risen from the woods just beyond the leaded glass windowpanes. She would have loved to wander for hours through this treasure trove, as each room revealed one more clue to the identify of the man they had all thought they knew.

The dining room walls were hand-stenciled with Ottoman patterns, and the living room walls were coated with a type of plaster that made them look very old.

"The kitchen is no surprise," Leigh remarked upon entering it and identifying the Gageneau oven and the restaurant caliber appliances. "How many gourmet cooks does it take to make dinner for one?" Her question was an admonishment.

"From this day forward, you will all be invited here as often as you like." His pause was deliberate. "If you like."

Leigh felt as though she were groping her way down a dark path full of wild things and perilous ravines. The sequestered house and the thick woods surrounding it added to the dark fairy tale in which she now lived.

"Please sit down," Sebastian said, directing them into the comfortable family room. It too was filled with antiques, exquisite rugs and personal photos in silver frames; all components of a life and identity her friend and mentor had chosen not to exhibit. Cynthia was noncommittal and quite obviously not sharing their state of awe.

Each piece held a piece of his history, whether it be the small ink well or the large Remington bronze "Bronco Buster" mounted on a black marble slab. Leigh would have liked to have the luxury of time to peruse them all, but the minutes and hours were now determined in Jude's time zone.

"The alarm system's activated and Cadigan is on his way, so we can be comfortably at ease for a while, at least. I believe I could use a drink. Anyone else?"

"Vodka on the rocks for me," Thrasher said, following Sebastian to the highly polished mahogany bar that filled one corner of the family room. "Leigh, Cynthia?" he asked over his shoulder. "What can I get for you?"

"Scotch and soda, jigger of gin," Leigh said with a fecklessness that astonished her. Any moment could be her last, and she was acting if this were a cocktail party hosted by the March Hare.

"Are you serious?" Thrasher asked.

"That was one of my father's favorite drinks. And favorite songs," she added. "I need something to remind me of a better time. Scotch and soda might just do it."

Leigh sat down on the buttery leather sofa; Cynthia joined her. "I'm so sorry."

Leigh frowned.

"Jude did such awful things to you," she said with a shame-inspired blush. "Someone should have stopped him."

"What do you know about him, Cynthia? You never once mentioned his name all the time I was living with you, even though Sebastian told you all about my horrible experience with the man. And you certainly were aware of my nightmares."

"I wanted to talk about him." Her blush had spread to her neck. "I should have," she said, lowering her head. "I wish I didn't have to tell you this."

Leigh steeled herself for what was to come.

Cynthia looked questioningly at Sebastian. He nodded his encouragement. She inhaled deeply. "Jude Orcus is my brother."

Leigh's mouth fell open. Thrasher dropped an ice cube on the floor and barely held on to his glass. Sebastian looked on with a strange detachment.

"That monster is your brother?" she cried.

"And the father of my children." Her announcement was devoid of any expression, either on her face or in her voice. She appropriated the bored look of someone totally uninvolved in the horror of the evil intimacy.

"So he wasn't killed in the fire, even though the body we carried out was positively identified as Jason Hardaway." Thrasher looked to Sebastian for an answer. "What in God's name?"

With gentle concern, Sebastian leaned down and put a glass of white wine in Cynthia's hand. "None of what you are about to learn was done in God's name."

Cynthia moistened her lips, looked about to say something, then instead took a long sip.

Leigh and Thrasher stared slack-jawed at them both, and then at each other, as if to ask, "When does one of you burst out laughing and tell us it's all a bad joke?"

The anger in Leigh's eyes shot out like blue bolts of lightening. "Sebastian, did you know Jason was alive and posing as Jude Orcus? Did you know he was Cynthia's brother?"

He remained silent as she tried to absorb the extent of the infamy.

"Answer me, Sebastian. Did you know all of this when you came to Minneapolis? Did you know when you were sitting next to me at his trial, commiserating, offering me sympathy and understanding? Offering everything but the truth?"

"Yes. Cynthia came to me when she found out he was alive and posing as someone else."

Cynthia raised her head feebly. "I was recovering in the hospital when my mother told me that Jason was not dead. I guess she must have been feeling something close to maternal at that moment and thought that it would make me feel better to know that my brother was alive. If she saw fear in my eyes instead of relief, she didn't show it. She was more concerned with Jason than with me. She made me promise not to tell my father that his plan to kill him had not been carried out."

"She didn't know anything about what he did to you?"

"No. At least I don't think so. I found out I was pregnant while I was in the hospital. The doctor told my mother, against my wishes. She never asked me who the father was. Her only concern was that I get rid of the problem as soon as possible."

"I can understand your not wanting to tell me all this, Cynthia," Leigh said, blinking back the tears. "But Sebastian, you were my friend, and yet you chose to tell me nothing, to give me no warning about who this man really was." With great deliberation she said, "Which makes me ask, what kind of a man are you?"

His voice was old and frayed. "Only God will be the judge of that. In some people's opinion, I doubt I'm much of one." He sunk his huge body into a large wing-back chair by the cavernous stone fireplace.

Cynthia rushed to his side, knelt at his feet, and clasped his hands in hers. "If you don't tell them, I will, Sebastian. You don't deserve their contempt."

"Leigh does deserve an explanation, Sebastian," Thrasher said.

Leigh watched in fascination as Thrasher's shoulders grew wider as Sebastian seemed to dwindle before her eyes. She felt something close to revulsion for the man who had claimed to be her friend. "You wanted to get to Leif Hardaway through Jude, and I supplied you with all the ways and means. You wanted to help Cynthia keep him away from her children and destroy her father, using me as your hired gun. And when it backfired and I got hurt instead, you generously offered me a job with your magazine. You're as much of a hypocrite as the politicians you so despise. I trusted you. I believed in you. What kind of idiot does that make me?" Then, to her shame, she began to cry.

Sebastian's expression held profound sympathy for her, but he made no move to comfort her.

Thrasher remained standing at the bar. Leigh's words had frozen every one of them in place.

"I think we should concentrate on Jude right now, try to figure out his state of mind, his next move. He's having way too much fun with us. He obviously wants to see a lot of squirming on his line before he pulls anyone in. His note was a teaser, so he's in no hurry to end his fun. His father will certainly play an important role in his game. From the first I knew that Leif Hardaway had something to do with the Channing Building fire. Its historical designation made it impossible for him to raze it and follow through on his plans for two square blocks of new construction. But I never believed for a second that the body we found there wasn't that of his son. Hell, I even felt some sympathy for Hardaway when I saw him at the funeral. He looked devastated. Now that I know the truth, I'd have to say he's one heck of an actor."

"He doesn't know anything about love or the truth." Cynthia's face and glass were both drained. She held the glass up and Thrasher quickly moved to refill it. "I saw no evidence of human caring. I suppose he would have rather found another form of cover-up than throwing his son into a burning bush, but when the opportunity arose to destroy both the Channing Building and the one person who could in turn destroy him, he took it. As for being an accomplished actor, he's not. He's an accomplished liar. So accomplished that I'm sure he convinced himself that his grief was not of his own making, that a cruel Fate had taken his son from him."

"So who did die in that fire?" Thrasher demanded.

Cynthia's eyes were focused somewhere back in a time and place she'd spent years trying to escape. "Somebody no one would miss. There's no paucity of candidates on the streets of San Francisco, so I don't think Jason spent much time researching. He took whoever was handy at the time. When life has no value, only expediency counts. Jason didn't have much time to find a substitute corpse; his father planned to kill him in just a few hours. No time to be picky." Her voice was cold, her shoulders hunched into her chest. "Jason was in luck. He almost rid himself of another pesky problem: me."

"He would kill his own sister?" Leigh gasped.

"No, he didn't know I was going to be there. I was scouting out the building for an upcoming fund-raiser. I knew the Channing building would soon be bare, so decorating would be simple. The social types were always on the lookout for new venues that would have a kind of reverse chic. Little did I know that my father had other plans for the building."

"Your mother must have been horrified that she hadn't warned you of his plans along with your brother?" Leigh cried.

"If she was, she didn't show it. She just told me how relieved she was that I was all right. End of concern, end of discussion."

Leigh threw up her hands in frustration. "Is it supposed to be comforting that I'm not the only one he's out to get?"

"Please let Cynthia finish, Leigh," Sebastian said. "She's been waiting a long time for her chance to tell the truth. Killing the messenger would be exactly what Jude would want."

The flesh on Cynthia's face was pulled back tightly. Her mouth was a flat line. Her eyes were unlit. "Jason had gotten to the point where he couldn't face me or himself. He had a chance to start all over, become someone else, maybe someone he could face."

Thrasher took a fortifying swallow of his drink. "So he let another man burn."

"Yes," Cynthia agreed softly.

"We had a lot of young recruits on detail that day. Johnny was the only one I could trust to save anyone in the building and not kill himself in the process. The prevailing theory in the department at that time was that fires were far too hot to fight from the inside. Johnny didn't share that view. Neither did I. When we heard the screams, there was no alternative but to go in."

Cynthia smiled. "I thank God every day for you and Johnny O'Regan, Thrasher."

"And on that one day, at least, heroes really did walk the earth," Sebastian said.

Cynthia went on wearily. "I'm sure my father was surprised. Garden variety heroes didn't hang out with the Hardaways. Men who break down doors with hatchets, breathe in killer smoke, and use their God-given strength to pull people to safety exist only when they are needed. When they aren't, they are relegated to the shadowy place where cab drivers, bellmen, gardeners, and waiters all go when they become unnecessary. They're convenience people," she said, bitterness coating each word.

"And your father still believes Jason died in that fire?" Thrasher asked.

"Yes. Unless Jason has chosen to have him witness his rebirth within the last few hours. My mother's intentions were good. When it was already too late, she became rather skilled at protecting her son. My father, on the other hand, was concerned only with protecting his reputation. Child molestors have not yet become sympathetic figures."

"But Jason never told anyone. No one knew?"

"His bedroom was far from mine. Jason had been coming into my bedroom since he was a little boy, needing more than a teddy bear to ward away the nighttime demons. I didn't mind, I was lonely and scared too. It was only later, much later, that he demanded more than comfort from me. He never told me what father was doing to him, but by that time I was old enough to figure it out. What I couldn't figure out was why he did the same thing to me."

Leigh now understood why Cynthia had been so desperate to share her memories, to wrap herself in their comforting warmth. Her own memories were abhorrent. She put her hand over her glass in refusal of Thrasher's offer of another drink, then changed her mind. All this was too much to take cold sober. "Thanks, Thrasher."

Thrasher read her mind and poured generously. "At least some good came out of that fire. Johnny O'Regan met his wife to be, and I assume they are living happily ever after."

Sebastian and Cynthia exchanged looks before he said, "It would be nice to have him on our side again, wouldn't it?"

Thrasher nodded.

"You'll soon have the chance to see him re-enlist, Thrasher." Sebastian paused before hitting them with another round. "They are together, but life is not as happy for them as it was before Jude's escape."

"Johnny and Gracie? Here?"

"They'll be arriving shortly, I hope."

"You're not going to tell me that they have some connection to Jude too?"

Cynthia burrowed, then seemed to shrink in the wing-back chair that Sebastian had just vacated. It threatened to swallow her up. "Johnny didn't want to leave the department, Thrasher. He had to. Johnny and Gracie are the adoptive parents of my children. Jude's and my twins," she added with great effort.

Neither Thrasher nor Leigh had the time to sort it all out before Cynthia continued wearily. "Jason merely did unto me as he'd been done unto. He ceased to be my brother. My father had turned Jason into Jude. And Jude, in turn, made me someone I found I didn't like very much. When I found out I was pregnant, I couldn't see any way out of the horror my life had become except to get an abortion." She looked tearfully at Sebastian. "It was at the clinic that Sebastian found me."

Cynthia's expression was rife with so many emotions that Leigh couldn't begin to identify them all. There was love and admiration, surely, but there was something else, something more.

"Sebastian saved me. And Bess and Buddy."

"How was Sebastian involved?" Thrasher addressed Cynthia, as if Sebastian couldn't or wouldn't answer for himself.

"He was there for me. That's all I think I need to say." Before he could ask for clarification, Cynthia moved on. "I decided not to have the abortion, but I knew my child, or as it turned out, my children, had to be kept safe from Jude. I was afraid he was more like my father than even he understood, so I told no one I was pregnant. I just took off, told everyone I was involved in a study program in France. That was fine with Leif and Lydia. One less child not to worry about.

"I lived with Johnny and Gracie in Mendocino until the twins were born. I kept in touch with my parents by posting letters through college friends of Johnny's who lived in France, so they weren't suspicious."

Thrasher's normally restless body was as rigid as a statue, his beard growing as dark as the day. "I knew Johnny was as disenchanted with the fire department as I, and they were both disappointed that Gracie wasn't yet pregnant, but when they left the area so suddenly and wrote so rarely, I didn't know what to think, except that we obviously hadn't been as good friends as I'd thought. Now I understand why they didn't want anyone to know where they were."

"I know they hated deceiving you, Thrasher, but involving anyone else could prove dangerous to us all. They agreed to move away from San

Francisco to make sure that my family never knew about them or the twins. They agreed to that when we signed the adoption papers. They would do anything to protect the children, they've proven that."

"I'm so sorry, Cynthia." Leigh rose and put her arms around her and hugged her as if she were the child needing protection. "Please forgive me. I've been thinking only of myself and the danger Jude, or Jason, or whoever he is, poses to me. I spent only a few hours as his hostage. I can't begin to imagine spending years as his prey. And now to have your children threatened as well. I had no idea." She remembered Sebastian's warning and felt a rush of shame color her face. The only thing she had been hearing since that awful day was her own pitiful cries for help and mercy, unwilling to offer it to others. "None of us has to fight him alone, face him alone. We're all in this together, Cynthia."

Sebastian put his arm on Cynthia's shoulder. "Cynthia did the right thing. She has nothing to be ashamed of." He gave her an encouraging nod. "I do, however. In my zeal to uncover Leif Hardaway's shady deals and connections, I made him very nervous. When he first began dealing with the Chinese Communists, I made it clear in my magazine that I was going to go after him; that I would probe like a laser surgeon. He probably thought that I, like him, would not consider ethics to be essential in investigating an adversary. Actually, I never would have brought his relationship with his son into the equation, even if I had found out sooner what that sick relationship was. If Jason had still been a minor child, of course, I would have had to intervene, but Jason was by then an adult and capable of bringing his own accusations against his father, if he so wished. But Leif was confident of neither my ethics nor his son's silence, so he felt he had no choice but to silence both of us. Of course, he didn't realize his son was privy to his plan of sending him up in flames."

Sebastian regarded Cynthia with a tender look, but one without pity. "Nor did he realize that from that day on Cynthia would replace Jason as his nemesis."

Cynthia elaborated. "I didn't want to hate my father, I wanted to honor him and love him. But he turned love into a disgusting four-letter word and turned honor into blasphemy." She laughed nervously. "I'm beginning to sound like a television evangelist, aren't I?"

Sebastian put his hand on hers. "You must have a passion for what you do and believe, my dear. And no one is asking that you hate your father, just that you don't allow him to do to the rest of the world what he did to your brother."

"He began the foreplay by selling secrets to China. If he isn't stopped, the whole world will be screwed." Thrasher admonished himself with a grim smile. "Just call me metaphorically challenged tonight."

"So we know to what lengths to which the senior Hardaway will go to perpetuate his wealth and power. We have to know how far his son will go to satisfy his needs."

Cynthia nodded and brushed back a white-blond strand from her eye. "According to my mother, Leif instructed Jason to go to the Channing Building to inventory some old office furniture they were going to sell before remodeling the building. Of course, father had no intention of remodeling and no intention of letting Jason live."

"But you didn't know you were you pregnant at that time," Leigh reiterated.

"No, I didn't find out until they examined me in the hospital, just before I learned that Jason wasn't dead."

"So Jason was never aware then that you were pregnant with his child," Leigh said.

"No."

"But he did find out?" Thrasher was in full lawyer mode.

Cynthia moaned. "Dr. Kelleher. Our family doctor. He was at the hospital when they brought me in. He read my chart, found out I was pregnant. Of course, he advised me to abort. When I resisted, he considered it his duty to tell my mother of my stubborn foolishness."

"But no one knew Jason was the father?" Leigh couldn't help but wonder what she would have done in Cynthia's place.

"Who would I have told? Why would I want anyone to know I was pregnant with my brother's child? But I just could not bring myself to kill something so innocent, so yet undamaged. Nor could I stay in my parents' house any longer. I hated them almost as much as I hated myself. I continued to hate until Sebastian finally convinced me that it was eating up my soul. He also pointed out that my mother was probably carrying more guilt around with her than Jason. Jason knows that. He uses that. I'm sure he adopted the name Jude to make sure she never forgot her treason."

"How was it that you were at the abortion clinic when Cynthia went there, Sebastian?" Leigh asked. She was afraid to hear his answer. She wanted to keep on believing that he could never be or do anything that went against his beliefs, because many of those beliefs had become hers as well.

Cynthia's smile was pleading as she looked at Sebastian and shook her head repeatedly. "It's not important why he was there."

Thrasher roused himself from the bar stool. "Do you believe it's not important, Sebastian? If we're going to be prepared for Jude, we have to know everything, know where everyone figures into his plan. Or vendetta. You first came to me after the fire in the Channing Building, when you told me of your suspicions of arson and Leif's involvement, but how did you know Cynthia? Striking up a friendship with the daughter of a man you are trying to indict, especially in an abortion clinic, is a little odd."

"I sent him my résumé," Cynthia answered for him.

His thick eyebrows met in the middle of his forehead. "How impressive can the résumé of a twenty-year-old be?" Thrasher had her back on the witness stand. "You certainly have turned out to be one heck of an advertising manager, Cynthia, but Sebastian hires only the best and most qualified people for his magazine. That wasn't you. At least, not then."

Sebastian had been quiet throughout the exchange. Now his voice boomed. "There's no need for a cross-examination, Thrasher. You're not here as a prosecuting attorney."

"Why am I here? Obviously not as a friend, or you would be honest with me. From the moment Leigh received that note, you have been portioning out little bits of information, clues as to your connection to this Jude character and innuendoes about your relationship with Cynthia. I don't mind telling you, you're creating more questions than you're answering."

Leigh's fear was growing. She could not lose the man who had become her second father. And yet she feared she was about to. "You've always been very close-mouthed about your past, Sebastian? I admired you too much to pry into something you obviously were not happy to discuss, but we're no longer playing *What's My Line* here, this is life and death we're talking. You met at an abortion clinic. Were you there with a wife, a girlfriend? You had to have a reason for being there."

"My wife left me almost twenty-five years ago."

Leigh's resolve to know the truth momentarily wavered when she saw the pain distort his features. "Why did she leave, Sebastian?" she asked.

Sebastian regarded each of them with unblinking eyes. "Like Jude, I am a cold-blooded murderer."

Chapter Twenty-Eight

Johnny kept his voice even. "I know you're both familiar with the word incest. We discussed it when we were studying the French and English monarchies and the family inbreeding that caused such horrible results, like deformity and insanity."

They both nodded, unsure of where this was all going and wary of tagging along.

"Bitti changed her name after your birth, just as Jason did. But she changed it only for us. She became a different person when she gave birth to you. She wanted you to know the person she is now, not the troubled person she was before. We and our friend Sebastian are the only ones who know her as Bitti. That's not her given name. Her name is Cynthia, Cynthia Hardaway. Her brother Jason, who calls himself Jude, is your father."

There were low moans of surprise followed by moments of strained silence, as they absorbed the portent of the words.

"Will we be deformed?" Buddy's calm had vanished.

"Will we go insane?" Bess cried.

"No, no, you were both born perfect in every way," Gracie nearly shouted.

"So this Jude dude doesn't want anyone to know the bad things he did?"

"No, Buddy," his mother explained. "We think maybe he wants everyone to know the bad things he did."

"Especially his father," Johnny added, wondering just how far back he should go into this hateful history lesson.

"Does Jason hate his father?"

"Most of all," Gracie said.

"Did his father get too close to him too?" Buddy was catching on fast. Too fast, Gracie thought, despising Jude for making her babies grow up so fast, forcing them to understand things they should not have to understand. At least not yet.

"Yes, Buddy, his father did get too close to him. But he didn't let anyone else get close; no family and friends or anyone who may have been able to help the boy see that he was not to blame for his father's actions. But after awhile, it was too late for anyone to help him. By then he didn't want help. All he wanted was revenge."

Only after her own brush with death had Gracie learned the value of life. And only after the birth of the twins had they both allowed the painful memories of the raging fire to fade to black and white instead of remaining a vivid blood red.

"She didn't have to have us, because we were an accident," Buddy charged.

There were some facts of life Gracie had hated teaching them. Like the fact that babies could be disposed of if their creation was untimely or inconvenient. "To God you were never an accident. Bitti heard God's voice and felt you growing inside her."

Johnny wanted them to understand the true miracle they were, not an accident. Cynthia would have had good reason in the eyes of many to abort them. They were, after all, a product of her brother's rage and forceful rape. Thankfully she had found a man who could deliver her and her babies from the hell into which she'd fallen. That man was Sebastian.

"From the moment you were only one cell old, every detail of the person who is you was already there; your sex, your hair and eye color, your height, and the color of your skin. And by the time you were nine weeks old you were sucking your thumb and doing the backstroke."

"You could also do the backflip and a somersault, according to Bitti," Gracie quipped.

"Did I have my penis then too?" Buddy asked with increased interest. That was the one distinction his twin sister could not claim.

"Not until you were about four months old," Johnny said, chuckling.

Bess was not so easily swayed from her initial fear. "Jason was sick and bad, and we were half his, half of him. Maybe we'll get sick too."

"No, Bess. You may have been created by a sinful man, but you were sent to us by a loving God. That's what you have got to believe. That's what we have believed since we first held you in our arms and felt your hearts beating against ours. You were gifts sent to us straight from God."

"Does Jason know we were sent to you?"

"No, he only knows that you were adopted, not by whom. At first he believed you'd been aborted, and when he found out you were alive, he wanted to see you."

"She was going to kill us?" Buddy's voice held an awe of what might have been.

"No, she couldn't do that, because she knew you were living inside her, that all your tiny fingers and toes, your heart and your lungs, were all there and growing with each day."

"You said Bitti found a man who helped her?" Bess asked excitedly, wanting the story to have a happy ending.

"Not in the way she had planned. And not even in the way he planned. But God was there with them, and His spirit moved them to do the right thing. And eight months later, you two were born. Bitti, I mean Cynthia, is going to be waiting for us at the house in Woodside. So will the man who helped her," Johnny promised.

"What's his name?"

"His name is Sebastian, Bess, and you're going to like him."

"Are we almost there, Dad?"

"It's a long way from Mendocino to Woodside, Buddy, but I think we should be there within the hour. It's been over eight years since we were last at Sebastian's house, but believe me, I'll never forget the road that led us there."

"What were you doing there eight years ago?" Bess's voice was smaller. She had heard too many answers she didn't like today.

"We were celebrating," Gracie answered, a smile in her voice.

"Celebrating what?" Buddy's curiosity overrode his fear.

"Becoming your parents," Johnny answered, watching his son's reaction in the rear view mirror.

"We were born in the house in Woodside, Dad?"

"No, but that's where we took you after Bitti gave birth to you in a nearby hospital. It was the safest place to be."

"Could you just take us out of the hospital without signing papers and everything? Legal stuff, I mean?"

"Very good, Buddy. Yes, of course everything had to be done legally. We didn't want anyone to be able to claim you didn't belong to us. Sebastian is a lawyer as well as a famous publisher and editor, so he drew up the papers, and we all signed them and had them recorded."

"If they were recorded, doesn't that mean that they become public information, that anyone can see them?"

Johnny suddenly had very ambivalent feelings about the diligence and thoroughness of their home-schooling. The children knew all about individual rights and the Constitution. They knew how evil people could use those laws and rights. Now that Jude was running free, he would have an opportunity to check the records, find out who they were and eventually where they were.

"Jude is a wanted man, Buddy, and his picture has gone out to all the police departments in the area."

"But you said someone is helping him, Dad. Couldn't that person get the records for him?"

"He might be able to discover our name, but then he would have to find us."

"Sometimes you get checks from the fire department, Dad. Would someone there tell him where you were if he was mean enough to them. Or nice enough to them."

Buddy's innocent assumptions made their blood run cold.

Chapter Twenty-Nine

Ed Cadigan was everything one would expect and pray a police inspector would be. His face was ruggedly handsome; his build was sturdy and manifestly capable of dispensing with any criminal intent on doing harm. His eyes were in turn steely and soft, depending on who and what he was addressing. When focusing on Thrasher and Sebastian, they were the shade of flint; while with Cynthia and Leigh they warmed to pewter. For all of them he inspired confidence that the good guys would indeed triumph.

"How long have you known that Jude Orcus is Jason Hardaway, Ed?" Thrasher asked.

"Sebastian wanted to know how to best protect Cynthia from the guy. I did a little bit of consulting on the subject."

"And I never had the chance to thank you for that, " Cynthia said.

Most people in trouble took comfort in the detective's bigness, his natural authority, and the fact that he seemed accustomed to people depending upon him. It was obvious to every one in the room that Cynthia was one of those people.

"I'm only sorry that I didn't know Jason was alive until my mother told me in the hospital. By that time she'd already made arrangements for a kind of safe house, then plastic surgery. She also set up an offshore account for him in some South Pacific Island that had no international treaties and no United States diplomatic reciprocity. From then on he could access money from any ATM in the world. She was almost delirious with joy that my father had been the one to show her how that could be done." She took a cleansing breath before she said, "Jason made his own arrangements for the replacement corpse, I believe. I doubt that mother would have had the courage to do that."

"Jason's staged death had to be kept secret if he wanted to survive, yet he allowed your mother to tell you?" Thrasher was impatient to have all the pieces finally put together.

"He learned through my mother that I was pregnant. That was even more important to him than his freedom. He wanted that child."

"Quite a gutsy move, Ms. Hardaway, choosing to have a child from an incestuous relationship. Especially when you knew your brother was so...unbalanced," Ed finished tactfully, his warm eyes thoughtfully appraising her.

She looked pointedly at Sebastian. "Even though I was frightened, I knew I was doing the right thing by carrying the babies to term. And I had the encouragement of a very good friend through it all."

Cadigan nodded. "Sebastian?" he encouraged his friend.

"What I did I did as much for me as for Cynthia."

When only silence followed his enigmatic remark, Cadigan pressed on. "Jude is very resourceful. He found out that Cynthia gave birth to twins and gave them up for adoption. I have my own resources; some in the institution where he was sent. I found out what he had found out and passed along the information to Sebastian, who in turn warned Cynthia. There wasn't much he could do while in the hospital, but now that he's out..."

Cynthia didn't allow him to finish. "He will kill everyone who stands in his way. Those children are his salvation. By borrowing their innocence, he can regain his own. He can live through them, exchange his own childhood for theirs."

"How do you know all this?"

"We shared a bed," she snapped. She quickly regretted her terse remark when she saw how Ed reacted to it. She felt her face grow hot with embarrassment and shame. "I know him only too well."

Leigh reached out tentatively for her hand and was relieved when Cynthia took it.

"I'm sorry to have to ask these painful questions, Ms. Hardaway."

"Cynthia, please," she said in apology. "I'm sorry too."

"Since this man causes a real danger to you all, I'd like to arrange for a twenty-four-hour guard."

"I don't plan to let the man put a hold on my life or the publication of my magazine," Sebastian snarled. "I'm sure he doesn't see Thrasher as a threat. The O'Regans, Cynthia, and Leigh are in the greatest danger."

"Not for long, hopefully. The police are conducting an all-out search for him. He's a danger to anyone and everyone who may cross his path."

"I hope it isn't too late." Leigh spoke what they all were thinking.

"Yes, he may already be close to finding Johnny and Gracie and the kids. I thought this would be the safest place for them, but maybe I was wrong," Sebastian remonstrated.

"I'll have one of my men posted here and at Leigh's house. I promise you, Jude will be arrested and put away. Permanently this time," Cadigan pledged.

"Yes. Contrary to their live-and-let-live philosophy, California citizens and the courts are still strongly in favor of the death penalty."

Leigh found Thrasher's words reassuring, especially since he may one day be in a position to uphold that penalty. She wanted him to be reassured as well. She could take care of herself.

"I don't want him in charge of my life anymore," Leigh announced. "I have an alarm system, and I own two guns. If he managed to bypass the first obstacle, I wouldn't have to give a moment's thought to shooting him right through his heart. Or the place where one ordinarily resides," she added. Immediately after she said it, she wished she had thought of Cynthia's feelings before issuing the threat.

She needn't have worried. Any brotherly love she had once had for Jason was long gone. "I wouldn't hesitate to shoot him either, Leigh, although I would aim for the groin area."

Her choice of target gave them all something to smile about.

"I want him put away, done away, gone from our lives. What he did was unconscionable, but Bess and Buddy are the result of it, so I can't hate him as much as I would like to."

"I think it would be wise for us to take the ultimate precaution and summon the best help possible. Let's hold hands and bow our heads," Sebastian said, his confidence in and reverence for his God as strong as the circle they formed.

"Dear Lord, our times are in your hand," Sebastian prayed, loosely quoting Psalm 31:15.

For the first time since they had entered the house in Woodside, a peace settled in.

Chapter Thirty

Leigh wanted to remain there until the O'Regans arrived, but Ed Cadigan strongly suggested either he or Thrasher escort her home. Thrasher was quick to volunteer, which left Ed free to drive Cynthia back to San Francisco. Cynthia's blush made it clear that arrangement was fine with her.

If Leigh weren't so bone weary and a little dizzy from the scotch and soda, she would have argued. Maybe. It was becoming harder to disregard Thrasher's masculine presence and the calming effect it was having on her. She'd forgotten how nice it was to have a man take charge. Also how addictive. A man's body created a powerful heat source found nowhere else. Contrarily, she shivered as she and Thrasher slid into the front seat of Sebastian's car.

"You cold, Leigh? Here, let me turn up the thermostat. I'm sorry, but I seldom turn these things on. My blood runs hot, I guess."

Everything he said and did seemed designed to lower her resistance and raise her awareness. "Thank you, I am a little chilly," she admitted, more tightly wrapping around her the hooded coat Sebastian had loaned her. She wasn't sure she'd ever be warm again. The primitive urge to tuck herself under his arm and bury herself in his bigness was almost overwhelming. Almost.

"Quite a day, wasn't it?" he said, backing the car out of the secluded driveway.

The moon's glow carved his profile in ivory, making his jawline seem even more firm and strong, his nose straighter, and his lips sensuously full. He would be considered movie-star handsome had this been forty years earlier. Today, most male stars were either androgynously pretty, or filthy and unshaven, not this irresistible hybrid of Cary Grant and Tom Selleck.

"Yes, quite." She couldn't remember. Had it been this hard to breathe normally when she was with Bill? Had she ever felt this intensely the need to be part of someone?

"I still don't have it all sorted out," he said. "It's like trying to find the grain of truth in a brimming silo. Tough job when you can't even find the silo."

"What is it Sebastian and Cynthia are still keeping from us?"

"Whatever it is, Cynthia doesn't want us to know about it. Notice how she shut Sebastian up every time he was about to come clean?"

"I sensed the same thing."

"It's hard to imagine Sebastian doing anything unethical or even morally questionable."

"He said the same thing about you?"

He scrunched up his forehead.

"He said you reminded him that saving a life was not merely one choice among many, but a moral mandate."

"Why do you think he needed a reminder of that? In all his books, columns, and editorials I never heard despair or negativity. Without his inspiration, I was the one who would have given up on the human race."

She paused, as if trying to remember Sebastian's exact words. "He told me he had once worked as a butcher, and like Pontius Pilate, he had washed his hands of the blood of the lamb, but the stain remained."

"What in the world did he mean by that? Are we supposed to take him literally?"

"You've known him a lot longer than I, but if you think about it, his life has been very episodic. It's possible he really was a butcher in one of his many lives, although I don't think butchers worry much about getting their hands bloody."

"After tonight's revelations I'd have to say anything he does or did do would not surprise me, but I don't think he meant it literally. I think he was alluding to something he did in one of those past lives, something he can't forget."

"Or forgive?"

"Sebastian doing something unforgivable? I suppose it's possible; he's his worst critic."

The sky was black, the road almost deserted at this hour — that time before dawn when it truly is darkest. Their silence was a companionable one, yet she felt a very strong sexual tension. Maybe that was inherent in any new and unexplored relationship and really didn't mean that much.

Thrasher looked over at her with a slight frown. "I really don't want to talk about Sebastian any more, Leigh. I want to know how you're doing."

With a valiant smile, she answered, "Thanks to you, better than I should."

"I never met Jude Orcus/Jason Hardaway, I'm happy to say, but he's got to be the worst nightmare one could imagine." He let his words sink in before adding, "I don't think you should be alone tonight." He hurried on, preventing her from answering before carefully considering what he was about to propose. "I know you have all that security in place, but sometimes it helps to have another warm body near by when you hear those bumps in the night."

"My dad used to say that?"

"What?"

"Things going bump in the night. That's how he'd explained away every scary thing: just a bump in the night." Suddenly she was crying like the scared little girl she'd been.

He stopped the car on the side of the road, pulled her over, and put his arms around her, drawing her so close she could feel the buttons of his shirt pressing into her breast.

"I don't know why I'm crying, Thrasher." She raised her head and bit her lip. "I'm not the weepy type; ask anyone. I learned long ago that tears don't wash away anything but mascara." She attempted a laugh. "I haven't made a very good impression since we were introduced, have I?" she said, pulling away only slightly.

He cupped her chin in his hand and studied her face. "You are a beautiful, brave, and intelligent woman, Leigh. I'm impressed. Very impressed." Then he smiled that smile she had first seen at the Hardaway mansion. It seemed eons ago.

"Did you ever see the play, *The Longest Day*?"

"I don't think so," Thrasher said, puzzling the question.

"I didn't think it would ever end. Just like this day. And the one I spent with Jude Orcus. How many more of my days do you think he'll stretch into eternity?"

"He's only human, Leigh. Even though I'll admit he has few of the normal characteristics. He can be stopped, you know. He wants to be stopped. And I'm more than willing to accommodate him. Keep in mind, Super Cop Ed Cadigan is on the case, so the creep doesn't have a prayer."

When she remained silent, he added, "But I have one," he said, taking her hand in his and folding them both together. "I pray that all the choices we make from now on will be pro-life." His smile was as alluring as his lips.

At that moment Jude Orcus didn't seem so formidable. The night didn't seem so dark. "Yes." His prayer ended with a kiss.

Chapter Thirty-One

Sebastian was just starting to get worried when Johnny called to say that he, Gracie, and the kids were at the gate. He quickly buzzed them in and rushed to the door to wait for them. Cynthia was right beside him. Ed Cadigan's hand was on his gun.

The children walked sleepily through the door. When they saw Cynthia their confusion was written clearly on their wan faces; they hesitated running to her as they normally did. Everything they'd been told had made her a stranger, someone of whom to be wary. Bitti had been so fun, so cool. Cynthia was serious and sad. She had seen and done things they were frightened to think about.

Sebastian welcomed the four into the house with a hug for Johnny and Gracie and a formal handshake for the children, who did not yet know him well enough to hug. Cynthia hung back slightly, smiling lovingly at the children. Ed slapped Johnny on the back and smiled at Gracie.

Gracie acknowledged her husband's friend but moved quickly toward Cynthia, grabbing her like a lifeline. "It's okay, Cynthia. They know everything now. It will take a little time for them to get used to the new you, but they still love you."

Johnny added his arms to those of the two women, and he held them both in his giant grasp. After giving his support, he turned to the children. "Give Bitti a big hug and a kiss. She's been very worried about us, and I think she needs to know how much we all love her."

Bess made the first move toward her, then Buddy followed. Soon they were all hugging and laughing as if nothing had changed.

Johnny waited for them to settle down, then he introduced them to Sebastian. "Kids, this is the man who is responsible for taking care of Cynthia and getting us together. Without him, we wouldn't be your parents, so we owe him a very big debt of gratitude."

"Thank you," they said dutifully, obviously curious about the bearded man who looked a lot like Santa Claus, except for the stiff gray suit and striped tie.

"You're welcome, Bess, Buddy. Now, I bet that long ride has made you pretty hungry, right?"

Their parents had taught them not to ask for things, but the question needed an answer. "Yeah, I'm starving," Buddy admitted.

"Some food would be very nice," Bess said, her stomach growling loudly in agreement, the sound bringing a welcome laugh from everyone.

"I just happen to be a very good cook, I'll have you know," he said, leading the way into his industrial-sized kitchen. "And my burgers and hot dogs are the best in the Bay Area. PacBell Park has been trying to get my recipes, but I'm holding out."

Very soon they were all pouring catsup, spreading mustard, and acting as if the bogeyman had already been disposed of.

For the sake of the children, the adults disguised their fear in flashy shows of hunger, taking great gulps of iced tea and coffee and big mouthfuls of burgers and chips. Dessert was a choice of apple pie and ice cream or left-over creme brulee, Sebastian's own variation of the delicious custard.

When they finished eating, Sebastian questioned enthusiastically, "Have you ever had a secret place to play hide and seek, a place no one else knew about?"

Bess and Buddy's eyes lit up. "Yeah, there's a cave near our house where we could hide for years and no one would ever find us," Bess cried.

"Except Mom," Buddy added.

"Well, I have a secret hiding place that not even your Mom could find. Want to see it?"

They followed him with eagerness, and he was struck by how easy it was to get children to follow. He cringed at the thought that Jude could also be successful in getting them to follow him, if given the opportunity to try.

Sebastian led them all down a long hallway, past the master bedroom, three enormous and well-appointed guest rooms, and into a paneled library lined with shelves of books all the way to the ceiling. A beautifully carved sliding ladder stood against one of the walls. "I'll go first and show you how to get into my secret hiding place," he said, climbing the ladder. Halfway up, he pressed the spine of a book of poetry. A large section of the wall opened to reveal a large room furnished as beautifully as the rest of the house. "Come on up," he said, stepping from the ladder onto the thickly carpeted floor of the concealed room.

Buddy followed next, then Bess. Johnny helped Gracie up the first steps and then he began the climb. They all fit easily into the sixteen- by twenty-foot room, in which there were two bunk beds, one double bed, several comfortable chairs and two end tables on which sat exquisite Tiffany lamps.

"Wow! I've never seen anything like this!" Buddy marveled, gazing around the room as if he had just stepped into Alice's Wonderland.

"I saw something like this in an old English movie once," Bess said, as awed as her brother. "I expect Miss Marple and Agatha Christie to poke their heads in any minute."

"Did you know this was here, Bitti? I mean Cynthia?" Buddy asked, touching everything, missing no detail of the wonderful room.

"Yes, I spent several weeks here once. I know it will be as fun for you as it was for me to have a place to go; one that's safe and comfortable for as long as you need it."

"How long do you think that will be, Sebastian?" Johnny murmured in his ear, careful not to let the children hear him.

"According to Cadigan, not long. Jude will have to make his move soon. Cadigan had an interesting talk with Lydia Hardaway. Fortunately, she was too distraught and guilt-ridden to continue protecting a killer, even if he is her own son. Although, she did insist that it was all her fault that her son believed murder was his only recourse, and admitted that she had helped him all along the way. But she also assured Cadigan that she wanted Jude captured, and in that way both her children and her grandchildren could be removed from harm's way. For Jude, that means either prison, the electric chair or hospitalization. She's still holding out hope that he can be helped, although that's very unlikely, and she knows it. She'll settle for stopping him and letting the law decide his fate. Without her aiding and abetting, I'm sure that can be arranged."

"Will he be able to find us here?"

"Lydia said Jude was going to see his father. Given the fact that Jason is supposed to be dead, I'm sure Leif will be a bit taken aback at first, but he's a survivor, and if his survival depends on helping his dead son find his children, he'll make that happen. He's got one hell of a lot of people who can grant him his every wish. With all the incredible technology at his disposal, he's a formidable ally to Jude."

"But a very reluctant one, I'm sure. He's got to be making plans to stop him too. Talk about a loose cannon."

"As am I. Leif's counting on us annihilating one other, so he'll be happy to direct Jude right to us," Cadigan explained.

"We had a heck of a time finding this place, even after having been here eight years ago. You think he could find it, Sebastian?"

"Yes, I'm afraid so, Johnny. But my security system is the best, so we'll have the advantage of knowing when he arrives. It will be soon, so I want you to stay up here. Ed and his men will make sure I'm okay. This room is just an added precaution, just in case."

"Just in case of what?"

"In case Jude is somehow able to pull off one more Houdini."

Chapter Thirty-Two

"You have a sofa? Or maybe a bearskin rug?"

For a moment she couldn't remember what she had, except for an increasing desire to watch Thrasher Cole's lips move. "I, well, yes, sure, I have a sofa."

"Mind if I bunk on it?"

"I met you only twelve hours ago." She tried to sound more incredulous than she felt, because she felt as if she had known him forever.

"Twelve hours ago Jude Orcus wasn't back in your life."

"I'll be fine; you don't have to baby-sit me."

He wasn't about to accept a no. "Twelve hours ago I didn't know anything about Leigh Barnes except that she writes a devil of a defense of the second amendment and looks a whole lot like the angel I once saw in a dream. And yet in twelve hours I think I've come to know you better than any women I've been with since my wife died."

She was desperate to have him stay, and at the same time anxious to have him leave. She was feeling far too much far too fast. She thought she had trained her mind well, convinced herself that loving someone offered only pain, not happiness. Loving Bill, loving her parents had proved that.

He was waiting patiently, unaware of the mental tug of war going on in her head. The day had been such an emotional one that perhaps she was reading more into this than was actually there. Maybe in the harsh light of day all the intensity would fade into normalcy and Thrasher Cole would turn into a nice but not thrilling guy. She offered a feeble answer. "I feel as if I know you too, but not well enough to sleep with." She rushed to her own defense. "I mean sleep in the same house with."

He grinned. "Writers aren't supposed to end a sentence with a preposition, are they?"

"You know what I mean. It just seems like everything is being fast-forwarded."

"Trust your instincts. They'll swear I'm harmless. Except if Jude Orcus comes anywhere near you, then I'm hell on wheels."

His guileless smile made her feel foolish for protesting what she herself knew was prudent.

"You must know Sebastian is counting on my staying with you."

"I suppose so, but."

"So is that a yes?"

"That's a yes," she answered, wondering if he could see the warm glow of her cheeks in the dim light of the car.

Once inside, she armed the security system and turned on every light in the house. He led her around from room to room, checking for anything out of the ordinary. The only thing that seemed incongruous in the softly feminine decor was a large gold frame on the living room wall. Mounted on a background of blue sky and white clouds was a large gold medal hanging from the end of a red, white and blue ribbon. He took a closer look. "Were you a runner, Leigh?"

She stared at the framed medal as if she had never seen it before. "I always believed Bill's death was just a horrible accident. But I should have known better, shouldn't I?" she asked.

She was looking at him as if she expected an answer, only he had no idea what her question was. "Who is Bill?"

"A man who would be alive today if he hadn't made the mistake of loving me."

She abruptly turned and punched a button on her answering machine. There was one message. He could tell by the look on her ashen face that the voice was a familiar one. "Moonbeam." The one-word message was a body blow that threatened to topple her. Her hand flew up as if hit by shrapnel. "Dear God!" Her fluttering finger was a divining rod, seeking out the erase button.

"Don't Leigh, that's evidence."

"It's Jude."

"He's indicting himself, don't you see?"

But she saw nothing but the offending machine. Not even Thrasher.

He gently removed her hand from the button, eased her back from the machine. "You can't let him get away with this, Leigh. We can't let him."

She blinked him into focus. "What am I going to do?"

"Not what he expects you to do."

"I don't know what he expects of me." Her slender arms hung limply at her sides. Her shoulders hunched into her chest. "I was foolish enough to think that because my number is unlisted he couldn't reach me." She shook her head angrily. "Why am I so stupid where he's concerned? Why do I always underestimate him?" The stylish suit she had slipped into so easily this morning was beginning to feel like a straight jacket.

"You aren't stupid, Leigh. Anyone who thinks like Jude is just as sick as he. You can't read his mind because it's indecipherable to anyone capable of deductive reasoning. There is no reason behind his actions, only hatred — of himself and anyone who obstructs what he considers a just revenge."

"I'm glad you're here, Thrasher." She raised her arms, her fingers so close to touching his lips. Instead, she backed away, turned, and started toward the linen closet in the hall. She brought out flowered sheets, a peach-colored blanket, and a down-filled pillow tucked inside a crisp cotton pillowcase. She placed them all in a pile on the cushioned sofa. Before he could say anything, including good-night, she disappeared down the hall.

Her bedroom door closed. A few minutes later her bathroom faucet was running, and then silence.

Thrasher remained awake and alert. Just as when he was on detail in the firehouse, sleep could come only when the alarm bells stopped ringing. Tonight the alarm bells would be continually going off, either in his head or in the reality Jude Orcus had forged. Jude would not claim another victim on Thrasher Cole's watch.

Chapter Thirty-Three

"I'd really like you in there with them, Sebastian." Ed Cadigan's wide-set eyes seemed to be encompassing the entire house at once, while his arms were poised slightly away from his body in readiness to defend or attack. Once he had satisfied himself that all was well, he turned his attention to Cynthia. "I'll agree that you can return to your house in the city, but only if I am personally in charge of your safety."

"Sebastian thinks that's best, so if he says I should be with you, who am I to argue?"

The frightened woman running from her parents' mansion, from her past, and from herself was nowhere in sight. In her place stood a woman on the verge of self-discovery.

"Just take care of her Ed, we'll be fine here." In answer to the cop's look of skepticism, he said, "You know my security system, Ed, it's as close to impenetrable as technology can make it. I do not underestimate Jude, especially with his father's techno-geeks providing another Number One Enemy with all their new toys of destruction. In our favor is that fact that he's spent years of his life in an institution, and he's not an expert on breaking and entering."

"The management and staff of two state institutions might disagree. A guy smart enough to weasel himself out of two state hospitals is smart enough to weasel himself into one private home."

"I don't deny his genius, Ed, which is why I'm taking the extra precautions with the O'Regans. I will not take any chances with those kids' lives."

"But it's okay to put your own in jeopardy?"

"I don't see it that way."

Ed's expression was dour. "After all these years I guess I should know that it's senseless to try to argue you out of something once you've made up your mind, but I don't think you understand the depravity of this man." He laid a sympathetic hand on Cynthia's shoulder. "Nor would anyone want to understand."

With a startling ferocity, Sebastian responded. "I have been that depraved man, Ed."

Cynthia stiffened and looked pleadingly at Cadigan, who was shaking his head.

"Not even close, my friend, not even close."

"You know what I did, and you can still say that?"

"What you did was not against the law, Sebastian, and I should know, since I am the law."

"An earthly law with loopholes and escape hatches built in. God's law is immutable, and I broke it thousands of times — intentionally and arrogantly."

"I hope you haven't made your false confession to anyone but me and Cynthia?" The detective leaned forward, his gray eyes darkened to coal.

"Not yet."

"Not ever, if you value all the work you've done, all the progress you've made in changing people's minds and hearts."

"It will all come out one day anyway, Ed. I'd rather be the one to 'out' me."

"You acted out of honest concern, Sebastian. You had your reasons, good ones. Hell, even I thought they were good ones at one time."

"Thanks, Ed, but you only thought, I acted."

"You know yours won't be the only reputation to be hurt," he cautioned.

"Yes. I've been thinking about Thrasher."

"And Leigh," Cynthia said. "If your past is revealed, so will hers. How do you think she's going to feel about you if she knows you've been keeping such an enormous truth from her all these years? How do you think the memories she has of Ellen and Larry Barnes will fare?"

The accusing words sunk in. "You're right."

"Now that that's settled, what we must be concerned with is that I have sufficient manpower to cover all the bases. It's only because of your sophisticated security system — and your stubbornness — that I even consider leaving you without human protection."

He took his wary eyes off Sebastian and directed them to Cynthia, who was at his side looking as if she would break into, *Stand By Your Man* at any moment.

"I'll be keeping an eye on Cynthia," he assured Sebastian.

"Tough duty, but someone has to do it, right?"

Cynthia blushed and Ed blustered, "Along with one of my best men, of course. She has to be watched particularly closely, since her brother will be after her if he decides he can't find his children by any other means." He spread his legs apart and took a macho stance. "Doesn't hurt that she thinks detectives are sexy," he winked at both.

As cavalier as he sounded, Sebastian was confident Ed would never allow Jude another chance to violate his sister.

Together, Sebastian, Ed and Cynthia made one final check of the secreted house guests, who had settled into their temporary digs. The twins were absorbed in a video game, giggling and fighting over the controls as if this were merely a great pajama party.

Johnny regarded his family and Sebastian uncertainly as he pulled back the covers on the twins' beds. "I'm not happy about this arrangement, Sebastian. Two angry men are better than one if Jude is contemptuous enough of the law to try to get into the house."

"It's your job to protect your family, Johnny. Besides," he said, nodding toward Gracie, "then she would insist on being downstairs too, you know that."

Gracie nodded vigorously and gave her husband a look that promised, "Defy my wishes at your peril."

"Then it's settled. Here's how you unlock the door from the inside. The intercom by the door here is our way of communicating. Just press this button if you need to talk to me. It will sound like a call on my cell phone to anyone in the house, but only I know where the call originates. Only when I tell you it's safe to talk do you utter a word. This also is hooked up to a police line, so Ed will also be contacted."

The children gazed wonderingly at the intercom, at Cynthia's worried eyes, then at their parents. Johnny knew what they were thinking and sought to reassure them. "Remember the parable of the Rider on the White Horse?"

Sebastian couldn't have chosen a better one himself. Johnny O'Regan was the kind of father he wished he could have been. He would give anything to have another chance to love better and longer. Not that he deserved a second chance.

"I saw heaven standing open and there before me was a white horse, whose rider is called Faithful and True. With justice he judges and makes war. His eyes are like blazing fire, and on his head are many crowns. He has a name written on him that no one knows but he himself."

The children didn't even notice when their three visitors began the climb down the ladder. Sebastian knew that Bess and Buddy would soon have the knowledge that would give them peace and comfort. Johnny would make it clear to them that God was a far more formidable foe than Jude Orcus. That Jude was *"treading the winepress of the fury of the wrath of God Almighty. On his robe and on his thigh he has this name written: King of Kings and Lord of Lords."*

As he closed the door, Sebastian was satisfied that the O'Regans were safe in his shelter and God's hands.

"This is it then, Sebastian. I'll be at Cynthia's house. The Hardaway mansion, Leif's office, and this estate will be carefully monitored for any abnormal activity. Any questions?"

"Yeah, how did you manage to so captivate my Advertising Director while you're wearing that ridiculous suit?"

Cynthia's fingers brushed the fabric of his polyester sleeve as if it were made of spun gold. "Clothes don't make the man. A real man makes the clothes."

Ed took her arm and hurried her out the door, but not before Sebastian got a glimpse of the "Aw Shucks" expression on his face.

For the first time, he was not afraid for Cynthia, despite the danger Jude posed for them all. She could somehow survive the physical scars each member of her family had administered, but she could not survive without the hope of a love eternal and everlasting. God had promised she would have that in heaven; soon, he was sure, Ed Cadigan would be promising her the earthly version.

Sebastian was exhausted, but before he headed for bed he checked the alarm, the motion detector, and all the arcane devices designed to keep intruders out.

The system was connected to the police station only a half a mile away, so if it was activated, the police could be there within minutes. They would be very long minutes, Sebastian had no doubt, but he still had some fight left in his aged bones; at least a few minutes worth.

He left a few lights on in the kitchen and family room, then headed for his bedroom. He was too tired to even brush his teeth. If, or rather, when Jude did gain entry to the house, he'd be momentarily stunned by Sebastian's foul breath.

He wasn't too tired to say a prayer. He could not put his faith in the security system or the police response, but he knew his prayers were immediately heard and answered. The only question was how would they be answered. Only God knew.

Chapter Thirty-Four

Jude was very pleased with the speed and capability of his father's minions. Up until now he'd always been on the wrong end of their expertise, unable to appreciate their skill in obtaining classified information, and slicing through Internet and computer safety nets. While in confinement he had learned as much as he could — given his limited resources — about his father's company and the amazing new technologies being developed every day. Utilizing his photographic memory and speed-reading ability, he had been able to devour everything made available to him within hours of receiving the material via his dutiful mother. She had sent him as many books and software programs as the hospital administrators would allow. When he wasn't reading, he was on the computer.

As much as he hated him, he had to admire his father's acumen in the skills normally found only in career thieves. In hours he had in his possession Sebastian's alarm code and a complete map of all the security devices around the perimeter and in every room in the house. This would be easier than he thought, he decided, as he perused the entrance to Sebastian's sanctuary. He hadn't yet come up with the most fitting place for the sanctimonious prig to breathe his last.

Covered with special overalls, designed to protect him from everything but nuclear fallout, he slipped easily through the thorny rose bushes and with the aid of the new, environmentally-safe clips mountain climbers used, so as not to permanently damage Mother Nature's favored rocks, he climbed the brick wall surrounding the estate. He clipped the nearly invisible barbed wire on the top of the wall and rappelled down the other side. Working out every day in the makeshift gym at the hospital had kept him as agile as a cat. The necessity of taking back what was his now turned him into a stalking tiger. He crawled on all fours past the van parked in the driveway and crouched in the forest ferns under the kitchen window. He saw Sebastian methodically checking to see that he had all his ducks in a row. The old fart hadn't changed all that much. The mustache and beard masked any aging that had taken place, and his body was as firmly rotund as it had been when he'd asked his questions so politely in Jude's jail cell.

Apparently satisfied that everything had been secured, the pompous ass headed toward what the architectural plans on the ground beside him indicated was the master bedroom. How delicious that he could predict the man's every move, every destination. Now that he was finally here, Jude wanted to delay the inevitable, savor the scene where the crime was about to be committed. With maximum mess and bloodshed, he would prove himself to everyone who had ever doubted his intelligence or his resolve. They would pay for taking away all the prizes that were rightfully his: his Pulitzer, his sister, Leigh, and most of all, his children.

They would soon be with him instead of under the influence of some civil servant with a low IQ and high regard for a God that doesn't exist. Johnny O'Regan had been rewarded for his bravery in saving Cynthia and Gracie with the precious fruit of Jude's loins. Jude would retaliate with all the ammunition in his vast arsenal of anger and rage. Of course he would need time for deprogramming the little tykes. Cynthia and her selected surrogate parents would naturally have poisoned their mushy young brains against him. They would not know that their father had been a noted newspaper columnist: a man revered, not reviled.

He adjusted his tool bag and reviewed his strategy. Sebastian Vanderhyde would be the first to answer for his sins. He had thought briefly of awarding his father that place on the roster, but that would be quite impractical and counter-productive. Jude needed the resources only Leif Hardaway could summon at a moment's notice. The pawns on his payroll would do his bidding without question or hesitation; the giant of industry had made sure that no one else could climb his beanstalk and knock him down from his perch. Leif Hardaway reigned alone at the top. Until now. Very soon Jude would be sitting right up there alongside him. Of course, it could become uncomfortable for two men to occupy the same rarefied space, especially if they despised one another. To make room, Jude might just have to lop off a chunk of the family tree, his father along with it.

He followed the slate path around to the back of the house where French doors opened into the library. The accommodating police chief on his father's payroll had cautioned Leif that this was the only weak link in this particular system: one Leif had led him to believe he was going to install in his own home. With the proper tools, this was the way in. Not many could afford them, but proper tools were his father's business. Selling them to the highest bidders allowed him to design even more proper tools. For all that to happen, one could not be sidetracked by scruples or swayed by emotions. Someday Jude would like to find out exactly what Leif's ancestors had done to eviscerate all those intricate circuits that connected the heart to the brain, leaving the body free to sin.

He reached into his pack. This tool was not yet even on the black market, but his father had assured him that it could disarm any security system currently known to man. Being a genius, it hadn't taken Jude long to master the technique. How stupid of Sebastian to rely so heavily on technology. Jude's passion for justice could overcome any circuitry the man possessed.

Within minutes the laser had carved a perfect hole in the glass. The calibrator had decoded and disarmed the alarm, and Jude Orcus was in the house and in business. He felt as light on his feet as Fred Astair as he soundlessly glided across the room. If he hadn't been wearing night-vision goggles, he would have resembled the dancer as well, with his lithe body and long, rangy legs.

The stage had been set exactly as the plans indicated. He knew every mark on which to land. He felt no fear as he inched open the library door and peered down the long hall. There was no light to alert any one to his presence while, at the same time, the darkness held no surprises. He heard no sound; not even the somnambulate snore of substandard sinuses or the conspiratorial whispers of rambunctious children.

For such an old house, the creaks in the floorboards were minimal. Everything was working for him and against Sebastian and his house guests. Sebastian, being a good host, would not want to rat out his guests, of course, but when the deadly mist from Jude's state-of-the-art water pistol began to eat his flesh, the old man would have no choice but to offer them up in exchange for a quick death. Jude understood the pain that his gun induced was guaranteed to loosen any tongue.

The master bedroom door was several feet ahead. The smell of his pompous prey was strong in his nostrils, the sound of Sebastian's ancient wheeze caught his ear. The man's great brain would soon be as pulpy as an orange.

The door to the room was open a crack. He couldn't believe it. The bastard was sending out an invitation to enter. Jude was careful to position himself at the side of the door where he could see in without exposing himself. Sebastian's bulk mounded the covers. His knees pressed his chest in a fetal position. How touching. He slept curled up like a helpless child.

His poisonous pistol was primed and ready to spray as soon as Sebastian's eyes opened and saw the danger before him. It was very important that he know who and what was the source of his undoing.

He moved farther into the room, until he could see the shock of white hair fanned on the pillow. "Time to wake up, Vandy Babe," he called sweetly, anxious to see the look of fear and smell the stench of his enemy's cowardly bowels; eager to duplicate in his enemy the symptoms of his own childhood nightmares. There was no response. Jude knew he had made an error in judgment just as he heard the crack of bone and felt his head explode with pain. He dropped the pistol, but still had enough strength to swing around and throw his body against Sebastian, who was struggling to maintain his balance while trying to land another blow. Jude had already pulled the knife from his belt. He plunged it deep into a fleshy target just below the ribs, and the old man fell at his feet. He had done damage, but was it enough?

An alarm blasted in his throbbing ear and sirens whined loudly in the distance. Sebastian was silent, probably dead. He looked around for the pistol. The weapon must have rolled under the bed or the dresser. There was no time to look further. He ran from the room, out the French doors and into the woods beyond. In a matter of seconds he was on the makeshift trail, in his jeep, and shooting down the bridle bath. The bumping of the wheels on the uneven earth carved tread marks on his aching head, but he continued.

Only when he was safely inside his father's Russian Hill love nest was he able to assess his injuries and his night's work. His father's personal physician, George Kelleher, who had treated everything in this apartment from genital Herpes to a gunshot wound self-inflicted by a disappointed lover, was waiting for him. They had quite a nice chat before Jude left for his job. In addition to the doctor's assurances that he would remain until Jude's return, he brought him up to date on recent additions to Leif Hardaway's little black book. The Doc hadn't been gender specific about the suicidal lover, why he or she was disappointed. His only concern, he said, was keeping his clientele alive and well. And quiet, if necessary, which he didn't say, but Jude was ready to counter any un-Hippocratic action the doctor may take against him.

"What's the prognosis, Doc?"

The physician did little to conceal his distaste for his patient. "That knob is the size of a grapefruit, but there doesn't appear to be a concussion, surprisingly. I'm not going to ask you how you acquired it," he said, putting his own proper tools back into his bag of medical tricks. "Take two of these every four hours for pain," he said, setting a small bottle on the coffee table.

The doctor differed from his father in one discernible way, Jude observed. He purposefully avoided any unnecessary physical contact with him. He wondered if the Doc knew or approved of his employer's *loving side*.

"Mr. Hardaway will require a report from you, I'm sure." Jude's smile had become a permanent and unadjustable sneer, his eyes a two-way mirror. With this new gift he could see things no one else could see, look where no man willingly allowed another to peek. Kelleher was a pimp like all the rest of the people on his father's payroll, long ago disavowing any moral oaths he had once taken, maybe even once believed, which served to reinforce Jude's belief in the evil inherent and irreversible in all humans. There were few if any left who played by the rules that long ago were concocted by some holy roller on a mountain top in a dessert of dust and roasting human flesh. How long would it take those few to realize the rules they lived by were invented by men who hadn't the guts to face the reality of death and the nothingness that followed? How could they not embrace the nothingness and use it to advantage? When there was nothing to fear, there was nothing that could hurt you. That was Jude's salvation.

He was proud of what he had accomplished, even it if was only a small part of his mission. He had shed no blood. He had left no trace of himself. There would be no fingerprints on the pistol. He didn't have to strain to recall the exact feel of the knife as it bored slickly into the soft flesh, so deeply that he was unable to easily dislodge the weapon he had been assured was untraceable. The fun had begun. Sebastian Vanderhyde was dead and unable to bear false witness against him ever again. Leigh Barnes would soon be twice dead, and then his children would be reunited with him and Cynthia. With the twins in his possession, Cynthia would have no choice but to join them, make theirs a real family. If that was not agreeable to her, well, maybe it was best that they all left this sorry world together. How could she object? If she truly did believe in her God and His heavenly mansions, she should be happy to arrive early and spend eternity there.

Chapter Thirty-Five

When the phone rang, Thrasher leapt from the couch and grabbed for his turnout coat. It wasn't there. He shook the sleep from his body like a Dalmatian shaking off water. He couldn't believe he'd fallen asleep. He grabbed the accusing instrument. "Hello?"

"Thrasher, it's Ed. Jude got Sebastian. You'd better get over here to St. Mary's. I don't know how long they can keep him alive."

"We're on our way."

The lights immediately went on and Leigh appeared, looking like an angel in her white robe, her face scrubbed to paleness. "What is it?"

"Sebastian is at St. Mary's. We have to get there as soon as possible."

She must have assumed the worst and the best, that he was hurt but still alive; because she didn't stop to ask any questions and went straight to her room. She returned only minutes later in jeans and a sweatshirt, carrying a pair of loafers. "I'll put these on in the car. You ready?"

He drove as fast as the early morning traffic would allow. For the first few minutes she was silent. Then the damn burst. "What did Jude do to him? How bad is it?"

"I don't know any of the details, Leigh. He got into the house, that's all I know."

She remained silent for the rest of the way to the hospital. So did he. He was out of practice assuring people everything would be all right when he knew it would not be.

Ed was waiting for them in the emergency room. Leigh rushed toward Ed, her hair disheveled, her eyes enormous. "How is he? Will he be okay?"

Ed addressed them both. "We won't know for a while. 'Cautiously optimistic' is the term the doctors used. Jude stabbed him. There was a lot of blood, but he somehow missed all the organs that would have caused immediate death. The bastard managed to slip in despite all the high-falutin' security. He must have had some pretty detailed plans of the property, because he parked his jeep on a bridal path that only the immediate neighbors know exists. It's very private property. No one has yet figured out how he got in and out without being spotted, but then it is a woodsy area, very insulated."

"Sebastian's security system was excellent," Thrasher argued weakly.

"Jude's tools were better. Thanks to his father, we assume."

"Why can't you arrest the guy? At least keep him from assisting his son in his murderous rampage." Thrasher's face was darkly shadowed by anger and a thriving stubble.

"Not only can't we prove he's helping his son, we can't even prove Jude *is* his son." Ed shrugged helplessly.

Leigh brightened. "What about all those new DNA tests? Once you establish that Jude is his son, then you can link him to everything Jude has done since he escaped from the institution. We know he and Lydia are his accomplices." She looked hopefully from Ed to Thrasher and back again.

Her optimism was short-lived. Ed's response was too cautious. "I hope that will be possible. But until we find him, you're in grave danger, Leigh."

She didn't flinch at his pronouncement. "I know my enemy. That's an advantage I didn't have before. Cynthia and the children are the ones you should be concerned about. And the O'Regans. They are his primary targets."

"They remain perfectly safe in the concealed room. Whoever provided Jude with the house plans was unaware of its existence. Sebastian did the carpentry himself, with a little help from me and my electrical engineering degree. Even the Woodside planning commission is unaware of his little addition."

"Kind of risky for you to be involved," Thrasher said in a lowered voice.

"Sebastian has done a whole lot of things for me that some people would not consider kosher, and I'll owe him till the day I die. A few nosy bureaucrats being kept in the dark never caused me to lose any sleep."

Leigh sagged and fell into a chair in a childlike position, her knees together, her legs slightly spread, her elbows resting on them, her hands tightly folded. "We can't lose him." She looked up at them pleadingly. "I can't lose him. I count on him. I didn't know how much until just now. After my mother and father died I didn't think I could ever expect anyone to care about me the way they did. Sebastian proved me wrong. Now it's too late to tell him, to thank him."

Thrasher's voice thundered. "Do not tell me it's too late, Leigh! Sebastian will not give up, and dammit, you can't either! Stop thinking about yourself and start praying for Sebastian."

Unexpectedly, she tilted her head to one side, studied him for a moment, and in a hoarse voice said, "I know what you're trying to do, Thrasher. It's the same thing Sebastian has been trying to do. Bring a dead woman back to life. But you can't perform miracles. Sebastian tried everything: he quoted scripture, he left Bible passages on my desk, he slipped inspirational messages into my e-mail. The last one was Psalm 3. It just popped into my head."

"Well, pop it out. We all could use some inspiration here," Ed quipped.

She closed her eyes and lifted her head, understanding the words for the first time. "*Oh Lord, how many are my foes! How many rise up against me! Many are saying of me, 'God will not deliver him.' But you are a shield around me O Lord.*" When she opened her eyes, they were wet. "That's all I can remember right now, but it helps. That's a small miracle in itself."

Thrasher's cell phone interrupted them. Not wanting to eavesdrop, Leigh asked Ed, "Where's Cynthia?"

"She's on the phone with her mother, trying to get any more information on Jason. She wanted Lydia to know immediately that he had tried to kill again, and that if she had any idea of where he is, it's essential she tell us."

"Yes, this is Thrasher Cole. What? Oh, damn! Excuse me, Senator Guttmacher. No, I do remember, and I'm very sorry. I'm at St. Mary's hospital right now. Yes, it is an emergency. Yes, I understand. No, I really can't do anything here, but..." He grimly agreed, "All right, I'll be there in half an hour. Good-bye."

Leigh and Ed waited for him to explain why he would consider something so important he would leave the hospital without knowing Sebastian's status.

"I won't be gone long. I wouldn't go at all, except Sebastian would kill me if I didn't."

Cadigan snapped his fingers. "It's about your judgeship, right?"

"It means as much, maybe more, to Sebastian than it does to me. It was he who got me this far. He's counting on one District Judge to get me the rest of the way."

"You have to go, Thrasher," Leigh said with firmness. "As soon as I can get in to see Sebastian I'll tell him where you are, and give him the news that you are officially Judge Cole. If that doesn't bring him to his feet, nothing can."

Chapter Thirty-Six

The Commission on Judicial Appointments consisted mainly of men who deemed Thrasher Cole too young, too extreme a Constitutionalist, too conservative in general, and far too much of a hero type for their taste. He had been surprised to find Senator Guttmacher joining the Chief Justice, the Attorney General, and the presiding justice of the district court. In fact, the senator seemed to be the one holding court. That was not good news.

He was probably as surprised as Thrasher that he had gotten this far on such a record, especially since the Justice Department was investigating pro-life proponents. To add fuel to their concerns, one of Thrasher's last cases had been representing a small businessman who was fighting his daughter's school over the hiring of a transvestite as her third-grade teacher. He/she was teaching a "human relations" course which included appreciation of the homosexual lifestyle. In the school's defense, they would be fined $150,000 if they didn't hire the teacher. To further frustrate the poor man, he was being sued by two lesbian lovers for creating a hostile environment at his small retail business, because he objected to their kissing in front of the customers.

"This will, I'm afraid, not be as pleasant an experience for you as you might have hoped, Mr. Cole."

Thrasher sat silently waiting for Senator Guttmacher to explain just why that was.

"Some very disturbing accusations have come to my attention. Accusations that I'm afraid we cannot ignore."

Okay, here it comes, he thought. He would be accused of being bigoted and promoting hate for defending his client. He was well aware that the Senator despised him and all he stood for, and against; namely, the Senator's propensity for using his office solely for personal profit. Thrasher's response remained one of silence, since he had no idea what the Senator was talking about. It seemed expedient to allow him to spell it out.

The senator cleared his throat and continued reluctantly, realizing that Thrasher's silence and look of innocent bewilderment had temporarily taken him off the offense and put him on the defensive. "I will explain."

"Thank you," Thrasher finally offered.

"We all understand that your wife and unborn child died tragically a year after your marriage."

He nodded. The mention of their deaths could still unbalance him. He couldn't trust his voice to remain steady.

"Can you explain to us the circumstances of their deaths?"

He had no choice now but to respond. "I would rather not. It's still a very distressing subject for me. And since their deaths are a matter of public record, I see no necessity in relating what you can discover so easily for yourselves without the distraction of my emotions."

"It's true that their deaths are a matter of public record, Mr. Cole; however, since new information has come to light regarding the facts surrounding their deaths, we would like to hear the exact details from you, so there will be no misunderstanding as to the circumstances."

He took a breath, but it was shallow and unhelpful in lessening his agitation. "My wife was killed by a hit-and-run driver as she crossed Union Street at 3:00 p.m. on Tuesday, March 4, 1996. No reliable witnesses could be located. The driver was never found. My wife and unborn child died at the scene." His grim recital of the facts was the only way he could manage to keep his composure.

"And previous to March 4, 1996, had your wife suffered any other ah, accidents?"

The Senator was having more fun than Heinrich Himmler at a blood purge.

"What do you mean?" He gripped the arms of his chair. It seemed preferable to the senator's neck. Only by hanging on to his chair could he keep from leaping up and punching him out.

"She stumbled and fell down a flight of stairs in our home. Unfortunately, I was not there at the time. She only suffered a broken arm and, thank God, the baby was unharmed."

"And when did that *accident* occur?"

To say that the senator was beginning to irritate him was nowhere near adequate. "Your emphasis on the word *accident*, Senator, is perplexing. Are you questioning the fact that it was one?" Thrasher wanted the weasel to come clean as to the reason for his patently offensive questions, and why exactly he felt compelled to ask them.

"Mr. Cole, several very reliable citizens have come forth with proof that you had, on several occasions, struck your wife in anger, and that the accident on the stairs was only one of many mishaps she suffered during your brief marriage."

He could hear Chandler's smooth voice cautioning him not to lose control. "I have no idea who these reliable citizens may be, but they could not possibly have proof of something that never occurred. My wife was not accident-prone, and I was not a wife-beater. The only time she had occasion to visit a doctor's office was for her normal check-ups, her regular pre-natal exams and, of course, the broken arm. She was a healthy and extremely happy woman, Senator, and I loved her more than I can say." His anger was so great that he was sure the veins in his neck were popping up. There was only one good thing about this line of questioning; it made him all the more determined to be in a position to see that men like the senator did not escape justice.

"I would ask you to present my accusers, Senator. I would like them to make these accusations to my face and in front of all of you."

"It is not for you to determine who we present and where, Mr. Cole. Your only concern should be honestly answering any and all questions this committee submits to you. We have proof of your wife's visits to various doctors in the city, Mr. Cole, obtained from reputable doctors who will swear that they treated her for a multitude of bruises and contusions."

He didn't know what was going on here, but he now knew that Leigh's mention of Psalm 3 had been a portent and no coincidence. His foes were rising up against him. What Leigh didn't remember was the seventh verse, which Sebastian had quoted constantly. "*Arise, O Lord! Deliver me, O my God! Strike all my enemies on the jaw; break the teeth of the wicked.*"

Mouths were being manipulated by a powerful ventriloquist; records were being expertly falsified, and Thrasher Cole was being set up big time. He didn't have a doubt in the world as to who was responsible.

What Thrasher Cole didn't know was that his wife had indeed been treated for multiple injuries. No records required falsification.

Chapter Thirty-Seven

Leigh could hardly contain her joy and relief when she saw Sebastian sitting up, a smile wrapped around his face like a bright bow.

"You can do it! You really do know how to smile!" She ran to him, then stopped short at the side of his bed. "I'm going to need to hug you, Sebastian. I need proof that I'm not dreaming, that you're alive."

He held up an index finer and waggled it. "My doctor has spoken. You can look, but you can't touch. You either, Super Cop," he intoned, waggling it at Ed Cadigan, who had one arm around Cynthia and the other on his hip. "Not until my doctor upgrades me from broken to fragile." He groaned and pursed his lips in serious cogitation. "But what does he know? He reads *Rolling Stone* and once voted for the Peace and Freedom Party. Come here, my dear. You too, Cynthia." He lifted his arms with only a slight grimace.

Cynthia smiled down at him as she waited her turn. Leigh gently put her arms around him, not caring that her tears were staining his face and blotching her already ravaged one. She didn't want to let go, for fear that he would somehow be lifted up to the Heaven where he belonged. It was selfish to want to keep him on such an unfriendly earth, but when it came to people she loved, she was extremely selfish and not ashamed to admit it. When she did finally pull away, she saw that he too was blinking back tears.

"How did he get through all that security, Sebastian? You had me convinced it was impenetrable," she scolded.

He looked out the window, cleared his throat, and fidgeted with his sheet.

"You knew he would get in, didn't you?" she accused.

He turned back to face her. His shame induced blush made him look quite healthy. "Yes, but what I didn't know is that I'm not quite as quick and sure-footed as my former karate instructor assured me I was."

"Tell her exactly how the former karate instructor was," Ed advised from behind her.

"I know it was before my time," Cynthia charged.

"Well, now that I think about it, I guess it had to have been about fifteen years ago that I took my last class. I guess it's not like riding a bike," he admitted sheepishly.

"But why did you expose yourself to him like that? You know he will stop at nothing to get what he wants. You were standing between him and his children. Surely you knew that those years of stocked up anger and hatred — and don't forget the daily workout in the prison gym — would give him superhuman strength?"

"My strength cometh from the Lord. And as you can see, it was sufficient."

"Thank God!"

"I already have."

How they could laugh while Jude was still on the loose was pure insanity, but it gave them a relief they all desperately needed.

"I'm hoping more thanks will be in order when we hear from Thrasher. I understand he's being interrogated by that rat pack of career bureaucrats. Have you heard from him yet?"

Ed shook his head. "No, but there isn't any reason to worry. What could possibly keep them from approving Thrasher? His record is so clean you could eat off it, as my mother used to say."

"Those men are very powerful, and as Edmund Burke once said, '*The greater the power, the more dangerous the abuse.*' "

"But he was appointed by the Governor. They'd have to have a felony offense to disqualify him," Leigh argued.

"And another thing *not* to worry about, Sebastian. Jude will not be breaking through this hospital's security. It's as tight as a....well, it's tight." Ed's flush was an apology for what he had almost said. He self-consciously shifted his weight. "I was hoping we'd get a report of a corpse with a giant lump on his head, but no such luck. He managed to survive your outdated karate chops without leaving even a trace of blood behind. For a genius, the guy has a very thick skull."

"Right now I'm only thinking about Thrasher," he said somberly. "Nothing must go wrong with his appointment. And the O'Regans, how are they doing?"

"It took a bit of convincing, but I finally persuaded them to stay put in their posh new digs. Even if Jude returns to the scene of his crime, my men will be there to greet him." Ed's hand moved instinctively to his gun.

Sebastian's frown smoothed and his eyes closed purposefully. When he opened them again his look was hopeful.

Leigh put a confident smile on her face, but her cheek twitched ever so slightly. Jude was not through with any of them. And now he had his father's arsenal of human and atomic weaponry to help him realize his dream. And her nightmare.

Chapter Thirty-Eight

The O'Regans had remained huddled together in the concealed room after being awakened by the intercom's recital of the battle being waged below them. They had been able to hear everything while their whispered words and careful movements went undetected. Johnny knew that Jude had gotten in when he heard the loud scuffling and Jude's terrifying taunts. When the alarm went off and there was no signal from Sebastian, it was clear that he had been the one felled, not Jude. Johnny followed his instructions and signaled Ed Cadigan by pushing the red button on the alarm board, even though he was certain help was already on the way.

"What happened, Daddy?" Buddy had awakened to Jude's voice urging Sebastian to wake up. Johnny knew Sebastian would not be lying in that bed. He also knew that Sebastian was no match for a man armed with sophisticated weaponry and a zeal to taste the blood of his enemies. Why hadn't he protested more loudly? Why hadn't Ed Cadigan? He was ashamed to look his son in the eye. He had temporarily lost the inviolate instinct that had previously moved him to save the lives of friends and strangers alike.

The police are on their way, son. We'll be fine."

"What about Dr. Vanderhyde? Will he be fine too?"

Bess and Gracie were holding each other and searching his face for the answer to that question.

"Dr. Vanderhyde is a very clever man. I fear his bones are in agony but his heart and soul are in very good shape, I'm sure."

"What about...him?" Bess asked tentatively.

"*'The Lord is known by his justice; the wicked are ensnared by the work of their hands.'* I know it doesn't seem like it right now, but everything will be fine. All of us will be fine."

The look that passed between him and Gracie was the same one they'd shared when he pulled her from the burning building. It was one of awe that their lives had been spared. Only this time it the ending may not be such a happy one.

Chapter Thirty-Nine

"Jake, I need your help."

"I can't hear you too well, Thrasher. Every chef, ever server, and every photographer in northern California has congregated here today in preparation for the auction. We're trying to figure out where the tables should be set up, which will probably be everywhere there isn't a barracks of portable toilets already designated."

"Damn, I forgot about the auction."

"Don't worry, we'll muddle through until you can tear yourself away from Sin City and truck on down to God's country. It's so beautiful this time of year that I pity anyone not living in the wine country. The wines for the barrel auction are all set, and the sit-down, six-course dinner is going to knock your socks off. You are going to make the auction, aren't you?"

"Some things have been happening here, Jake. I didn't want to bother you with any of this when you're so busy with the auction, but you're the only one who can help me."

"Are you in some kind of trouble?"

"Plenty. Sebastian's in the hospital with a stab wound that should have killed him. The maniac who did it is on the loose. And I'm being accused of being a wife-beater."

The former football star receiver was momentarily stunned, but true to his character, he didn't let it slow him down. "What do you want me to do?"

"I'm not sure. Maybe nothing, at least not until the auction is over. But I do need some advice."

"I give advice to novice wine-tasters, Thrasher; I give help to my best friend. We've been through way too much together for me not to know when you've got your ass in a ringer. You need help and right now, and I'm going to give it, even if it means shucking the winery."

"Thank God that won't be necessary, Jake. All I need from you is for you to make a few calls."

"I've got my pen and pad right here. Shoot."

"When you were in the Senate, how well did you get to know Senator Guttmacher?"

"As well as I could tolerate. That man is so corrupt he should be the poster boy for term limits. Of course you probably know he's tight with Leif Hardaway. Hardaway probably financed fifty percent of his last campaign."

"Yeah, and I'm sure Guttmacher is repaying the favor by sabotaging my judgeship. I think this calls for some pretty drastic measures, Jake. Measures that can be taken only by the high-powered team of patriots who helped us bring down another set of corrupters eight years ago. I'd call them all myself, but I've got a lot of fires to put out and my skills aren't what they once were, I'm afraid. I know I'm being followed, and my house and office are probably bugged."

"You give me the list and tell me what you want us all to do. We won't fail you, buddy."

"You never have."

An hour later he called Jake again. His relief at hearing his friend's reassurances was only momentary. Just as he left the phone booth, he spotted the rack of newspapers. Both the San Jose and San Francisco papers read: SEBASTIAN VANDERHYDE: PRO-LIFE, RIGHT-WING MAGAZINE PUBLISHER ABORTION CLINIC OWNER.

In slightly less bold print lower down on the page of the *San Francisco Globe* was: JUDGE NOT. THRASHER COLE'S NOMINATION HELD UP BY ACCUSATIONS OF SPOUSAL ABUSE AND MORAL TURPITUDE.

He blinked several times, hoping his eyes were as deceiving as the headlines. His hand shook as he shoved the coins in the slot of both racks. His heart was an anvil banging away at his chest. His temples were throbbing and his legs wobbled like an old man.

He ducked into a coffee shop, had the presence to order a cup of coffee and an acid-eating rasher of toast, and began digesting the newsprint from the top:

> Sebastian Vanderhyde, the ultra-conservative author and publisher, was the former owner and director of a southern California abortion clinic which performed 50-60 abortions per

> day. According to several former doctors and nurses working at the clinic, at the time Vanderhyde retired from the business, his clinic had 75,000 abortions to its credit, many of them late-term, third-trimester fetuses. One of his clients, according to appointment records, was his own wife, Sonja Vanderhyde. Cynthia Hardaway, his Advertising Manager and constant companion for the past eight years, was also a client. Mr. Vanderhyde could not be reached for comment.

This couldn't be true. This could not be the man he knew. The sanctity of life was all-important to Sebastian. To him the truth was sacrosanct. He could not be capable of living such a lie. He couldn't.

His eyes moved down the page:

> Thrasher Cole, former fire department captain, attorney, Deputy Attorney General, and appointee for the 9th District Court of Appeals, has been accused of spousal abuse, child endangerment and moral turpitude. A doctor who treated Chandler Cole for injuries suffered as a result of this abuse has come forth with records of two visits to his office, where she was treated for bruises and lacerations. There is a report from her regular physician regarding a broken arm, suffered when she fell down a flight of stairs in the family's home. The child she was carrying was miraculously unharmed.
>
> Also coming forth is Delia Packard, estranged wife of Glen Packard, editor of the *San Francisco Globe*. She has stated that she and Mr. Cole had an ongoing affair during Cole's marriage. In her statement to this paper she claimed her confession came as a result of deep soul-searching. She has suffered from a guilt that Cole's feelings for her may have contributed to the altercations in the Cole marriage. She also feels strongly that only the most moral of men should preside over others in our courts.

Leif Hardaway was pulling out all the stops. Ruining two men and sacrificing his mistress was apparently what it took to appease his son and insure his own escape from prosecution — in the courts and in the press. Thrasher knew all of it was a lie, and he could prove it. Only probably not soon enough. But what about Sebastian?

He drained his cup and shakily replaced it on the saucer. What would this do to his friend physically and mentally? If it was as fabricated as the exposé on him, Sebastian would be able to fight back. If it was true, he may just decide to give in to his injuries, his disgrace, and his age. Thrasher had to know the truth.

Chapter Forty

"Sebastian, I'm going to the office, make sure everything is okay."

"I'd appreciate that, Leigh."

"I'll go with her, Sebastian," Cynthia said, giving him one more kiss on the cheek. "We don't want to miss a deadline just because the boss decided to take a sabbatical. Besides, I need to keep busy." Her blond hair was in disarray, without luster, but her eyes were bright gemstones.

Ed Cadigan looked down at her with the look of a man seriously smitten. "I'll be going along with you, young lady." At six foot, five inches, he made even the statuesque Cynthia look diminutive. "I don't intend to let you out of my sight unless there are two of my men replacing me. Until Jude is brought in, you will be under my personal surveillance at all times."

"I like the sound of that," she answered, taking proud possession of his arm.

Ed proceeded to escort the two women, via squad car, directly to the lobby of the building in which the suite of *America in Review* offices occupied the ninth floor. Ironically, the building was one of Leif Hardaways earlier real estate acquisitions.

"Why don't I get you some coffee and the morning paper?" Ed suggested.

"Sounds great," Leigh said, as she headed straight for the elevator. "Why don't you help him, Cynthia. You know what I like. I'll meet you upstairs."

She pushed the button and waited for the floors and the remainder of her anxieties to pass. Seeing that everything was ready for press would help keep her mind off the more vital problems. This was the first time she had played chief instead of assistant chief, and she intended to reward Sebastian's confidence in her by getting the magazine out on deadline.

She turned on the computer, anxious to see if she had any new e-mail messages. There was one sent from her own office. Who could have been in here? No one was allowed in the office except the executives. The message was from Jude.

"*By now you should have seen the newspaper headlines. If not, perhaps you should peruse them before you read on.*"

She disregarded his instructions. She would not take orders from Jude Orcus. But the further she read the more confused she became. She reluctantly decided to do as he said.

Two daily papers were sitting on the receptionist's desk. She didn't have to look far to discover what Jude intended her to see. She picked up one, then the other. Mesmerized by the headlines, she made her way back to her office, bumping into several chairs and a door knob on the way. Once she'd read and reread the articles, she returned to Jude's e-mail message.

"You now know the real Sebastian Vanderhyde, a hypocrite in the worst sense of the word, a liar who delights in condemning others while committing the acts he defines as mortal sins."

His words, as well as those in the newspaper, assaulted her and threatened to buckle her knees. The two men she revered most in the world were described as villainous, traitorous, and blatantly hypocritical. The headlines may as well have read, "Armageddon has come. The world as you knew it has ceased to exist."

With her brain hobbled, she had difficulty comprehending Jude's final words.

"Sorry to be the one to defrock the sainted ones, but a quote comes to mind. No doubt a favorite oldie but goodie. 'Do unto others as you would have them do unto you.' You destroyed my life without a second thought. I have given a great deal of thought to how best to destroy yours. I have decided the best way to do that is to bring down your golden idols, Sebastian Vanderhyde and Thrasher Cole. You will see them for the sinners they really are. The world will no longer see them as heroes, but purveyors of lies and false promises of love, peace, and the soul's salvation. Tit for Tat!

I will spare you, Leigh, because I want you to live a long and unhappy life. I will give you detailed instructions on how you will earn your survival. I have attached instructions as to where we will meet to discuss the particulars. Oh, and by the way, there is one item that did not appear in the papers. Sebastian Vanderhyde is your father."

Chapter Forty-One

The urge to run anywhere but back to the hospital was compelling. Trying to recognize the distorted faces of the people she loved, the people she had thought loved her, would test her in every way conceivable.

When she walked into Sebastian's room they were all assembled. While she had been driving around the city trying to compose herself and the resignation letter she now held in her cold hand, Ed and Cynthia had driven straight to the hospital. They met her her just inside Sebastian's hospital room.

"When we got to the office with the coffee, you were already gone, and we knew you'd seen the papers. You should have waited for us, Leigh. I know how upset you must be," Cynthia cried, her words tripping over themselves.

Thrasher appeared calm, but dark half moons bulged under his unblinking eyes. He was one arrogant SOB. How could she have ever been so gullible, so unquestioning? Her career had been forged through investigative reporting, yet she allowed a man she barely knew to spend the night in her home. *Sleeping on my best cotten sheets*, she silently raged.

"Leigh?" Sebastian called out. A doctor was leaning over him, obstructing her view of his shamelessness.

"These pills will help, Sebastian, but this roomful of people will not. Some of you will have to leave," the doctor ordered, brooking no argument.

"Cynthia and I will wait outside," Ed said, taking Cynthia's hand, putting an arm around her sagging shoulders.

Cynthia pulled away and went to Leigh. "Please let Sebastian explain all this, Leigh. Give him a chance to tell you what an enormous load of guilt he has been struggling under all these years. Let him prove to you that he is the man I know you love, the man who saved my life and thousands of others. Let him save you too, Leigh, from Jude and the Devil who has guided his every action."

Leigh said nothing.

Cynthia smiled a sad understanding. "I'll be just outside if you need me, Leigh."

Leigh's expression remained set. Cynthia's words had done nothing to move her.

Thrasher pulled out a chair and set it next to Sebastian's bed. The doctor nodded to his patient, but signaled a warning glance before leaving the room. Leigh remained standing just inside the door, regarding both men with a scorn that only deceit and betrayal can elicit.

"Please sit down, Leigh, dear," Sebastian pleaded. "I know you don't want to be here, but you know you have to be. You have to know the truth."

"Neither of you would know it if it was personally delivered to your door with a blast from the Archangel Gabriel's horn."

"Please let Thrasher talk first, Leigh. His is not a complicated explanation. None of what they said about him is true."

"And all of what was written about you was true?"

His hanging head was the only answer she needed.

"Thrasher?" She stood, letting him offer his version of the truth.

He pulled up another chair and placed it so that they could face one another at the edge of Sebastian's bed. They both took their chairs, as reluctantly as children forced to sit at a table full of relatives and leafy green vegetables.

"I'm *hoping* that your anger is with the story of my supposed affair with Delia. I'm praying that you could not believe I would ever hurt my wife or anyone else. I loved Chandler very much, and she loved me. My accusers are right about only one thing. I do carry a great deal of guilt for her death."

Leigh's eyebrows shot up.

"She begged me not to continue publicly suggesting arson was the cause of the Channing Building fire. She warned me that if that was the truth, whoever was responsible would do whatever was necessary to cover it up, to discredit me. I didn't know until today just how perceptive she was. Leif Hardaway arranged to have his own son killed in that fire so his crime of child molestation would never be discovered, and in the process he was able to acquire the property he could not get any other way. I wish I would have had proof of that at the time. I only had my instincts and experience to tell me what no one else was willing to divulge. Anyway, I did promise her, and when I saw how relieved she was, I also saw how desperate she must have been. I would not jeopardize her health, so I fully intended to keep my promise."

His pause was solemn. "That same day Senator Jake Malloy, my best friend, called to say he had been sent an anonymous letter, accusing Hardaway of causing the fire. He'd already given it to the police, but he thought I should know, since I had been so badly burned in it. I was on my way to the police station when the police paged me. Instead of finding the truth about Hardaway that day, I lost my wife and child. Chandler and our baby were gone." He swallowed with difficulty. "So was the letter. It had mysteriously disappeared from the evidence room."

"What about the doctor's reports of Chandler's injuries?" Her voice had not softened.

He fixed his eyes on the ceiling and blinked several times. "When I think back on it I can see things now that I couldn't then. What I thought was only normal concern for me, for us, was really stark fear. The bruises she successfully concealed from me were certainly not due to clumsiness. Chandler was anything but clumsy. I can also see the panic in her eyes after her fall down the stairs, fearing that our baby had been harmed. I believe now that she was being threatened, and those accidents were proof of the seriousness of those threats. I knew my wife; she would have gladly suffered any pain to save me and our baby. I'm sure Leif Hardaway managed to convince her that he'd kill all three of us if she didn't succeed in persuading me not to pursue the arson angle. And he or one of his 'enforcers' backed up his threats with their fists."

Her eyes were as wet as his. "I believe you," Leigh said softly. "I know Jude and now I know his father. I'm sorry I doubted you. I know you are not capable of such a heinous thing."

"But I would be capable of adultery?"

"That's not a fair question," she protested.

"You're wondering, and so am I, what possible reason Delia Packard would have for saying she had an affair with me if she didn't? What could she expect to gain from such an admission? She had a lot to lose — like her husband. I expect each of the newlyweds has already hired a cutthroat, grossly overpaid divorce lawyer by now."

Sebastian, who had been cautiously quiet, explained. "Delia Packard has been having an affair with Leif Hardaway for years. Ed Cadigan did some digging and found that Leif owns a pied-a-terre on Broadway, where he and

Delia did their trysting. He either convinced or threatened Delia into making that statement to the press. In talking to the manager of the building, we also learned that Jude may have been there as well. A man of his description was seen several times, as well as Doctor Kelleher, who was seen toting his bag up to that particular apartment. Jude's not there now, of course."

"Of course," she said dryly. Leigh knew exactly where he was, but she wasn't about to share her information with anyone just yet.

"Do you believe me, Leigh?" Thrasher asked in a quiet voice, leaning forward and placing his weathered hands on her knees in a beseeching manner.

"Yes, I do."

She knew he wanted more from her than those few words, but she was not yet ready to offer more. Not yet. She turned to face Sebastian, who had the expectant look of a man on trial, about to receive the verdict on his guilt or innocence.

She wanted to blurt it out. "Are you my father? Did Ellen and Larry Barnes let me live a lie for all these years?" But she didn't. She wasn't sure why.

"You don't have to ask, Leigh. I did own an abortion clinic." He looked down at his wrist. "This Rolex is the only thing I salvaged from my previous life as a well-paid assassin. It serves to remind me of all the valuable time I squandered doing the devil's work."

"How could you do it? How could you see all those babies killed and not want to kill yourself?"

"I couldn't. At least not once I saw for myself the reality of the operations being performed there. Believe it or not, I once thought of abortion as a kindness, as a solution to a myriad of problems: over-population, unwanted and uncared for children who grow up to produce more unwanted and uncared for children. A lot of people still believe that wholeheartedly. I thought I was doing the world a service. And I was making a fortune at it," he spat. "Can you imagine how much money can be earned by performing sixty abortions a day, every day, all day, year after year?" he accused himself. "I became a very rich man."

He had aged at least ten years since she had seen him this morning. Not even the battle with Jude and his knife had done as much damage as the newspaper article. His lips were chapped; there were even traces of dried blood on his lower lip. He seemed to be having some difficulty breathing, but perhaps it was she who felt a tightening of the chest.

"I was happy, Leigh, or so I thought. My wife Sonja was beautiful. She loved the luxuries I was able to provide. She'd come from a very poor family, and although she was quite thrilled to marry into a wealthy family, she was ecstatic when I compounded the family fortune after my parents' death. She had ten sisters and brothers, all of whom she had cared for at one time or another. Ironically, we never discussed having children. I just assumed we would have at least a couple. It was only when she became pregnant that we were forced to have that long-delayed discussion. She told me she never wanted children, that she was planning on having an abortion. It was then we both realized we'd made some terribly false assumptions. She assumed that since abortion was my business, I would have no objection to aborting my own child in the interest of population control or whatever I chose to use as a reason to snuff out a life. I assumed she loved me enough to bear our child."

Was Sonja her mother? She wasn't sure she could wait until Sebastian got to the end of his story to find out. Before she could ask, he continued.

"That was when I really took a look at the abortion procedure. I had never done that before. I left that part to the competent doctors and nurses I hired. The day after our discussion, Sonja made an appointment at the clinic. Since I couldn't talk her out of it, I decided to view a procedure myself. The first one I saw was called a laminarium, in which seaweed is inserted into the cervix. It swells and dilates the neck of the womb. The bag of water is broken. Then there's a swirl of blood." He grabbed a tissue from the bedside table and wiped the moisture from his upper lip. "I was nauseated by the procedure. Then it got worse. The doctor cut the umbilical cord and proceeded to dismember the child. First, he pulled away the extremities: the back, the spine, the torso. Then he neatly stacked them on the table for reassembling. I was horrified at what I'd been condoning. No, what I had been profiting from. When I expressed my horror to the doctor, he gave me the 'It's only a fetus' routine, but he finally conceded that the *tissue mass* actually does react to the sound, to the pain."

He started to gag, and both Thrasher and Leigh leaped up. He raised his hands, fended off their help. He shook his head, wiped his mouth, swallowed, and took a breath. "I'm sorry, but I can still see so clearly that human pile of rubble stacked up on the table. I can see the doctor grasping the head with a clamp, crushing it like a ripe melon, then removing it in pieces. Finally, he took a curette and scraped out the remaining human scraps. It's important to get everything in order to avoid infection, you see. It's also mandatory that all the body parts are reassembled to prove that there actually was a baby to abort. The government demands proof that the procedure isn't being done unnecessarily, you see. A baby must be killed, otherwise there could be lawsuits and such. No one running a business wants messy lawsuits."

"How did you manage to keep your past a secret for this long? You ran a very large and lucrative clinic. I'm amazed no one dug into your past and published it before now," Thrasher said.

"The people who knew me then, who knew what I did, were not inclined to talk about it to anyone. Many people say they not only condone abortion but applaud it as a new and needed woman's right, but when it comes right down to having the procedure, it's still a dirty secret."

Leigh had to know if Jude had told her the truth about her birth. "Did your wife have the abortion?"

His forehead smoothed as if by magic, and he looked more like the Sebastian she had known yesterday. "No, she did not. I had the means to persuade her to carry the baby to term. Once the baby was born, I gave her what she wanted more than me and our child: several million dollars and a quick divorce."

"Is she still alive?"

He looked at her strangely, and she was afraid she had given herself away by not asking first about the child.

"No. She died several years later. Complications from an abortion."

The sad irony of it took her breath away.

"What happened to the baby?" Thrasher was the one to ask the definitive question.

"The baby was adopted by two wonderful people who I had known for some time. They had tried unsuccessfully for years to have a child. I knew they would give Sonja's and my child a better chance for happiness that I could alone. A child needs a mother and a father." His hands lay still on his chest but his legs were twitching under the sheets, like hers sometimes did when she was half asleep and trying to run away from a nightmare.

"What about the clinic?" Thrasher persisted.

"I turned it into another kind of clinic: a pregnancy clinic. No abortions were ever performed there again, but many pregnant woman passed through those same doors. Instead of abortion doctors and nurses, we had doctors and nurses who volunteered their services to those women who chose to keep their babies, so they could have free medical treatment for the first three months of the pregnancy and someone to help them make a decision they could live with for the rest of their lives."

"Quite a change," Thrasher understated.

"Quite," Leigh said. "That was a transitional time for you, Sebastian. Are you still happy with your decisions?"

"As far as the clinic is concerned, yes. I doubt that I'll live long enough to see as many children born as I destroyed, but I'm pleased with the results so far. We've assembled a team of well-trained counselors who discuss all the options a pregnant woman has: carrying to term, adoption, whatever can help both mother and child survive in a very tough world. The child's as well as the mother's well-being is vital."

"How many choose to go somewhere else and proceed with an abortion?" Thrasher's question made Sebastian's legs twitch even more.

"Too many, perhaps a third of them. But God sent them all to us instead of directly to Planned Parenthood, so at least they had an opportunity of discovering the real Father, of knowing how much He loved them and the child they were carrying."

"It's important to know one's real father, isn't it, Sebastian?" Leigh watched closely for his reaction to her question.

"Yes, I believe it is."

Those woeful eyes brimming with tears gave her the answer for which she had come. The details would have to wait.

"I'm sorry," she said, addressing both of them. "I have something very important to take care of. I'm going to have to leave."

"Not alone!" Thrasher ordered.

Her smile was enigmatic. "I won't be alone."

She turned, and was out the door and down the stairs before they could stop her.

Chapter Forty-Two

The flight had been as pleasant as possible for someone who so little understood the dynamics of aviation. She caught a glimpse of two uniformed men in the cockpit as she passed by the flight attendants, whose first class smiles promised it would be a smooth and pleasant flight, despite the detailed life-saving instructions they always gave to the contrary. The one she assumed was the captain looked starchly confident that he could keep the tons of metal in his command from plunging to the earth; a drop no more deadly than what Jude had planned for her, she reminded herself.

She settled into her first class seat, the only one she could get at the last minute. Her fear of flying took her mind, at least for a few hours, off her fear of landing. Jude hadn't been specific as to what he had planned for their reunion, but if it meant no more people would be hurt, she was willing to do whatever he considered necessary.

Her cell phone had rung constantly from the time she left the hospital until she boarded the plane. Finally, she had just turned it off. This was something she had do alone.

The man seated next to her by the window was typical of most of the other pampered passengers. He was more interested in sipping his cocktail and addressing his laptop computer than engaging in conversation with her, which was a relief. Making small talk would only distract her from the important business of planning how to stay alive.

The flight was smooth, the lunch unusually digestible, and the landing uneventful. There had been nothing but her own anxiety in those three and one half hours to prevent her from constructing a plan as well as a contingency plan. She was surprised at her own calm in devising the various scenarios she could expect Jude to present. She was the author of the thriller and Jude was, of course, the protagonist. If she were clever enough, she could end the story as thrillers should end — with the bad guys pushing up daisies and the good guys riding off into the sunset in a luxury car, boat, or private jet.

Even before renting a car, she made the call that would determine the success or failure of her hastily devised plan. It went far better than she thought. She was grateful she'd kept in touch with her old friends. She was grateful her old friends had not changed a bit.

She rented a Lincoln Town Car. Force of habit. Her mother and father liked "comfortable" cars, which to them meant one as long and large as the road and the driver could handle. The tears came without warning. She didn't bother to brush them away. There would be more to follow.

She had come home again, in spite of Thomas Wolfe's warning. He was wrong, but maybe that was because his home wasn't Buffalo Falls, Minnesota. She had returned — this time in a conscious state — and everything was exactly as she'd remembered it. The sleek and civilized airline terminal, the blast of hot and humid air that lurked just outside the door and sucked the water out of her body like a giant syringe.

The memories of Minnesota were not old and faded like sepia prints in a cherished album; they were vivid and alive, as were Ellen and Larry Barnes. Her parents were here with her one last time. They were sliding into the roomy luxury car, enjoying the company of their daughter, and the ease with which she steered them all back home. The life she had loved living for so many years was still there in Buffalo Falls. If it be God's will, it would end where it began.

She could see them so clearly. The two people who had loved and raised her had not changed at all. Of course, they hadn't lived long enough to develop the aches and pains that crop up like dandelions after age sixty. Nor had the lines in their faces been etched too deeply. She had not dared look for them until now, never dared hope she would see them again. But now that death held no fear for her, now that she knew so much more about them and about herself, she saw everything much clearer; even their reasons for not telling her she was adopted. To what purpose? They knew Sebastian and what kind of man he was. They knew her family health history. They knew the mother who sold her child for considerably more than thirteen pieces of silver.

She looked at the speedometer, but the numbers were blurred. She dabbed at her eyes and realized she had pushed the accelerator so hard she was going twenty miles over the speed limit. She slowed down, despite the fierce desire to hurry to her destination. Jude would be waiting for her. He said he had a lot to say to her. She had a lot to say to him too. She couldn't wait to assure him that he would get everything he deserved for sparing Ellen and Larry Barnes the ravages of old age. She would point out to him that because of his brutal actions, they had died prematurely and painfully, their hearts too hurt to catch the next beat. She swallowed her grief and took a deep breath, wishing fervently that she had been there to say good-bye, to tell them how much she loved them. And to forgive them for lying to her for her entire life.

But she had been unavoidably detained in a coma that doctors predicted would last until the plugs were finally pulled. Her father had gone first, her mother a week later, neither one of them believing that their daughter would remain on the earth to mourn them. She finally understood that they left because their belief was so strong, their love so great. They knew the Lord would reunite them all in paradise. Perhaps it would be today.

She drove almost an hour, seeing little but wheat fields, pastures, and lowing cattle. Barbed wire fences raced alongside her on the smooth ribbon of road. The monotony was unbroken, until she reached the outskirts of Buffalo Falls. She'd forgotten how lovely the initial introduction to this small farming community really was.

She slowed down to thirty. There was a discreet sign at the entrance to a tree-lined road on her left which read, "Buffalo Falls Country Club." She smiled at the innocent deception. The term "country club" evoked images of an elegant clubhouse with long mahogany bars and waiters bringing ice tea or wine coolers to an affluent lunch crowd. Quite a different atmosphere from that which pervaded the redwood clubhouse, whose only architectural redemption came from the picture windows that invited the vibrant greens and gaily-colored flags into the inexpensively paneled dining room. The country club was the venue for high school reunions, bridge clubs, wedding receptions, and any other social activity that required a big square room with lots of tables and no diversionary decor. There were no snobs allowed. Only people who enjoyed laughing, loving, and playing together, oblivious to anything but how joyous life can be when you want it to be.

How odd that life suddenly was more full of promise and beauty than ever before. How could she have ever doubted for a moment the existence of a God after living and coming of age in Buffalo Falls?

The flat land that had led her to this point now rose into gentle grassy hills, then dipped into sparkling streams that meandered through the pines and cozied up to the river's shore. The old canning factory around the curve and at the top of the hill was now only a cracked and graying shell. The Green Giant Company had closed it just after they'd moved away to Beaver Lake, which meant that hundreds of teenagers could no longer experience the thrill of being pelted by corn kernels splattering their sticky juices from the moving conveyor belt. They could no longer experiment with ways and means to make themselves look macho or glamorous while wearing a hairnet, overalls, and a face full of corn. Did young people still understand that money earned shucking corn and shelling peas meant an old beater of a car plumb full of gas, a movie date finished off with a burger and fries, and a pizza with everything on a Friday night in nearby Fairview? The only alternative to summer employment then was an endless night at home with the folks watching Lawrence Welk. Life had been so simple. Choices had been few and easy.

The sign ahead said, *Buffalo Falls, Population 1500.* Either the sign was out of date or the population hadn't increased in more than twenty-five years. Maybe the miracle was that it hadn't decreased either.

She rounded the corner and passed the Bluebird Cafe, the scene of so many flirtations, breakups, and tearful reconciliations. And all done to the tune of the jukebox in the far corner of the long, booth-lined, vinyl-floored restaurant. It was the only one in town that had managed to stay in business from year to year, despite the scandalous behavior of its owner, Ralph Dibble. At the last high school reunion she'd attended, the few friends who had remained in Buffalo Falls had assured her that adultery was still considered a sin in their little town, even though, as in larger cities, it had become as common as the cold.

The scandal de jour then was the stuff of which movies are made. More than a few of the Bluebird's regular customers were switching their allegiance and their after-game, after-church dinner reservations to the recently opened Main Street Cafe. Engaging in idle gossip was unchristian, but so was the burgeoning belly of seventeen-year-old Kelly Robinson, who was unable to change her status as an unmarried, pregnant home-wrecker until Ralph divested himself of his long-suffering wife, Thelma, who unfortunately for Ralph was also the cook at the Bluebird. As a testament to the Christian ethic of forgive and forget, Thelma agreed to continue on as cook, even after the divorce became final and young Kelly replaced her in Ralph's bed, which was right above the kitchen where Thelma deep-fried and cut up through the lunch and dinner hours. She was no martyr; she'd just worked too hard and too long making a go of the restaurant to let it go under.

And it surely would have if Ralph had done the cooking. Following Thelma's example, the former customers continued to hate the sin but love the chicken fried steak, and they slowly returned to the Bluebird.

So did Leigh. The minute she walked through the door she saw him. He was sitting in the last booth, smiling as devilishly as ever, looking as recklessly handsome as he had in the ninth grade. It was a testament to Bill's charms that she had never succumbed to Grady Johnson's. The closer she came, the easier it was to see his darkly tanned arms, striped midway up his biceps as only a farmer's could be. Even tans were never a concern to people who worked in the fields and made their meager fortunes by turning dirt into golden corn, juicy red tomatoes, and willowy wheat.

Their meeting didn't take long. In ten minutes she was back in her car. If she was lucky, she and Grady could reminisce about the days of cherry cokes and pink carnations later. If she wasn't lucky, and if there was any justice, Grady would be rewarded with a bumper crop of corn this year.

She turned right on Main Street, driving slowly down the eerily vacant, wide street, which was now overlooked by brand new, old fashioned lamplights. At sundown they would cast their glow on the VFW Club, the municipal liquor store, and Johnson's jewelry store. Next in line was Hanson Motors, where for decades the townspeople had taken their Fords and Chevys to be serviced. It hadn't changed, nor had the sturdy brick building at the end of the block; the Security State Bank of Buffalo Falls. The act of returning to the scene of the crime was essential to Jude's master plan. The only reason she could think of was that he not only wanted to finish what he'd started, but further humiliate the kind people who had put their life on the line to do the right thing.

Not knowing what to expect, but following instructions, Leigh parked in front, got out, looked up and down the street, then walked through the wide oak doors. Before she had reached the first teller's station, she was grabbed from behind and shoved into a side office.

"What the…!"

Joe Towson turned her around to face him, his burly arms still holding her in place. "Sorry, ma'am. We couldn't afford to take any chances. This here is the vice president's office. It's safe."

His eyes searched the perimeter like a secret service agent. He probably wasn't aware of it, but he was doing a perfect impersonation of Clint Eastwood. He had everything down: from the squinty-eyed stare to the "make my day" chill in his voice.

Once the shock of being manhandled by the policeman wore off, she demanded, “What’s this all about? Who are you?”

“My name’s Joe Towson, ma’am,” he answered respectfully, his hand still on her arm.

Her attitude softened, her back lost its stiffness. “I’m sorry I’ve waited so long to come and see you, Officer Towson.”

“Actually, it’s Captain Towson.” He released his grip on her arm and stood back slightly, studying her shyly. “Apprehending Jude Orcus got me a few promotions.” He looked suddenly sheepish. “Sorry, ma’am. That was very unfeeling of me, sounding like your tragedy was my ticket to fame and fortune.”

Leigh would hardly have thought being a police Chief in Buffalo Falls constituted fame and fortune, until she reminded herself where she was and what was really important in life. Joe Towson loved his job and did it well. He was a very successful man. How long would it take her to learn? How long did she have?

“Lots of people have been looking for you, Ms. Barnes.”

“I think you know me well enough to call me Leigh, Chief Towson. After all, you saved my life.” She couldn’t have chosen a more appropriate hero; one who hadn’t the vaguest idea he was special.

“No, ma’am, my promotions never went that far. God was the one who stepped in. No one in this town doubts that for a minute.”

“You’re right, but thank you for so ably assisting Him.” She smiled warmly, not trusting herself to say more. Another episode of *Touched by an Angel* had just been wrapped up.

He pulled out a chair from near the highly polished desk and offered it to her. She shook her head and remained standing.

“Mr. Cole and an Inspector Cadigan got wind that you’d be coming here. I’m not sure how they knew or why they think you need protection, but they want me to keep you safe until they get here, which shouldn’t be too long, the way I understood their call.”

They must have seen the e-mail. In her haste, she’d forgotten to delete it. Now they knew as much as she. But they wouldn’t get here in time to keep her from doing what she knew was right, what was necessary.

“I’m guessing their concern has something to do with Jude Orcus. Am I right?” His eyes were narrowed, but they didn’t lose their softness.

“Yes. I’m supposed to meet him here.”

“Why?” he entreated. “You want to give him another chance to finish you off. Forgive me, but that's plain foolhardy. It surely isn't God's intention to save your life only to have it taken away again, I know that."

"Do you?"

He cocked his head to one side and instinctively pulled on his mustache, allowing him time to figure out what she was asking. He failed. "Do I what?"

"Do you really know God's intentions?"

"Well, no, but…."

"Neither do I, but I do know Jude Orcus's intentions. I believe I can stop him from doing further harm to the people I love, and I'm going to try, no matter how many good people try to stop me."

He let his mouth hang open slightly. Then he closed it with decisiveness and put his hand on his belt, close to his holstered gun. "I can't let you do this, Ms. Barnes."

She clutched her purse tightly, reversed it to her left hand, her right hand on the clasp. "You really must let me go. He knows where I am. I agreed to give him the opportunity to face me, to tell me what he wants from me in exchange for the lives of the people I care about."

His tone took on a severity that was foreign to him. "I can't allow you to put yourself in harm's way."

Her smile momentarily disarmed him. "I'm afraid you must," she said, reaching into her purse and pulling out the seven-shot Smith and Wesson revolver she had moments ago received from her old friend, Grady. She pointed it at his startled face. "I wouldn't kill you, Joe, but I would wound you. You would most likely still be able to subdue me, but I would have already committed an act for which I will have to pay dearly. You don't want me to go to prison, do you?"

She felt sorry for him. His was a dilemma she would not have known how to handle if their positions were reversed. He had proved that he was not an indecisive man in the course of doing his job, but now he was perspiring, and his hands were clenching and unclenching at his sides.

Just then, the phone on the vice president's desk blared. "Would you mind getting that, Joe? I think it might be Jude."

He stared at it for a long moment before finally picking it up. "Yes?" His face turned a light shade of purple and his jaw muscles twitched violently. "Yes. Yes, I understand. You bastard," he finished through clenched teeth.

"Where does he want me to go next? This little scavenger hunt must be proving amusing to him."

"He wants to talk to you. He threatened to kill you immediately if he sees you are being followed."

She took the phone, still aiming the gun at him and keeping her distance. "Yes. Yes, I will but… Okay, I'll be outside in exactly one minute."

She cradled the phone, gave Joe a sympathetic smile and said, "I'm going out the back door. I don't want you or anyone else to try to stop me from exiting. I'm counting on you to save my life again, Joe. Please don't disappoint me."

Reluctantly, he remained. He'd had no time to ask for help. Leigh Barnes had entered the bank only seconds after the call from Inspector Cadigan had come in. The bank employees had been cleared out until further instruction from the Captain. As soon as the door closed behind her, Joe made a bee-line for it, just in time to see a car racing down the alley. It was a black Mercedes, and Jude Orcus was behind the wheel. Leigh was beside him, as she had been on that day. When it disappeared around a curve, Joe's hope of saving her disappeared along with it.

Chapter Forty-Three

The gun was safely tucked into the waist of her skirt, her loose-fitting jacket concealing it nicely. Only the click of the doors being locked broke the eerie silence of the car's interior. She studied his profile as they twisted in unison with every sharp turn. She had never seen this side of him, literally. The cavernous cheeks had filled in somewhat, and the gushing oil glands had gone dry. Even his lips seemed of normal shape and size. He must have once been an attractive man, she thought, amazed by her objectivity.

When they reached the highway he lowered his speed for several miles, then turned off onto a dirt road on their right.

She knew where he was taking her. She wondered at his choice of what could be the final destination for both of them. Or was it his choice? She had become certain of one thing in the last days. No human being was ever in control of his life.

Leigh could not even hear Jude breathing. Her own seemed to be suspended as well. However, his truly brilliant mind would be working hard. He did his homework and meticulously planned his moves, like an expert chess player. Certainly she was a pawn in the game he had been playing for so long, but it no longer seemed important to him that he win. That she could tell. He was resigned. But to what?

Her heart was beating normally, her breathing was unlabored, despite the fact that both the man and the car had driven her to edge, then over it. Whether she lived or died was neither hers nor Jude's decision to make. Peace warmed her soul like a steaming bowl of oatmeal on a bleak, winter day. All the memories that had flooded over her since her return had cleansed her of all doubt.

He had not looked at her all the while they were driving. He said nothing. She asked nothing.

Then she saw it in the distance, its steeple still as high as the sky, the American flag clapping its approval from twenty feet below. Bethany Church had for one hundred fifty years stood boldly against the harsh assaults of weather and the unpious who sought to bring it down. It stood dignified, immaculate, and holy. Within those sturdy walls there was stored a constant and inexhaustible source of hope and strength to those who sought it. It was in this old church that her parents had married, where she had been baptized, and had received communion. Behind the massive headstone of the church's original pastor, near the plot where Larry and Ellen Barnes now lay side by side, she had received her first kiss.

The reddish-gold of the bricks darkened as the car followed the shadows that were stretching lazily over the rough surface. The bejeweled windows radiated vibrant purples and reds and blues onto the long, curved walkway sloping gradually up to the wide front steps. It was on that sloping walk that her father had sweltered in his dark suit under the summer's scorching heat and penetrating humidity. It was on that sidewalk that he received a weekly whipping from the wintry wind and blustery snow storms that reddened faces and numbed fingers at least six months out of the year.

"I've brought you home again, Leigh."

"Yes."

He drove the car through the side gate and up the narrow road that gave access to the elderly and handicapped members who could no longer trek up that treacherous path to God. She didn't object when, after turning off the engine and getting out of the car, he took her hand and helped her out. He continued to hold her hand when he opened the intricately carved doors that led into the narthex.

Then, without consulting her captor, Leigh released his grasp and walked slowly down the aisle, noting all the changes that had taken place since she had last worshiped there. The seats of the wooden pews were now covered with thick padding. The congregation was aging like the church itself, and modifications were necessary to alleviate the creaks and cracks the years had wrought.

The pulpit was as high and formidable as it had been when she was looking up at it from a stance much closer to the floor. While most things shrunk with time, that pulpit seemed to be even larger now.

She knelt down before the altar and bowed her head. She heard the music of comfort and love sung by birds swooping and soaring just beyond the stained glass windows. She had almost forgotten Jude was there when he knelt down beside her and asked, "Why you? Why not me?"

She raised her eyes level with his. They startled her with their iridescence and clearness. There was no sign of the blood that had stained them, no evidence of the hatred that had hardened them and the despair that had deadened them. She shook her head slowly, trying to comprehend what he was asking.

"Why were you given parents who loved you and wanted you? Why were chosen to be blessed and not me?"

"I can't answer that, Jude," she answered, her hands still folded, her soul still peaceful. "But it's not too late. It's never too late to find answers."

His voice was as gentle as the breeze that glided over them from an open window; his words as blunt as a headstone. "We are all given free choice. That's fine, but I didn't choose to be sodomized by my own father. I didn't choose to be ignored by my mother. I didn't choose to be driven from the one place where I finally found admiration, respect, and yes, even love. You didn't know that, did you? You didn't know that I really was who my readers thought I was," he said stridently. Then, the stridence was gone. "For a while, at least."

She kept her eyes locked on his, knowing that nothing she said or did would stop him from baring his soul in this place where he finally felt safe to expose it.

"There was a young woman. Julie Benson. She was the receptionist at the newspaper. She had pale green eyes like Cynthia's. She looked at me like Cynthia used to look at me....once. She saw something in me that no one had ever seen, or even bothered to look for. I saw it too. For a while, at least. I began to think maybe there was a God. Because there was a Julie."

"What happened to her?"

"She died."

"I'm sorry," she said, and genuinely meant it.

"I'm not. If she'd lived I would have hurt her too."

"Why?"

"Because I have to. I wasn't meant to be happy. I wasn't supposed to be loved. I've known that since I was three years old. So, I have to even things up."

"Is that why you abused Cynthia as you had been abused?"

"I had taken all the abuse, while she remained pure and holy."

"And when she was no longer pure and holy she stopped believing in her goodness just like you did. But she found Him again, even after all the bad things that were done to her, that she did to herself. You can find God again too, Jason. There's still time."

He shook off her words. He wouldn't let her confuse him. He had things to say. "You had everything I wanted: a mother and father who adored you and a perfect life you took for granted. It was unfair that you were the one who was smiled upon while the rest of us were put through a reign of torture that made death look like a damn good alternative!"

She expected to see the evil torture his eyes and body back to what it had been before, but the cancer she had seen infecting him and everyone around him now appeared benign. All his torture was now directed inward, filling his face with a pain Christ must have felt when he said, "My God, My God, Why Hast Thou forsaken me?"

"Did making others suffer make it all fair?"

"Yes, damn it, it did. For a while, at least," he said once again. "Until yesterday."

Her eyes urged him to continue.

He turned and looked up at the heavenly body hanging from a crude wooden cross. "I broke into Cynthia's apartment. I saw a picture of them."

"Them?"

"The children. My children."

"They're beautiful, aren't they, Jude." She prayed they were still alive.

"They looked so innocently happy. And safe. And loved. They looked like kids should look. The four of them together in that picture, they looked like a…" his voice broke, and the sound was like the deadly whir of a tornado as the world he had always known spun around him.

"Like a family," she finished for him.

"I wanted a family. Was that so much to ask?" he cried unabashedly

She stood and pulled him up with her. "I'm not the one you should be asking, Jason. God is the only one who can give you the answers you need."

"How?" he pleaded, his body caving in with grief for what he had never had, and what he had thrown away.

"Just ask. Ask and you shall receive," she said, with a smile that came from a well of hope bubbling up inside her. "I know it sounds too easy, but it's true."

"You didn't ask for that ride in my Mercedes, but you received it," he countered.

"A very good friend once told me that I was not smart enough to know how God answers prayers or directs our lives, that I had never had a glimpse of the

Master Plan. Only faith in Him can help you now, Jason. I think you knew that when you brought me here."

"I'm not going to hurt the children, Leigh. You don't have to worry about that any more. And the rest of them: the O'Regans, Thrasher Cole, Sebastian, they will have nothing more to fear from me. But it's too late for me to be saved. You know everything I've done, Leigh. Such atrocities can never be forgiven"

"I don't know."

"How can you forgive me?"

"I don't know."

At that moment the church's doors burst open and what seemed like an army of uniformed men raced down the aisle, guns and voices raised. "Give it up, Jude! You're surrounded! You'll never make it out of here alive!"

The brief smile he offered her was profoundly sad. "You think Moonbeam and I will hit it off?" he asked, as he pulled the gun from his waist band and shot himself in the head, its contents splattering the sacred altar and her anguished face.

Chapter Forty-Four

The weather was mild and sunny. The wine was flowing from barrels, bottles, glasses and any other receptacle worthy of the holy water of the Napa Valley.

Although it had only been a month since she and Jude had knelt at the altar in Beaver Falls, it seemed a lifetime ago. And it was, really.

"Well," Thrasher asked, spreading his arms out to encompass the valley, the vast fields of vines, and the great numbers of people enjoying the fruits of those vines. "What do you think of the Golden Bridge Winery?"

She had never seen Thrasher in a mood as bubbly as the brut champagne she was sipping from an exquisite crystal flute. "You witnessed my lack of expertise at the wine tasting today. I can't tell say for sure if it was caressing my taste buds or puckering my palate, and there's a certain panache required for cork sniffing I haven't acquired."

"Golden Bridge tannins are never puckery, merely sufficient to keep our wine from tasting flabby," he intoned, sniffing pretentiously.

They laughed with the giddiness of teenagers just discovering the taste of young love.

"I'm no Robert Mondavi, of course, at least not yet. Jake is the one responsible for the successful barrel auction yesterday, and for securing the best chef in the Valley — or the entire bay area — for the dinner here tonight."

"I'm glad I finally got to meet him. He's exactly how you described him. I feel as if I've known him for years. Too bad he opted not to run for a second term in the Senate. We need a lot more like him in Washington."

"I agree, but I'm glad he wasn't in Washington when I needed his help in rounding up all the forces that finally took Hardaway down. And saved my bacon, I might add. Without his connections, his formidable clout, my name would still be a dirty word and Leif Hardaway's would be golden."

"But will all the charges against Leif stick?"

"There are a lot of people trying their damnedest to see to it they do, including his own daughter and wife. Cynthia is determined to see that her father pays for what he did to his family and to the country. Although it remains to be seen if that damage can ever be undone. I guess we won't know for sure until the ballistic missiles are guided right to our nation's doorstep."

Even though he spoke to Leigh with some bravado, Thrasher would never stop worrying about Leif Hardaway, even if he was locked up without a hope of getting out on bail. Tony Angelico had more tricks up his sleeve than the sorcerer's apprentice.

If Leigh sensed his worry, she didn't let on. "Let's hope our military defense is not in as bad shape as Jake says. It was fascinating talking with him about all the things the American people don't know. I guess if we did, there would be panic in the streets. " She sipped her champagne. "Did you read the article I wrote in last week's magazine?"

"Are you kidding? I'm your biggest fan."

She wriggled in her chair. "I'm not fishing, really."

"Don't change your hat size for me," he teased.

"Arrogance was my undoing. Never again will I think I'm calling all the shots."

"There's no danger of my thinking I'm the judge, either."

"But you are, thankfully."

"Which is why Senator Guttmacher is shaking in his boots about now."

"Even the faithful Dr. George Kelleher is scampering to save his own pitiful hide. Ed Cadigan says Leif's lackeys are coming out of the woodwork pleading for immunity if they tell all. We're going to find bodies that have been buried since Leif's first dirty deal thirty years ago. The really sad thing is that Jason wasn't the only young boy he used. Once the story came out in the paper, several young boys came forward to testify that they had been raped. Apparently the trysts he had in that apartment building of his were varietal."

She cringed at the term she had heard so much in the last few days. The word varietal didn't sound nearly as appealing in that context.

"Those revelations alone should put him away for a long time. That is, if he's put in solitary confinement. Child molesters are not looked kindly upon by the prison population, and tend to have a short shelf life." Thrasher took another sip of the fine Merlot, a look of immense satisfaction suffusing his face.

Leigh noticed it and emulated it. At this moment, things were very much right with the world. "Not even his media pals could help him this time. A murder indictment, child molestation, and treason are pretty hard to gloss over, even with the media's experience at skewing the news to accommodate their viewpoint. Believe me, Sebastian and I will make sure nothing is overlooked in our coverage of Leif's career of corruption and his undignified demise."

"I still think the local papers would have tried to hide it on the back pages. Bad luck for Leif that he so publicly duped the publisher. Even in San Francisco it's considered bad manners to bed a man's new bride, especially if the bedder might be HIV positive."

"Let's hope his legacy doesn't include that. Delia deserves a dip at the box office for her attempt to discredit you, but I wouldn't wish that disease on anyone."

Leigh let the flavory bubbles of her champagne tickle her taste buds and return her euphoric mood. She wouldn't have thought it possible, but the unforgettable events in Buffalo Falls had given her hope for the entire human race. If Jude could seek and find God, any lost soul could. "I never thought I would say this, but Jason… or Jude, was neither one that day in the church. I saw him being reborn as the child he had never been allowed to be. His eyes were filled with the reflected light of something inside him I couldn't see but could feel."

"Too bad it came too late to do him any good."

"I'm not so sure about that. God's time is so much more complex than our seconds and minutes. I know because He's stopped it altogether several times for me." She could tell he couldn't yet comprehend what she was telling him. "Who's to say that in the moment it took for Jason to die, he didn't see the face of God, beg His forgiveness, and follow Him home?"

Neither the wine nor Leigh's hopes of redemption for Jude had diluted Thrasher's desire to see the guilty punished and justice achieved. "I'm not about to forget all those people he killed, all the lives he altered forever."

"I won't forget either, Thrasher, I promise you that. But I'd like to think that Sebastian's right. None of us can see the Master Plan. If we could, life would be merely a useless exercise instead of an expedition into our own immortality."

"Profoundly put," he said, putting his arms around her. "Wish I could brag that it was my wine talking, but I don't think we can claim it increases intelligence. Although I might talk to Cynthia about that as an advertising angle."

"I doubt you'll have the chance to pry her away from Ed Cadigan," she said, observing the two as they happily ignored everyone else.

"Just look at Sebastian over there, critiquing our Chardonnay and Beaujolais," Thrasher pointed out. "I'll bet he's wowing those oenophiles with descriptions they've never even thought of."

"Before I met him, words like peach, anise, herbal, and grassy were not adjectives I'd use to describe wine." Her gaze drifted. "Before I met him there were a lot of things I didn't know."

As if once again reading her mind, Sebastian ambled over to their table and sat down. "Did anyone ever tell you you're the most beautiful daughter in the world?"

"Actually," she said, coloring slightly, "yes."

Sebastian took her hand in his. "Of course Larry would have told you every chance he got. He was never afraid of wearing his heart like a red badge of courage. Most men, especially in those days, would have wired their mouths shut before they would publicly say the L word."

It all seemed so natural to Leigh. Gaining a father had not been something she'd thought possible after losing one. But she'd felt something move deep within her the moment Sebastian first spoke her name, took her hand. At the time she believed it was merely awe at meeting such an extraordinary and famous writer and thinker. Now she knew that the connection between them had been forged the day she was born, no matter how brief their union as father and child.

Thrasher could tell that Leigh was choking back all kinds of emotions. He'd give her some time. "It must have seemed a little strange, releasing your child for adoption to a woman you once loved. Ellen must have been a very special lady."

Sebastian's eyes went all soft, as if he were being caressed by many fingers. "She was beautiful. And totally unobtainable, or so I thought until Larry captured her and carried her away to Minnesota. I was a real slow study when the three of us met in a freshman English class at Stanford. I wish it had been a choice between brain or brawn when Ellen was scrutinizing us both, but Larry was as smart as he was brawny. He was a linebacker for the Cardinal football team, a superior student, and so good looking he made every gal on campus blush just by saying hello."

"And my mother, I mean, Ellen?"

"Your mother. Yes, she was as delicate as baby's breath and as robust as a geranium. She looked so fragile, yet she would stand up to professors every time they questioned the veracity of her reasoning. Nor did she ever hesitate to stand up for anyone too weak or scared to stand up for themselves."

"Did she stand up to you too?" Leigh asked, trying to imagine her mother with anyone but Larry Barnes.

"I was scared to death of her. Every time I tried to talk to her I'd stutter and stammer like an idiot. I truly think that if she didn't know I had to have some brains to get into the school in the first place she would have considered me unteachable."

"So you never asked her out?"

"Only when it was too late. I asked her to go to a movie with me the day after Larry proposed to her. She sounded genuinely sorry. Not for the engagement, of course, but for the poor boob standing before her looking like he'd been hit by a freight train."

"But you said you three were best friends? How could that be if both you and Larry loved the same woman?" Thrasher was fascinated by the new Sebastian, the love-struck romantic who could be intimidated by a pretty young girl.

"I loved them both. Larry turned out to be more like a brother to me than a friend. I couldn't begrudge him for going after what any man with half a brain would have gone for. But after we graduated I lost track of them for years."

"And you met Sonja." Leigh could still not say the name without getting an acidic taste in her mouth; the same taste that followed a bout of nausea.

"She was also beautiful, Leigh. You look very much like her."

Leigh knew he was only being honest, but she didn't want to look like Sonja, she wanted to look like baby's breath and geraniums.

"Like so many young men in heat, I didn't look beyond her beauty. I assumed so much about her that was never, ever there. Including intelligence. I'm afraid she did likewise about me."

"But with you there is a there there," she said, loosely quoting Gertrude Stein's description of Oakland, California. Or was it Alice B. Toklas who said that? She could never remember.

"Not if you consider what I did for a living. How much there could there be in a man who thought nothing of destroying perfectly good babies."

She too had to be honest. "I don't know."

"So you see, Leigh, I was not the man Larry Barnes was. Nor was I the man

I was yet to become. I'm glad I didn't see Ellen again until I had made the transformation from beast to man."

"Did you immediately think of Ellen when you were trying to convince Sonja to choose adoption instead of abortion?"

"I had attended a reunion at Stanford several years earlier and heard that Ellen and Larry were still in Minnesota, and that they were disappointed not to have children yet like most of the other classmates. When Sonja finally agreed to adoption, I called them, said I was going to be in Minnesota on business, and could we get together. The rest is history."

"My history," Leigh said thoughtfully.

"And there's a lot more to come," Thrasher said, kissing her on the cheek. "You think there's a chance we could make it together? History I mean," he said with a Jake Malloy laugh.

With an almost old world formality, he took her hand, kissed it tenderly and said, "You do know I've fallen in love with you, don't you?"

She smiled. "You're not a very good actor."

"I never aspired to be one. Being a lawyer is bad enough."

"If a lawyer is bad, wouldn't a judge be rated on an even higher scoundrel scale?"

"There's only one sure way of finding out," Sebastian pronounced, kissing her on the other cheek.

"I'm hoping it won't take you too long, either," Thrasher said.

"Having a new father is enough of a responsibility for now, gentlemen, but I kind of like two men wanting me in their lives for the rest of mine."

"I can wait, Leigh, but I wouldn't mind shortening the engagement period so we can beat Cynthia and Ed to the church."

As if on cue, the inspector and his equally enamored date joined them at the table situated in the center of the bougainvillea-draped gazebo. "There's way too much consumin' going on here, folks. I think I'm going to have to confiscate some of this wine," he said pouring a glass for himself and Cynthia from a bottle of Merlot. "I'd like to make a toast."

They all raised their glasses and clinked them joyously. The crystal goblets rang like church bells, evoking laughter and prospects of happiness. "To the women who make us the men we were meant to be."

"Here, here," Cynthia and Leigh cried out.

"Am I going to have to roll out more barrels?" Jake was approaching with a beautiful woman on his still well-muscled arm.

"We may need to plant some new fields, partner. I think we're going to be doing some major celebrating in the near future." Thrasher could take his eyes off Leigh for only the seconds it took to be polite to his friend.

Jake raised his eyebrows. "Have you an announcement to make?"

"Not yet," Leigh answered before Thrasher had the chance. "We still haven't properly celebrated the appointment of Judge Thrasher Cole," she said, lifting her glass. She leaned toward him and kissed him soundly, oblivious to the hoots and hollers of the rest.

Waiters milled around them, filling their glasses, offering dessert trays for inspection, and making sure the winery owners and their guests were being properly pampered.

While they were celebrating the new wonders in their world, wine aficionados were whispering like conspirators, not about the voluptuous and volatile varietals, but the juicy scandals that had come to fruition in the last month.

Former close associates and social acquaintances of Leif and Lydia Hardaway were unusually close-mouthed, except when eating or supping. They knew they could very well be the subject of future scandals that could rise up ominously from the pages of Leif's appointment books and financial ledgers. His allies would no longer remain invisible or blameless. The domino effect was already taking place, and there seemed to be an unlimited number of blotched bones yet to fall.

The clearing of Thrasher's name and his recent appointment to the bench had brought loud cheers from readers of *America in Review*, but only low mutterings from Senator Guttmacher and his merry band of pickpockets who could no longer depend on the Hardaways to guarantee their cut of the government's take.

"We've got the best seat in the house," Sebastian said, looking out on the mountains, the field of harvested grapes, and the tinted tile roofs of the Golden Bridge winery and the elegant main house where Jake would later entertain the cream of the crop with after-dinner port and sherry.

"You've got quite an audience, Thrasher. Better be careful what you commit to." Jake warned, apparently nonplused that his date was now flirting with a former 49er at another table.

"I have no intention of being careful. I love Leigh Barnes and I want to marry her and have as many babies as she'll consent to."

"You have a nice round number in mind?" Leigh asked.

"Four has always been my lucky number." His eyes were actually twinkling.

Sebastian's exhalation of breath was loud and agitated. Red wine bubbled from the side of his mouth as he searched his breast pocket for a handkerchief.

"Dad!" It was the first time she had said it aloud and in public. "Are you all right? Here, let me help you," she cried, dabbing his beard with her napkin.

"I'm sorry, please forgive my clumsiness. I guess I swallowed too quickly," he apologized, concealing his agitation behind the handkerchief.

"I think I should take you inside. Perhaps it's too warm for you out here," Leigh said with concern. "I don't want to take any more chances on losing you just when I've found you."

"Yes, let me bring you into the main house, Sebastian," Jake offered.

Sebastian held up a hand in denial of his distress. "I am perfectly fine. In fact, I really would like to take a leisurely stroll around the estate, if you don't mind," he asked, addressing both Jake and Thrasher. "Kind of get the lay of the land, since I would imagine Leigh is going to be spending quite a lot of time here." His color had returned and his heartbeat was almost back to normal.

"Let me go with you," Leigh said, rising quickly from her chair.

"That would be lovely, Leigh. But right now I think I'll just wander off on my own and leave you young people to keep up the festive mood. Digesting too much good news and good food at one time gives me heartburn."

Leigh reluctantly sat down again. "Are you sure you don't want some company?"

"Have you ever seen me not sure about something?" he asked rhetorically.

"No, I guess not," she answered, still solicitous.

"I'll join you later," he promised.

In the midst of the laughter, the pouring of good wines, and the outpouring of love, Sebastian nodded to the people he had come to cherish, and began the arduous task of doing the right thing. He had to be quiet and listen. And if God said nothing, he would say nothing.

He sat down on one of the stone benches that had been placed around the estate. He thought about Jude, the sad young man who had with such grief and devastation brought Sebastian to the happiest place in his life. The Lord did indeed work in strange and wonderful ways when humans ceased to question and just believe. He would soon to able to see the Master Plan if, indeed, the doctors were correct in their diagnosis.

He should be eager to learn all the secrets of God's universe. But he was not. He could wait a little longer. Maybe long enough to hold his grandchild? God would make that decision for him. But that wouldn't stop him from praying, "Just a little longer, Lord."

Printed in the United States
23909LVS00003BA/25